Enchantments

A South Pole Santa Adventure
Book 5

BY

JingleBelle Jackson

Copyright © 2016 JingleBelle Jackson
All rights reserved.

ISBN: 1537223402
ISBN 13: 9781537223407

For my guy Glen – always my biggest fan

Choose
Kindness

A Note to Enchantment Readers:

Thank you for reading **Enchantments** *the fifth book in the South Pole Santa series. My intention with this book was to wrap up the series but it seems Sandra and the gang felt otherwise and it is likely there will be a sixth book. There are still so many adventures ahead for them all! For some readers, I know it can be frustrating to have a story that continues. If you're one of those, I encourage you to simply skip the epilogue in this book. I tried hard to write the last chapter in a satisfying way for those who like a wrapped up story. I hope you all agree - whether you choose to end the story at that point or push on through the epilogue. Either way, my fervent desire is that you enjoy this new adventure of Sandra and her friends! Chase your dreams!* - JingleBelle

Character List:

- **Santa** – The main man, the big guy, the elf in the red suit
- **Cassandra Penelope Clausmonetsiamlydelaterra... (Sandra Claus...)** – South Pole Santa
- **Cappie** – Also known as Captain Margaret Richmond. Sandra's legal guardian since her parents disappeared when she was eleven.
- **The *Mistletoe*** – The tugboat Sandra and Cappie call home
- **Squawk** – Sandra's beloved talking macaw
- **Rio** – An emerald-colored dolphin that is loved by, and travels with, Sandra and Cappie
- **Ambyrdena "Birdie" Snow** – Sandra's best friend, daughter of a water wizard and African princess mother. Birdie can talk to birds.
- **Spencer Mantle** – Sandra's super smart best friend, son of two humans
- **Sanderson "Sandy" Claus...** -- Sandra's dad, of elf and human descent; tragically lost at sea
- **Cassiopola "Cassie" Claus...** -- Sandra's mom, of human and royal elfin descent; tragically lost at sea
- **St. Annalise** – A remote island in the Caribbean Sea that is home to St. Annalise Academy where Sandra goes to school

- **Christina Annalise** – Headmistress/director of St. Annalise Academy and mother of Jason Annalise
- **Jason Annalise** – Adopted son of Christina and purported King of Fairies
- **Gunderson "Gunny" Holiday** – A runner-up for South Pole Santa from the great state of Texas. Now assists the two Santas.
- **Thomas Jackson** – A retired St. Annalise Academy professor living on St. Annalise and Cappie's new husband.
- **Crow & Ghost Holiday** – Gunny's younger twin brothers
- **Zinga** – An elf and executive assistant to Santa
- **Breezy** – An elf in charge of weather reporting and friend to Sandra. Breezy, like many elves, can read thoughts.
- **Toby/Tug** – A very clean house elf
- **Emaralda "Em"** – A "delgin elf" with a special ability. Em assists Sandra as her transportation.
- **Calivon** – the current elfin ruler and chairperson of the Magical World Council
- **Zeentar and Selena Snow** – Birdie's parents
- **Samuel** – Birdie's fiancé
- **Wistle** – A shan fairy
- **Reesa** – A shan fairy
- **Quisp** – A tiny shanelle fairy
- **Clementine** – A new family member
- **Tamblor and Kilt** – Frightening saneer fairies

- **Beatrice Carol** – A World Wide News TV reporter from London, England
- **Nicholas Navidad, Redson O'Brien, Klondike Tannenbaum, Rollo Kringle** – Runner-up competitors for South Pole Santa

Prologue

They're Real!

Location: The Mistletoe

They held Sandra so tight she could barely breathe. It was her parents! In person. Not the illusion she thought they were when she first saw them standing there on the deck of the *Mistletoe*. This hug was real. She had felt them around her almost since the day they went missing and had always believed they were still alive. And now, here they were, proving her right, holding her and crying. All three of them. Tears of joy. Tears of disbelief. Tears for all the years apart. Tears pouring until finally they ebbed enough for Sandra to stammer out the one thing she most wanted to know.

"How?" There was so much to know but at that moment, how they had managed to get there was her most pressing question.

Her mother held Sandra back away from her and brushed her daughter's hair out of her eyes. "Darling, could we go in and talk?" she asked as Sanderson, Sandra's dad, scanned the area around the big tug with anxious eyes.

Sandra could see the urgency in both their eyes and hurried them into the big galley of the boat. Her exhaustion from the busiest day of the year delivering gifts followed but the beautiful day of Christmas had been replaced by a decade of built-up exhilaration. Her parents were alive and they were here! Of course she was awake!

"Oh, darling, how we have dreamed of this moment," Cassiopola, Sandra's mom, said as both parents reached in to hug her again as soon as they were in the galley. Too tight, really, but Sandra didn't mind. It meant they were real. "The *Mistletoe* looks so wonderful! You and Cappie have taken good care of it."

Sandra just nodded her head as she wiped away tears.

"Cassie," Sandra's dad said to his wife. "We need to begin." Sandra saw something pass between her parents as her mother nodded her agreement in response.

"Come, Sandra," her mom said, pointing to the galley table. "Let's sit down and let us tell you where we've been and what you need to know."

CHAPTER 1

So Much to Know

Location: The Mistletoe

It's too much, Sandra thought again as she lay in her bunk reviewing the night before. Losing them once was too much. Too painful. Too hard. "Too unfair," she said out loud to herself. Losing them again was simply more than she was afraid she could handle.

They had told her so much that she needed to know, and now she willed her brain to remember. It was imperative that she didn't forget a single thing.

"Where have you been?" Sandra had asked, needing to understand for her own mental health. She had spent nearly a decade without the parents she loved so much. Why had they stayed away and why were they here now?

"It's a long story, darling, that we will spare you for now," said her mother. "The short version is we've been held in a place far away guarded by dark magic. In the beginning, we thought for sure our hearts would break from being taken from you and having no way to communicate. Almost immediately, though, we realized there were some guards who sympathized with us. Through practice, my powers have grown and we've found small — very small, really — ways to get messages to you."

"I knew it!" Sandra said. "I knew there were times you and dad were talking to me!" She smiled and both her parents beamed with pride that she had figured it out. They were also pleased with themselves that their efforts had been successful.

"But who's been holding you? Is it the fairies? That would not surprise me at all! And how did you escape finally?" Sandra asked. She was full of so many questions.

"Well, technically, my beautiful daughter, we haven't," Sandra's dad said as her mom seemed to choke up. "We're only here now thanks to your mom's powerful magic and your dad's charming ways." He smiled.

"This may be terribly upsetting to hear but it hasn't been the fairies," her mother said, wiping her tears and sounding stronger. "I don't know if you will find this surprising or not, but we have been held by none other than Calivon — one of our own kind."

"CALIVON!" Sandra burst out, now shouting. Calivon, the leader of the elfins and therefore the whole of the magical world. Sandra had always felt uneasy about him.

"Shhhhhhhhhhh!" Both her parents said at the same time as her dad shut the galley door completely.

"Yes, Calivon," her mother said with sadness and distaste rimming her words.

"But why?" said Sandra, knowing the answer as fast as she had asked the question. "For power, isn't it?"

Her parents nodded.

"He wants to remain ruler of the elfins and can't be if they know an heir to the Leezle line is still alive – let alone two of us," Sandra's mom confirmed.

"That's why he's always quizzing me and looking at me. Trying to trick me into saying who I am and who my parents were."

"Yes, and why you must be careful – as you are – around him!" her mother said. "Your locket kept you hidden but now that its magic spell has worn off, he can uncover you. How we worry about that! He suspects you are our daughter but he hasn't been completely sure and he doesn't believe you know your birthright. That is the only reason, we believe, that he has not moved to capture you as well. If he believes you stand in his way as the royal leader of the elfins and the magical world, you would be in even greater danger."

"But I have no interest in leading the elfins," Sandra protested.

"Neither did I," her mother said bleakly. "That's why we chose to live topside here on the human plane of reality and raise you on this wonderful tug, seeing and experiencing, the

JingleBelle Jackson

world. I have never been so happy as those times." Sanderson reached out and held his wife's hand.

"Calivon didn't care that your mom wasn't interested in ruling," Sandra's dad said. "We have pleaded with him many times to look at the proof and see that we were choosing a different life than the one he wanted. We didn't care if he was leader! We just wanted to be left alone, but he, and others like him, refused to be convinced. They insist it doesn't matter what we want. Their position is that your mother's birthright requires her to step-up, and that if he could find her, others who wanted the royal Leezle line to continue to rule could find her too."

"He was right, of course," Sandra's mother said bleakly. "I knew that my lineage was not something I could escape despite how hard I tried. I never should have put your father and you in danger as well."

"Nonsense!" said her father, pacing a bit. "We were meant to be together and, even with all that has happened, I would never have made a different choice.

"Sandra," he continued, changing the subject just a bit and smiling at her broadly now. "Can I just say how incredibly happy you have made us since the day you were born and how proud we are of who you have grown up to be?"

Naturally, those words set Sandra to crying again but her dad wasn't done.

"And you becoming South Pole Santa," he continued, shaking his head. "Such an achievement! No parents anywhere could have beamed more than yours did when we heard that

Santa saw your kind heart and knew that was exactly what the world needed as the most important quality to being the second Santa. It was a very hard day when we knew you had been selected and we couldn't be there. It was also one of our best days ever as parents. You're a beautiful daughter inside and out and we could not be prouder of you."

"Oh, Dad, I love you so much," Sandra said, hugging him.

"In addition, practically speaking, you getting selected as South Pole Santa has helped to keep you out of Calivon's reach," her mother continued. "He may suspect you are a Leezle and not like it, but if he were to take you, as he did us, the entire world would be looking for you. That would put a great deal of attention on the magical world, which, as you know, is against magical laws. As long as you seem content in your role and oblivious to who you likely really are, it seems he is, begrudgingly, willing to let you be, and for that we are very thankful. But you must never let down your guard with him! Not for a minute."

Sandra nodded, understanding that about Calivon without even knowing why. Now that she knew why, her vigilance with him would be more constant. The tricky thing she knew now would be to keep herself from harming him for taking her parents. For the first time ever, she knew what it was like to truly feel hate toward someone, and the feeling wasn't comfortable.

"No harm, dear. You mustn't," her mother said to Sandra, looking at her knowingly. She knew Sandra's thoughts because they had been her own for many years. "You mustn't let this one dictator take your happiness. He has taken enough from all of us. We will not give him that too."

Sandra listened and said nothing. She loved her parents, but on this topic, she would need to decide for herself how she felt and what she would do. Thinking about Calivon and all he had taken from her, right now doing nothing was not one of the options she was willing to consider.

Cassiopola chose to ignore her daughter's silence and moved on. "We need your help, darling," she said, and Sandra again gave her mother her full attention. Helping her parents was her top priority at any time on any day.

"This will be hard to hear but we were only able to escape today because, well, it was Christmas and Cappie was getting married," she paused her original thought, smiling happily. "Can I just say how happy we are for her? Tell her that for us, please. We will never be able to thank her deeply enough for raising you when we could not, and we are so pleased she has found love."

Her smile disappeared as she continued.

"Those two things – Christmas and Cappie's wedding – happening today apparently allowed Calivon to feel that everyone was preoccupied with the wedding and the festivities enough that he reduced the guard level on us for this one night. We were down to just one guard who has been kind and sympathetic to our situation. Your dad, using the charming ways that he mentioned earlier," they all smiled, "convinced him to look the other way for us to have a break outdoors for a change. After all, it was Christmas and an occasion worthy of such a rare treat. Once outside, I was able to use a masking spell to make it seem we were there still in his mind, and use my locket," she paused and showed Sandra her locket that looked just like Sandra's "to get us here on the *Mistletoe* for this incredibly wonderful moment of time."

"Moment of time! Please Mom and Dad, don't go back! Please!"

The two parents looked miserable.

"Sandra, that's where you can help," her mother said. "You must be very careful but there are allies willing to set us free. Calivon has many opponents. We've had confirmation recently that there's a parchment that is part of a book of ancient elfin history. There's always been a rumor of its existence but now we know absolutely that it's true. Thankfully, the parchment is impossible to destroy. It includes words that when spoken by a Leezle, on behalf of a Leezle, will release all chains or harm that has befallen any living Leezle and will keep them always protected from wrongdoing. If you can find that document, and read the words, then we can be released and never kept under capture or harm again. We know it's far too much to ask of you, our precious daughter, but there is no one else who can do this."

It felt big and scary and impossible, but Sandra knew she would search for it. She had faced danger before.

"Do not say 'yes' in haste, dear daughter," said her dad. "Calivon watches you already. He will watch you even more if he suspects your intentions. You would have to do this while doing everything else you do as well. He has spies everywhere! They must see you as you are every day. Do you understand? We don't care if it takes years as long as you stay safe."

"I understand, and it won't take me years," Sandra said, feeling in her bones that the words she spoke were true. She would set her parents free and no one would harm them again. Least of all Calivon, who as soon as her parents were free, would face her ire. She would be patient and hold her anger for him in check in deference to her parents. *But after that, he should be scared*, she thought only to herself. Though, looking at her mother, Sandra suspected her mom knew what Sandra was thinking.

"Of course, there are elfins who know where the papers are kept but none of them can be trusted," Sandra's father said. "We believe there are fairies who may know as well. That is the only lead we have. No matter who you talk with on this, you must be extremely cautious. Calivon cannot hear anything about what you are seeking. He believed, rightfully, that we were searching for it and hid us away as a result."

Sandra was barely listening to him. Something far more pressing and more important had to be said.

"Never mind about all of that! Don't go back! We can hide together! You can hide on the South Pole Village barge while we figure out what to do next. Or at the North Pole Village where Calivon would never think to look for you and the elves would never tell. Please stay here! I need you so much." Sandra was pleading with them, knowing her plan made more sense than their awful plan to return to wherever it was that Calivon had them locked away.

Sobs escaped Sandra's mother as her father held her. "Sandra, this is very hard for both of us, and especially for you, our treasured daughter, but there is something else we haven't told you yet and why we must go back." He glanced at the clock on the galley wall. "And soon, Cassie," he added, tipping his head to her at the clock. She nodded. "It's time. The spell will be wearing off and we must not put our guard in harm's way by having anyone find out we've escaped."

"Who cares about this guard?" Sandra pleaded. "He'll be fine in the end! Please don't go back, you've hardly been here!"

"We must, Sandra," her mother said softly, now looking at her with eyes begging her to understand. "We must because you have a sister and she's still there."

# # #

A sister! Sandra had a sister. A nine-year-old sister named Clementine. Her parents called her TinTin.

Sandra's feelings were so mixed about the news. Joy at the thought. Neutrality at believing the news, and even some jealousy, if she was being honest, that this TinTin was with her parents and she wasn't.

No matter how she felt about this news of a sister, though, she understood why her parents had to go back and why they hadn't been able to escape. Sandra's mother had been pregnant when the two had been taken so they had had TinTin almost the whole time they had been gone. Calivon had used the baby as a way to be sure her parents were compliant, making sure there was time each day when TinTin was held away from them so they would know how easy he could take her. The young couple missed their first daughter in a way that only parents who had been wrenched from their child could possibly understand, but they knew she was safe with Cappie on St. Annalise where they had managed to get the two of them to go. TinTin, on the other hand, had no one but the two of them.

A sister, Sandra thought, again and again. There was so much to remember from her parents' visit, instructions on where to start looking for the elfin document, who to seek out, and words of love and regret, but it was this news of having a sister above everything else that she kept coming back to. A sister that she had never met and didn't even know existed. The news was like a gift. It seemed right that Sandra had learned of TinTin on Christmas night.

Calivon had taken too much from her. She fought back her anger to keep it from igniting a fire inside that could not be quelled. She had to be calm, centered, cool even, if she was going to get her parents freed and meet her sister. Already plans for where to start her search were brewing. She would stay focused on her goal of setting them all free and then she would shift to making sure all of the magical world knew of Calivon's duplicity.

CHAPTER 2

Tossing, Turning and Finally Talking

Location: The Mistletoe

It had been three days and Sandra had not told anyone about her parents' visit. She had asked for a little time to rest, which everyone understood. Even without the surprise visit and the big wedding she had just celebrated with Cappie and Thomas, she usually needed time to rest the week after Christmas. Being South Pole Santa was a big job year round but a gigantic job in November and December. To be honest, all of her friends were tired as well, and everyone, including Squawk, welcomed the extra time to rest.

This year, unbeknownst to others, after the visit from her parents, Sandra felt emotional and raw, and simply not capable of talking with anyone without sobbing. Her parents' visit had brought up feelings of grief and despair that

JingleBelle Jackson

she thought she had let go of a long time ago and she knew only Cappie would truly understand. When her parents had first disappeared, the loss had been devastating to her and Cappie but, eventually, they had found a new normal and their happy life on St. Annalise had helped make the abrupt, severe loss more bearable. Since then, thanks to Cappie, and Sandra's own tendency to always having a positive outlook, she had lived a happy life. She had kept a belief deep inside her that her parents were still alive and still watching over her. That belief had given her confidence and allowed her to be joyful despite the loss.

Despite her need to be alone, Sandra knew she couldn't keep her friends away long. She suspected the only reason Squawk and Em weren't there already was most likely due to Birdie and Spence holding them back to let her rest for a few days. She wanted to tell them all her news, as the friends shared pretty much everything with each other. She wanted to be joyful and confident when she talked about it all, though, and, day after day, those feelings were eluding her. She found her days to be consumed by her thoughts, which went round and round in circles without any answers or solutions. When she wasn't thinking of the Christmas night visit, she was sleeping. A lot. She would move from the elation of "my parents are alive!" to the despair of "I may never see them again" in seconds. It was exhausting and she would handle it by heading back to sleep some more where she blissfully didn't have to think about any of it. She finally recognized

12

she was getting nowhere on her own and needed to talk to someone. She planned to find Birdie but it was Gunny who came walking up the dock that day and Gunny who she knew she could safely tell.

"Hey, my favorite Santa," Gunny called out as he walked up, looking at her a little puzzled as he got closer. She looked pale and disheveled. He had only seen her look that way one other time – the week after his least favorite guy on the planet, Jason Annalise, broke her heart. "Everything okay with you, Sand?" he asked, watching her carefully. "Something happen? Have you seen fairy boy lately?" He didn't want to ask, wasn't even sure his own heart could stand it if she was this upset over that guy again, but he had to know.

Sandra burst into tears.

Gunny felt anger, and maybe even some jealousy at Jason for causing this hurt, but he would deal with that later. For now, he needed to keep the Santa he cherished from collapsing as she had before.

"Oh, Sandra, he's not worth it. He's just not. You deserve so much more than him." *Or me*, he thought ironically, but kept that part to himself.

Sandra managed to dry her tears pretty quickly. *Maybe I'm just all cried out on this,* she thought, finding some comfort in the idea.

"No, Gunny, it's not about Jason. I haven't seen him." Gunny's heart returned to its normal beat. The guy grinded on him but right now Gunny was the one holding the girl.

Sandra took a deep breath. "I haven't been able to tell anyone about this but it's about my parents. They were here."

"You mean like in a dream?" Gunny asked carefully, not wanting to upset her but knowing it was impossible.

"Nope, I mean as in physically here on the *Mistletoe,* after the wedding, holding me after all these years away. And now they're gone again." Her voice quivered but she held it together and said flatly all in one breath for great effect, "It was great and hard all at the same time and, it turns out, that, if that wasn't enough of a shock already, I have a sister. Named TinTin."

"Let's go sit down in the galley, okay? And I'll make you some lunch?" Gunny suggested, realizing he was hearing far bigger news than he could possibly have anticipated. Holding her, she felt too thin. He knew she hadn't eaten. Feeding her and listening were his top two priorities.

She nodded while he got her seated and headed to check out what she had in the fridge. Eggs, some cheese, some fruit – he could work with that. "I'm going to make you the best omelet ever," he declared. "Now start talking."

CHAPTER 3

A Big Tale From a Tiny Source

Location: The Mistletoe

Sandra had talked and talked and talked and talked. Gunny had mostly just listened, asking only an occasional question for clarification, usually while she paused to take some bites of the omelet he had prepared along with some cinnamon toast and slices of fruit.

Her story was so much bigger than he could have ever guessed and his heart tugged, understanding how hard the last three days must have been for her trying to process it all on her own. Now, having heard it all, his goal was two-fold: get her back to her happy place and help her free her parents. Oh, and kick Calivon's butt. You mess with Sandra and her family and you mess with him and the Holiday family.

"So, where can we start?" he asked her, not even considering she would do it on her own. For once, she didn't object.

15

This was too big and important for her to even pretend she could do it by herself.

"That's the part I'm not sure about," Sandra said hesitantly. "My parents said they thought that the fairies would know so I'm going to start with Jason. As the new king, he should have access to everything, including any helpful, secret information."

Gunny didn't like the idea but he said nothing. He was sure Jason, like himself, would be happy to do anything he could to help Sandra and he was pretty sure Sandra was right that Jason could likely use his power as king to get her some answers. *Why did it always have to be Jason?* he thought. He wanted help for Sandra from any source but that guy.

"He won't be able to help." Though he had wanted to say as much, it wasn't Gunny who had spoken.

"Quisp?" Sandra asked, surprised to hear the little fairy's voice. Sandra looked all around before she finally spotted her pretty face peeking out from behind a pineapple on the counter. "How long have you been there?"

"Two days, Sandra. I'm sorry for not telling you but I've been worried about you and I was afraid you would make me go away," the tiny fairy said tentatively. Sandra had first met Quisp on a visit to the South Pole outpost where Quisp had been living and helping the elves there. She had been very shy, maybe due to her tiny size, but was becoming more self-assured as she spent time with Sandra and her friends.

"So, you heard what I told Gunny?"

"Yes, I know I shouldn't have listened but I love you, Sandra, and want to help. And before you say it, I won't tell anyone."

"You absolutely can't, Quisp. It would put me and my parents in danger."

"I know! I would never do that! I can help, Sandra. I know something about this. Jason Annalise won't. The fairies who know where to find the book of elfin knowledge are not shans or shanelles. They're saneers." She whispered the name and came closer to Sandra and Gunny to talk even softer. "They're a secret order of fairies that most fairies believe are only a myth or maybe they just prefer to believe the saneers are a myth. I don't blame them but the saneers are the keepers of secrets and spells, and very real."

This was the most Sandra had ever heard Quisp say. Since the sky writing she had done before Christmas, the tiny fairy had become surer of herself and less scared. Now she was speaking quietly but with knowingness. Gunny and Sandra were locked on every word she was saying.

"Quisp, how do you know all of this?" Sandra asked.

"My mother said she knew one a long time ago," she said. "The saneer made me little."

"What?" both Sandra and Gunny asked loudly in unison.

"Fairies seek out saneers when they need a favor. My father was missing and my mother sought out a saneer for answers. In exchange for the help finding my father, the saneer took my size for his own. This is rare but possible in the world of

17

JingleBelle Jackson

fairies. My mother said he took more than he had said and just smiled weirdly at her when she objected. She told me many times that she would never have used the saneers if she had known the true cost ahead but, truly, I don't mind being this little, knowing it meant my dad returned."

Sandra felt a huge new love and respect for her tiny friend. Quisp was very brave to trust anyone after what her family had been through.

"Sandra, you cannot seek out the help of a saneer lightly! They always require a heavy price and they cannot be trusted! They seem nice on the outside and they hold, and know, secrets but they are also spell casters and enchanters who love to practice and manipulate."

"I will be the one to contact them," Gunny said. "You are far too important to the world, Sandra, and they will find it harder to trick or manipulate me."

"Gunny, no! You're important to me and this is my burden to bear," Sandra said, alarmed at his suggestion.

" . . . *squawk*! . . . it's all of ours!"

"Squawk! What are you doing here? Where did you come from?" Sandra had questions for the big macaw as he flew into the room.

" . . . *squawk*! . . . couldn't stay away . . . *squawk* . . . stayed quiet . . . heard it all . . ."

"And so did we," Sandra's best friend Birdie said, as she and Sandra's other best friend, Spencer, stepped into the galley from the deck, looking sheepish. "I'm sorry, Sandra, but we saw you go inside with Gunny and were going to surprise you but then overheard what you were saying and instead decided to be quiet and listen instead of interrupting."

Sandra looked at all three with a little frustration before she motioned them all in. First Quisp eavesdropped and now all the rest of her friends! "You shouldn't have listened without telling me, but I would have told you all anyway and now I don't have to tell it again. I know you love me so I forgive you. But don't do it again!" She wagged her finger sternly at them all.

"We won't, promise, but you should have told us," Spencer said, coming up to his friend and hugging her. "We're more than your best friends, we're your family, too."

" . . . especially me . . . *squawk*!"

"So did you also hear what Quisp was telling us?" Sandra asked.

"Most of it. We agree with Gunny. One of us should seek out these saneers. Not you, Sandra, definitely not you," Birdie said.

Sandra was already shaking her head, listening to the words. That was not negotiable as far as she was concerned. Her parents, her sister, her problem, her risk. But she didn't want to argue right now.

"We'll talk through a plan," was all she said to them. Gunny knew that was code for "I'm going to do it myself" but he kept quiet. He felt just as firm that he would do it himself. Having her in danger was not acceptable.

"For now, I'm feeling much better knowing you all know what has happened. My parents are alive! I wish Cappie was here to tell but I'm so glad I have you all to tell," Sandra said, smiling through tears that welled up.

"We couldn't believe the news! It's so great," Spence said.

"And a sister, Sand?! No way! Seems unbelievable. What a Christmas night you had!" Birdie said.

"Isn't that wild?" Sandra said with not quite as much enthusiasm as telling them her parents were alive. "She's nine!"

" . . . TinTin . . ." Squawk said. ". . . like a can . . ." The group all laughed a big, hearty laugh that was more about relieving a little pressure than from how funny they found Squawk. They all needed a moment of levity.

"Sand, not to change the subject, but part of the reason we're here is that Santa and Mrs. Claus are done with their visit here on the island and heading back to the North Pole this morning. We thought you would like to see them off," Birdie said.

"Oh, my sand dunes! I've been so caught up in my own drama I've forgotten to check on them!" Sandra said, moving to the door. "I need to get a shower and change my clothes. Run ahead, everyone, and hold them here so they don't leave without me."

None of the group moved. Not one of them was sure she should be by herself. She looked at them and understood.

"I'm okay," she said. "Thanks to all of you, my dear friends, I really am. I needed to talk things out and I needed your love and support. There's a big challenge ahead of me," she paused as she saw they all were about to object so she amended it. "There is a big challenge ahead for *us* and a big fight, too." She didn't say who the fight would be with – they all knew it was Calivon. She had sparks in her eyes now thinking about it.

"Now go!" Sandra finished, being firm with all of them.

South Pole Santa could be bossy, Gunny thought, feeling a little amused. He liked Sandra to feel more sassy then sad. *Calivon should be scared.* He smiled at the thought.

CHAPTER 4

Tucking in For Slumber Month

Location: Next stop: North Pole Village!

Sandra had caught up with Santa and Mrs. Claus in time to not just see them off but to go with them. Yes, there was drama going on in her life, but talking with her friends had given her renewed hope and that had helped her shake her mood. Well, that and being around the elves. She helped round up all the remaining elves on the island for the trip back to North Pole Village for Slumber Month. It was important to her that they all get their much needed rest and she wanted to be there to tuck them all in. Even more than that, she was lonesome to see Em. Santa had sent her back to North Pole Village with some of the other elves earlier in the week to help with the after-Christmas clean-up.

The feisty little delgin had become much more than Sandra's perfect mode of transportation. Em was family to

23

her. A little sister. A tiny mentee. A giant-sized hero. Em filled all those roles for Sandra, and she loved her.

"Redwood, there you are! I knew you were here still! C'mon, let's go. You're the last one. Everyone else is already loaded in the coaches," Sandra said to the tall elf sitting on one of the beaches watching the waves. "Everything okay?" she asked as she got closer.

"Everything is really great, Sandra. Just feeling a little lonesome for home," Redwood said. "It's the first Christmas I've ever been away from my family in Iceland. It was great and all, just a little different."

Sandra felt terrible for forgetting that Redwood might be homesick! He had chosen to move to the North Pole and help build toys but that didn't mean he wouldn't miss his friends and family.

"Oh, Redwood! How awful of me to forget such a thing. Has it been okay? Did you get to talk to your family at least on Christmas?"

"I did and I wouldn't trade this experience for anything! I love making toys for the children. You and Santa have been great to me, and the North Pole elves are fun. I just have a minute now and then of homesickness."

"You ready to go back then?" Sandra asked.

"More than ready!" The lumbering elf jumped up and went running limberly down the beach to where the Reindeer Express coaches were ready to go. He and Sandra piled in and the coaches lifted off.

"Next stop North Pole," Zoomer called out cheerily and they zoomed off into the sky.

At the Pole, as usual, as soon as they landed, the elf marching band led by Ellen and Buddy came marching in formation down the street playing a new song for them. The musicians were playing "Mele Kalikimaka", a popular Hawaiian Christmas song with a happy tropical beat. Both Santa and Sandra enjoyed hearing a new carol in the line-up and were particularly happy seeing the smiling elf faces. The band stopped mid-song as soon as they saw both Santas and rushed them at once in a big elf hug. Every care Sandra had melted away like butter in the hot sun, under their cheerful attention.

"Ho Ho Ho!" Santa boomed, loving all the attention as well and making no move to wiggle out of the big hug.

"SANDRA!" came the loudest shout possible from down the street. Anyone who didn't know Em would likely never believe that much sound could come out of that size of an elf. Em, though, was nothing if not more than she seemed at all times. The group there that afternoon knew to make a path between where the sound was coming from and Sandra. In far less time than seemed possible, the little delgin had flung herself into Sandra's arms.

"Thank you, Em, for such a warm welcome," Sandra said sincerely and hugging her back. "It's only been a few days but I'm lucky to be so loved and missed."

Mrs. Claus had gotten in on the hug too as every elf loved her like a mom and now she worked to get unwound and bring out the practicalities of what mattered to elves.

JingleBelle Jackson

"Who is hungry?' she asked, already knowing the answer.

"I am!" every elf and Santa and Sandra hollered at the same time with their hands in the air.

"Then follow me for a homemade dinner with homemade cookies and cocoa for dessert before Slumber Month begins for all tonight!"

"Hooray!" the elves all shouted, following Santa and Mrs. Claus down the street. All but Em, who pulled on Sandra, keeping her back.

"Sandra, I'm going back with you," Em said with her hands crossed, looking serious.

"Now, Em, we've had this conversation," said Sandra carefully. "You need your sleep just like everyone other elf. Maybe even more so because you work so hard for me and the world's children."

"I can sleep at St. Annalise. I promise," Em implored with a whine to her voice that proved to Sandra how tired the little delgin really was.

"You could, but not as well as you will sleep here. I promise you, young lady, that nothing real exciting will happen and I'll come get you as soon as you are awake," Sandra said, hoping to calm her.

"It's not fair. Squawk doesn't have to sleep."

Ah, so this is the real issue, Sandra thought. Em and Squawk were very competitive about everything, but especially about getting Sandra's time and attention.

"Squawk is not an elf or a delgin. Being just a bird, he doesn't need as much rest." Sandra was glad he wasn't there right now. Squawk would be very upset with her if he had heard her call him "just" a bird. She didn't really mean it as much as she was trying to calm Em's concerns.

"You're right. Delgins are very special," Em said, yawning and rubbing her eyes.

"Em, you are the very most special delgin I have ever met." *And the only one*, Sandra thought. "I am so lucky to have you in my life and I already can hardly wait until you and the others wake up and we can start on new adventures."

"I'm hungry," Em said in return, yawning again.

Sandra took her little friend's hand, and the two ran to catch up with the others so they didn't miss out on Mrs. Claus' dinner and, most especially, her cookies!

CHAPTER 5

Beach Talk

Location: St. Annalise

"Here you are! Happy New Year, bestie! We missed you at the party last night," Birdie said, plopping down next to where Sandra sat, beach sand sifting through her hands, as she stared out to sea in contemplation. She always went to the beach – any beach – to think through her next steps in challenging times. Being by the water helped to calm her and the sea air blew doubts and fears right out of her mind.

Sandra gave Birdie a quick smile and patted the sand next to her for Birdie to sit down. "I meant to go, Bird, I really did. But then I just couldn't. I'm just not in a party mood lately, thinking about my parents, and I didn't want to bring people down. Plus, I just got back from tucking the elves in. They were all so tired but it took me extra time to convince Em to stay and get in her needed rest too. You know how she

JINGLEBELLE JACKSON

always wants to stay with me. Being a delgin and a Northern Lights elf, though, she probably needs her sleep more than most of them." She paused thinking of her wonderful delgin with great affection.

"Anyway, when you put it all together, I really just wanted to sleep more than stay up last night. Did you kiss anyone at midnight?" Sandra teased. She knew Birdie's main squeeze, Crow, Gunny's brother, was still back in Texas, giving Birdie some space from their relationship.

"Of course not!" Birdie said, alarmed at the very idea. "I tried to talk to Crow but he's still not taking my calls. He should have answered. I had something big to tell him! Listen to this." She dug out a piece of paper from her back pocket and read it to Sandra.

"My dear daughter, you have been given a reprieve. Sam will not be arriving this month. He is in service as a medical apprentice at a regional hospital where they are shorthanded, and he has asked that he be given more time so they can locate a temporary replacement for him. I have agreed to a start date of March 1 for you both but not a minute later. With fondness and great affection, your mother."

"He's not coming?" Sandra asked, just to be sure she understood what Birdie had read. Birdie's mother had surprised Birdie with a fiancé named Sam Dalon. It turned out the two had been promised to each other when they were toddlers and the time had come for the marriage as far as Birdie's parents were concerned. Birdie had protested that she didn't even know "this Sam guy" so her mother had relented to giving them a month to get to know each other before their engagement was officially declared. Birdie wanted nothing to do with any of it but had agreed to meet Sam – with no intention at all of honoring the engagement – in order to keep peace with her mother.

"Well he is, but not till March," Birdie answered hesitantly, still looking at the paper as if it held more answers.

"That's great, isn't it?" Sandra asked, not sure how Birdie felt about the news. "Maybe, by then, he won't come at all."

"Sandra, you know my mother. That is never going to happen."

Sandra nodded. That was probably true. "How do you feel about the change in date?" she asked.

"Confused, to be honest," Birdie said, knowing she could share her deepest feelings with her best friend. "I'm happy about it since I really have no interest in meeting some guy I was promised to – and him to me – when we were both so young. And I miss Crow so I'm glad this means I'll get to see him. At the same time, I feel frustrated that it's been put off and I'll still have to deal with it. And weirdly, I think I feel . . ."

Birdie's words trailed off and Sandra had to push on her to finish.

"You think you feel what, Bird? Don't leave me dangling here."

Birdie turned and faced her friend before she blurted out, "I think I feel intrigued."

"Intrigued?" Sandra asked, feeling confused.

"Maybe that's not the best word but I am definitely impressed that this guy – Sam – would stand up to my mother and for such a good reason. He's working to aid people in need! That's a pretty cool thing to do. I don't want to like him at all, but I have to admit that I find that part of him to be, well, interesting and intriguing."

She flung herself back flat in the sand dune with her arms wide open. "And now that I think about it, liking that about him, liking anything about him, makes me like him even less!"

Sandra laughed out loud. So did Birdie. Sometimes relationships of any kind at all, since they were always about feelings, could be so full of conflicting emotions.

"Well, you have time to think about it all and March is not that far away, really," Sandra said. "Maybe we could work on the Academy of Kindness full time this month since it sounds like we'll both have time," Sandra suggested.

"I love that idea!" Birdie declared, sitting back up with enthusiasm. "I have lots of suggestions. But first, have you heard anything from Cappie and Thomas?"

"Nope." Sandra said simply. "Which is exactly how it should be with the two of them on their honeymoon. I made them promise to keep the time just to themselves."

"Six weeks away is a long time for you and Cappie not to talk though, isn't it?" Birdie pushed a little bit, wishing Cappie would call and, if she didn't, hoping Sandra would try to reach her.

Sandra nodded her head. "The longest ever. I'm not sure we've even done six days not talking, but we both know we need to get used to a little more space. This is the perfect time to begin. She's on her honeymoon and the elves have Slumber Month so I have time off. She knew it was the calmest time to go." She couldn't help but give an ironic laugh at the end and roll her eyes a little bit at Birdie. It was only hours after Cappie and Thomas had left on their trip that Sandra's parents had appeared. Still, she was glad she and Cappie had agreed they wouldn't talk till they were back. Sandra would never forgive herself if she had interfered with the couple's special time away. Even this really big news could wait until they were back.

"Have you decided what you're going to do next?" Birdie asked. "Have you talked to Jason about it yet?"

Sandra shook her head. She had planned to talk to him about it, she still was planning to talk to him about it, in fact, but he had been pulled away for fairy business and she thought it was just as well. Quisp had said he wouldn't be able to help her anyway, that only a saneer could, so she wasn't sure how much she should even tell him or when. Jason being away gave her time to think and she found that a plan was starting to form.

"I think I'll have Quisp help me meet a saneer," she said, talking straight ahead, knowing her friend would prefer she didn't.

"I don't like it, and I wish you wouldn't, but I'm pretty sure I would do the same thing," Birdie said, reaching out and

JingleBelle Jackson

giving her friend's hand a quick squeeze of love and support. "Please don't meet with any of them without us, though. You know we are all for one and one for all."

Sandra smiled at her friend and her three musketeers' bravado. She also changed the subject as she pushed up off the sand.

"What fun can we have while I'm off this month and you don't have to entertain your suitor?"

"He's not my suitor!" Birdie protested, getting up too.

"Okay, your Romeo-from-afar. Your wanna-be-boyfriend. Your husband-in-waiting. Your 'intriguing'," she paused and made parenthesis signs in the air, "medic."

"Quit it, Sand!" Birdie said, tossing sand at her friend who was laughing out loud over her clever teasing. Sandra reached down and tossed some sand back at Birdie, who tossed even more at her before they both broke into big laughs and headed down the beach toward home, brushing the sand they had just thrown out of each other's hair.

CHAPTER 6

Quisp Has a Lead

Location: The Mistletoe

"I can't help you, Sandra. Seriously, I cannot." Quisp sat high on a shelf out of Sandra's reach with her arms crossed uncharacteristically.

"Quisp, you're my only link to them!" Sandra declared again to her tiny friend. "You're the only one I know who has ever even mentioned the saneers, let alone actually had some interaction with them. I have nowhere else to turn."

"Yes, you do! Turn away! I should never have said anything. I don't even know why I did." The little fairy was clearly in distress. "It just came out and now I don't know how to undo it."

Sandra rushed to calm her friend. "Quisp, will you come down here with me? Please? I can't stand to have you upset and I like it so much better when you are close by."

35

Quisp fretted back and forth and finally buzzed to a shelf closer to Sandra.

"Okay, let's review the situation," Sandra said. "Like usual, you have helped me. You've saved me so much time trying to figure out where I could get help and you already knew I could get it from the saneers. Thank you. You must know I won't stop till I have answers. These are my parents! And a sister. I can't stop. If you can't help me, then I have to find someone who will."

"Okay," said Quisp quietly.

"Okay you'll help?"

"No! Okay you can find someone else."

"Quisp!" Sandra blurted out exasperatedly. Her outburst chased Quisp back up to the higher shelf. She had been going round and round with her tiny friend for days on this topic and making no progress. "Who am I supposed to find? You know you're my only lead! Just give me one clue." She stomped around the room, beseeching the fairy to help.

Finally, the tiny fairy could carry the burden her friend was putting on her no longer so she shifted it to another.

"Wistle knows the saneers too," she whispered almost silently but Sandra heard her.

"Wistle knows? Thank you, Quisp!" Sandra blew a kiss to her tiny friend, headed out the door and off to find the fairy who was a sort-of friend. More friend now that she was dating

Crow's twin brother Ghost but, nonetheless, not necessarily a friend to be trusted. But, right now, knowing Wistle knew something Sandra needed desperately to know, Sandra felt they'd be getting a lot closer.

"Tell Squawk when you see him that I might be late," she called back.

CHAPTER 7

Fairies that Fairies are Scared Of

Location: St. Annalise

Sandra had headed over to the St. Annalise branch office of the United Fairy Organization (UFO) near the school where the island-based fairies liked to hang out.

"Wistle? Wistle?" Sandra called out from the empty lobby area into where she could see fairies beyond the front desk.

The fairy came buzzing out, looking irritated, when she heard Sandra's voice.

"Uh, excuse me, Sandra, but per Christina Annalise, this club is for fairy folk only. Yes, you may be a Santa and yes, for some totally unknown reason, our King of Fairies may think he is crazy about you, but that still doesn't mean even you can come barging into this off-limits area."

"I know, Wistle, and I apologize. I wouldn't have come, of course, if it wasn't really important." Sandra sputtered out, feeling uncomfortable as all the fairies gathered there looked her way with clear fairy disdain.

"I can think of nothing this important," Wistle said, stating out loud what the others seemed to clearly feel as well. Some seemed to be more than just annoyed with her. Did she see glimpses of pure dislike in a few eyes? A shiver ran down her spine and she lowered her voice.

"I need to know about the saneers," she said, leaning in to Wistle.

"What?" Wistle sputtered, sparks of fear flying through her eyes as she saw that a few of the others were now looking their way suspiciously. "Why, Sandra?" Wistle asked, now going to full-size and taking Sandra strongly by the elbow. "I don't believe I heard you correctly with all the noise in here. Let's go somewhere more private that is not here." She practically shoved Sandra out the door, down the path, over the island meadow, across two beachy areas, and down the dock until she got her clear to the *Mistletoe* and locked the galley door before she spoke again.

"Are you mad?" Wistle stated, pacing the floor. "You come into the UFO and start spouting about saneers! Do you know the new level of crazy that is? No fairy in their right mind would even say the word out loud and half of them don't even know who or what a saneer is — and they're fairies!

Enchantments A South Pole Santa Adventure

The rest are likely to report that someone was looking for one and I'm not sure I can keep them from that." Wistle was already thinking ahead and scheming on how she might help her clearly-gone-mad-mostly-a-friend friend.

"You think they heard me?" Sandra asked. "I was speaking low."

"Yeah, right," Wistle said with sarcasm dripping in her voice as Sandra looked hopefully at her. "They're fairies, Sandra! We hear everything!" Sandra knew that was true.

"They'll report me?"

"Yes," Wistle replied, looking worried and pacing.

"To the saneers?"

"Yes."

"And then what? Will they come looking for me?"

Wistle didn't want to worry her friend, there were still some things they could possibly do, but she answered honestly.

"Yes."

"Good! I wish I had known that," Sandra resisted looking up to where Quisp was hiding and giving away what took her over to the UFO looking for Wistle in the first place, "so I could have bothered you all sooner."

Wistle said nothing. She slid onto a seat and took in what Sandra had said. She had always felt like this Santa was overrated by many and now she had proof that Sandra simply was not of sound mind.

JingleBelle Jackson

"Sandra," Wistle said carefully. "*No one* wants a visit from the saneers." She said the last word very quietly, almost as if she wasn't even saying it but just implying it.

"Wistle, I don't want to tell you why, but I need their assistance with a pressing matter."

"There is surely another way to resolve whatever you think you need them for," Wistle said glumly. "But it probably doesn't matter now, anyway, since someone will clearly tell them what just happened at the club. They will come." She said it resolutely and sadly.

"They'll send more than one?"

"I don't really know," Wistle said. "I try never to think of them, as every fairy who knows of them has been trained to do. For most of us, they are just a myth. Fairies that are not even safe for fairies. A myth we would prefer wasn't of the fairy realm.

"Please, Sandra, as your friend, do not meet with them. And if they insist, please tell them nothing and for fairy globes sake, do not ask anything of them!"

"Wistle, I have a matter of urgency . . ."

"It's getting dark!" Wistle interrupted her. "I'm sorry, Sandra, I must go. I dare not be here if they come. There are a few things for me to tell you. They come only at night and can be seen only in the dark. They are charming but often speak around a matter. They collect things that are precious. Things that are priceless. Things that have almost no value to

42

them but great value to the one giving. Be careful, Sandra. Be careful!" She said the last as she orbed out the window.

Things like Quisp's size, Sandra thought, as she looked out the galley window. Wistle was right. The sun was setting. Sandra felt nervous but determined.

"Quisp?" Sandra called out. She knew the fairy was there somewhere hiding and had heard the conversation with Wistle. "Quisp, you mustn't stay here. They have taken enough from you and I need a favor. Go and find where Squawk is and help me keep him away from here and any of my other friends that might come this way. I know they're bigger than you but find any way you must to keep them away. This meeting is to be only between the saneers and myself. Do you understand, Quisp?"

The little fairy flew down close to her, crying. "Yes," she sputtered, heading toward the open window without hesitation. "Oh, Sandra, I'm so sorry."

"Nonsense," Sandra said, sounding stronger than she was feeling. *What had she done?*

CHAPTER 8

Meeting the Saneers

Location: The Mistletoe

No saneer appeared that night.

At least that was what Sandra thought when she awoke from dozing off waiting for them. It was just after midnight and she was stretched out in one of the big lounge chairs on the back deck of the *Mistletoe*. It was one of her favorite places to sleep and she never felt afraid. Until about five minutes after she awoke. She had a sharp feeling of fear and she jumped up out of the chair to shake it off. That's when she saw the two glow-in-the-dark orbs approaching the *Mistletoe* from the starboard side – the side away from the dock. Sandra knew it could only be the saneers. She took a deep breath and felt her parents' energy around her. "Yes, we're here," she heard her mother whisper in her ear. "We do not like this but you do not face them alone."

45

Sandra felt stronger immediately and was able to put a smile on her face as two glowing fairies transformed to full-size in front of her on her deck. She realized they were not quite fairies as she knew fairies. Despite their glow, they had a dark inner side to them. Their mouths were smiling but not their eyes. Most fairies she knew simply never smiled – not with their mouths nor their eyes. Jason was the one exception she knew and even he had never been much of a smiler. He had gotten better but most people would likely describe him as more "intense" than "friendly."

"Hello to you, dear one," the first saneer to land on her deck said in what Sandra would later describe as a monotone cheerfulness.

"Hello," Sandra said in return, wearing her own fake-a-smile expression. *Two could be good at this,* she thought.

"Greetings to you," said the second saneer. *Better make that three could be good at this,* she amended in her head.

"I am Kilt and this is Tambler. We understand you have asked for us."

"I believe you know that I am Cassandra Clausmonetsiamydelaterradotdotdot." She said her full formal name to help set the tone of this as a business meeting and to buy a little time to help calm her racing heart. She hoped it helped with the first because it hadn't done anything for the second. Her heart continued to beat at an uncomfortable speed.

"Ah yes, the Santa girl with the intriguing last name," the one called Kilt said, still smiling. "We understand it comes from a game your parents played with you?"

"Not a game, exactly," Sandra said, happy to explain her name. "We lived all over the world and they added on to our last name in tribute to those places. When we left France, my dad picked Monet. When we left Thailand, he selected Siam. For Vietnam, he selected Ly and my mom picked de la Terra when we left living in several Latin America countries. I added the dot dot dots so people know it will grow again."

"I see, I see," said Kilt, this time actually looking amused as if Sandra was something unexpected to them. "Well for Tambler and me, I fear you will find us lacking as we each have only one name." Tambler giggled at that.

"They both seem like fine names," Sandra said generously and meaning it. So far this seemed to be going fine.

"Was there something you needed from us, fine lady?" Tambler now asked of her. "We heard you had asked of us."

Done with the chit chat, Sandra thought. Fine with her if they got right down to business.

"Perhaps," she said. "First, I would like to secure your word that our discussions here will remain private to just the three of us. I understand that the saneers pride themselves on guarding confidential inquiries and information, and it is of the utmost importance to me that that is indeed the case." She had actually not heard this from anyone but she hoped setting that expectation would help to prevent any chance Calivon would hear of this meeting. "Do I have your word?"

She looked at them both as they nodded and Kilt spoke for both. "You have our word."

Sandra was stubborn. "From you as well, Tambler?

The saneer looked surprised. He gave a look to Kilt and then verbally agreed as well. "Yes, from me as well."

"Thank you both," Sandra said. "Then I feel we can continue." She came right to the point. "I desire to see the ancient documents of the elfins. I understand that, for reasons I am completely mystified by, as being part elfin myself, that these historical documents – the pride of the elfin people surely – are kept away from us and held in a secret location. I simply need to be provided the location or even just copies of the documents themselves, I really don't need the actual originals to satisfy my curiosity regarding my kind's history and beginnings." It wasn't entirely the truth but it was partly true.

"You are just curious?" Kilt said with disbelief evident in his voice.

"I am. From my human side, I have access to papers from almost any country regarding how it was established. For instance, if I was from the United States of America, I could read their Declaration of Independence. I also have access to many versions of the Bible and of many very old documents from the beginning of humankind. But from my elfin side there are no historical documents available for reviewing?

That does not seem right." She spoke loudly and realized this issue, regardless of why she had started down this path, was one she believed in. History and facts should not be controlled by a few but available to all. "So I ask you for your assistance, though this seems like an unimportant matter to you both, which I understand as it is not your history," She took every chance to put it in as small of a light as she could. "It is quite important for me and my kind. Can you help?"

The two said nothing but turned from her and orbed to a place above the *Mistletoe*. She stood still and firm, leaning just slightly on a deck chair to calm any shakes she might have so they would not see them. They returned to full-size standing again on her deck.

"We can provide you with information regarding what you seek," Kilt said. "Naturally, we will need payment."

Careful, Sandra heard her mother say, but Sandra ignored her. She was prepared to pay.

"Of course," she said in return. "What is your price?"

"We require this vessel."

CHAPTER 9

A Disagreement About an Agreement

Location: The Mistletoe

"This vessel!" Sandra wasn't even angry as much as she was truly incredulous. Of course she was not going to pay for the information with the *Mistletoe*. Her parents would understand that choice. She would work toward another option.

"That is not an acceptable payment," she stated in return. "Let us continue with our negotiations. I am prepared to offer you a sizable amount of money." She didn't know where she would get it from but she knew she could get it for something so important.

"Money! What need do we have for money?" Tambler said. "This is not worth our time."

"Then would you appreciate property? There are some fine lands available, away from all others where you could

51

JingleBelle Jackson

live topside without interruption from humankind." Sandra was now thinking of some of the special atolls near to St. Annalise. She didn't particularly like that they were so close to her home but was prepared to live with the discomfort for such an important prize.

"We have no need for land," Tambler said. "I suggest again, Kilt, that this meeting should end."

Kilt, though, seemed to be mulling the choices while looking directly and unwaveringly at Sandra.

"You could pay us with time," he finally said. "We like time."

No, Sandra! That is not acceptable and surely a trick! Her father now was shouting so loud at her she couldn't believe the saneers didn't hear him — even though she knew the voice was heard only by her. She herself struggled to dismiss his voice.

"Tell me more about what a payment of time looks like to you," she said to the smiling saneer.

No, Sandra! Both her parents were shouting now.

"Why, it would barely be anything you would notice," said Kilt with his best sincere insincere voice. "We simply would take a little time here and there that you barely would even miss, I'm sure. Simple little minutes, hardly any kind of payment at all when you think about it for something as important as what you are asking for from us." Tambler was now smiling again and nodding his head in agreement, which made Sandra more nervous than ever.

Enchantments A South Pole Santa Adventure

"And if I were to agree?" she said louder than needed but in an attempt to drown out her parents' strong objections ringing through her head. "When could I receive the documents?"

"That, we could not say for sure for we can only provide you the information on where they are kept. When you accessed them would have to be left up to you."

"I would like several days to consider this," Sandra said carefully. She was young with a long life ahead of her and inclined to believe she could afford to give up minutes of her time, but she knew she needed to give it careful consideration.

"You cannot," Kilt stated. "This is our offer. Time from your life in exchange for information on what you have asked of us. You need to decide now. We will not return."

Sandra was feeling unsure. Her parents were screaming in her head, her own good sense was shouting "no", and she knew her friends would disagree, but she knew no other way.

"Yes, I will – " Sandra was interrupted with a flash so bright that it blinded all three of them on the tug.

"What is the meaning of this?" Jason Annalise, king of fairies, looking more stern and regal than any king had ever appeared, demanded, as he came to full-size on the deck of the *Mistletoe*. Sandra couldn't remember a single time when she had ever been happier to see him. The feeling, definitely, did not seem mutual.

"Sandra, you're talking with saneers?" Jason looked at her completely confused before turning to the two, who seemed

53

nonplused to see him there though he was their king and it was an honor to be in his presence.

"You two, what business do you have here?" Neither said anything while Jason stared at them until Tambler finally spoke. "You would have to ask her. She requested this meeting."

"Either way, frankly our business with your beauty here is completed," Kilt said. "I do believe we received a yes from her on payment." Sandra went to object and state that she was only going to say, "Yes, I will need more time. We cannot complete this transaction, as your costs are too high," but the saneer pushed on.

"Sandra, this has been our pleasure and in 'time,'", he smiled as he stressed the word, "we will be in touch with you to deliver your request and collect on our payment."

"No Kilt, you have misunderstood – " Sandra said, but with barely a look at Jason, the two saneers changed to their orbed states and floated away.

"Sandra, what have you done?" Jason asked bleakly as soon as they were off.

"Saved my parents," she whispered.

CHAPTER 10

A Hero Just in Time

Location: St. Annalise

While the saneers were strong, insincere, and insolent toward their ruler, it seemed their ruler, Jason, was still stronger. He had been away from the island but, as luck would have it, had returned that evening and his royal sense had alerted him to the energy of saneers being on the island. In his wildest imagination, he had not expected to find them with Sandra on the *Mistletoe* and he wanted answers.

Jason listened to Sandra's complete story regarding her parents and sister. She left out nothing. She knew that despite the differences held between the elfins and fairies that she could trust him with her story more than she could trust many of her own kind. Jason disliked Calivon as much as she did and was not surprised to hear of his treacherous ways. Even understanding all of that, however, he was unhappy

JingleBelle Jackson

with Sandra for calling on the saneers before she had talked with him.

"I needed their help, Jason," she said several times in an effort to get him to understand. "They are the only lead on where the elfin documents are held and I must get to that information. And why shouldn't I be able to see those documents anytime I want to see them? It's outrageous! Do the fairies keep their historical documents away from fairies?"

Jason shook his head.

"Of course not!" Sandra said pacing. "Because they're documents that belong to all as these should be."

"There were other ways to explore getting the information," Jason said, not giving her any agreement about her choice to contact the saneers. "You don't fully appreciate how dangerous the saneers are." He was honestly worried about her.

"Jason, I told you. I didn't really agree to their terms. You appeared and cut me off and they only felt I had agreed. Before they deliver the information to me, I will clear this up and we will either continue to negotiate," Jason shook his head so hard at that statement that Sandra hurriedly added, "or, I will tell them no thanks and we will find another way."

"You make it sound so easy but I'm telling you, with a saneer, nothing is as it seems and nothing is as easy as you state." As much power as he had, Jason wasn't sure even he would have been as brave as Sandra had been to meet

56

with not just one but two saneers on his own. She always impressed him.

And she also worried and annoyed him. He was still completely besotted over the Santa in front of him, not to mention he owed her his very life. He would use some of his powers as king to assure none of her time would be taken from her in case the saneers tried to make good on her non-agreement.

"Sand, no argument on this. I am going to cast a shield of protection on you that no saneer will be able to pierce as long as I am alive and that is going to be a very long time. Fairies, I am happy to report, like all magical beings, live very long lives indeed."

Sandra made no objection. In fact, she felt relieved. The two saneers had scared her and she was concerned they would try to hold her to a contract she hadn't agreed to. Jason's shield would be of great comfort to her.

"Ah, my king," she said and went to kneel in front of him. He prevented her from doing so.

"You never kneel to me, Cassandra Penelope Clausmonetsiamlydelaterra dot dot dot," he said quietly, firmly, and with pent-up emotion evident in his voice. "You always stand by my side as my equal and me as yours. It is my honor to do so and I hope to act in such a way as a king, and your friend, to earn those same feelings from you."

"Jason, you have always had my respect," Sandra said.

"Maybe so," he said, now talking not as a king but instead as the guy who had loved and lost her, "but I have not always deserved it. I'm working on changing that. For you, and for the realm I govern as well."

He placed his hands on Sandra's head then and she felt a spark run through her before he stepped back.

"There. Done," he said, rubbing his hands together. Establishing the shield was a more powerful act of magic than he had made it sound to her and he could feel the need to recharge.

"Sand, I need to go and I believe you're safe for now," he said. He held her by her shoulders and looked seriously at her. "Do not meet with them again. Do you understand me? This is not a request from your friend but an order from a king. Maybe not your king directly but your king I hope in here." He tapped her on her heart and then reached around with his strong arms to hold her close.

She felt safe. A feeling she hadn't had with him in a long time.

CHAPTER 11

Making Changes to the AOK

Location: The Mistletoe

"I'd like to call this meeting of the Academy of Kindness Board members to order," Birdie said in as an official voice as she could muster. "We have present here today, Spencer Mantle, Christina Annalise, Sandra Claus..., and Birdie Snow. Missing today is Crow Holiday." Birdie had actually called Crow to explain about Sam not coming until March and to please come back to St. Annalise until then. In fact, none of the Holiday men were currently on St. Annalise but instead were all home at Holiday Ranch for some time off from their responsibilities helping the two Santas. There was plenty for them to do at the big Texas Ranch, and Sandra knew the rest of their family would welcome them being there but they were missed on the island, too. Especially by two young women and one sassy fairy. Sandra, Birdie and

59

JINGLEBELLE JACKSON

Wistle had the month off and time spent with the brothers would have added to their fun.

In fact, this was the quietest month Sandra could ever remember having. Gunny was gone, Jason was busy with all his new duties as fairy king. The elves — including Em — were all in slumber, and Cappie and Thomas were away on their honeymoon. It was really just her, Squawk, Rio, Christina Annalise, and her two best friends for a change. Christina was Jason's mother but more than that, and so important to their meeting, she was the headmistress of St. Annalise Academy. Her knowledge made her invaluable to the development of the new Kindness Academy that Sandra and her team were developing.

After a little time of adjusting to the quieter pace, Sandra was beginning to relish the quality time they were getting together. They had been doing some of her favorite things like yoga and surfing and, best of all, planning the new Academy of Kindness. The time to think on it all, undisturbed, had brought a huge new idea to her that she was anxious to share at that morning's meeting.

"... *squawk!* ... I'm here too! ... *squawk!*"

"Why, yes, you are, Squawk, and pardon me for not noting that," said Birdie in her usual inclusive and kind way. Birdie and Squawk had a special friendship. Squawk preened at her words.

"*eeeeeeeeeeee eeee,*" came from the side of the *Mistletoe* right before the beautiful emerald green dolphin jumped high out of the water and deliberately splashed them all.

"Rio!" Sandra admonished while laughing with the rest. "Yes, we will note for the record that you were in attendance at this meeting too but then that means you better stick around."

The happy dolphin slapped at the water in reply.

"Alright, then," said Birdie, laughing at the antics. "Let's try again to pull this meeting to order. We have in front of us the big task of launching the official Academy of Kindness this year, and if that is going to happen, we've got to get busy deciding on some specific items."

She paused to pull out a whiteboard and picked up a pen to write.

"When will the academy start?" she stated as she wrote "when?" on the board.

"How often will the kindness sessions occur?" said Spence.

"How many days will each session last?" Christina Annalise suggested.

"Yes," Birdie said, writing.

"What will the children do?" Spencer prompted as Birdie wrote "activities" on the board.

"Where will they stay?" Birdie said, as she wrote "where?"

". . . *squawk!* . . . what to eat? . . . *squawk!*"

"Yes, Squawk, very good," Birdie said, acknowledging the big bird's suggestion. "What to eat?" went on the board.

"Anything else?" Birdie asked, reviewing their list.

61

"Who will teach the lessons?" Christina Annalise suggested. It seemed natural that a headmistress of a school would make that suggestion.

"I think there might be more," said Birdie, setting down her pen. "For now, this list feels like plenty to keep us busy for several meetings."

The group all nodded their heads in agreement.

"So where shall we begin?" Birdie asked. "Sandra, you talked earlier of having an idea you wanted to talk with us about?"

"I do. A big idea that I'm really excited about and I hope you all will feel the same."

"Well, c'mon," Spencer said. "Don't keep us in suspense."

That was all the encouragement Sandra needed.

"Okay, here's my idea. I want to permanently host the Academy of Kindness on the South Pole Village barge!" Sandra could hardly contain her excitement about the idea and was grinning from ear to ear.

Her friends, while not quite as excited, having just heard the idea, nonetheless, jumped in to support her thinking.

"That sounds incredible!" Birdie exclaimed

"Are you sure?" Spencer asked. "Would there be room?"

"I like what you are thinking, Sandra, but I want to be sure you know that I don't mind hosting it here at St. Annalise at all," Christina Annalise said.

"I know, Christina, and I appreciate that so much but there are some really wonderful reasons for hosting it on board the barge.

"First, the barge is mobile – or it will be soon - so we can take it to different parts of the world and go to the children rather than them having to come to us."

The group members nodded their agreement.

"Second, it would help us get closer to the countries we serve and let them see a Santa village close-up and in operation, helping build an even closer bond between children and the elves. Even adults could reconnect with the magic of Christmas and power of kindness."

She was on a roll now and moved to the whiteboard herself to write down each point.

"Third, it really is the most spectacular place to have the academy! The barge isn't done so we can still make the tweaks on it that hosting the kindness camp would require. I'll have to break the news slowly to Gunny since I keep asking for changes, but I think even he will be willing to remodel some rooms again for such a good cause."

She wrote on the whiteboard, "Convince Gunny."

"And finally, it means so much to me to start this academy and promote kindness around the world that I can't really imagine having it being held anywhere else. Keeping it on the barge means I can combine two things I love so much in one moving location. It means I can be part of every session rather than missing many because of my Santa duties on the barge and being away from St. Annalise.

"I even have thought we could change the name on the side of the barge to read: *South Pole Village: Home of the*

Academy of Kindness." She wrote it in big letters in the space left on the board.

"So what do you all think?"

"Everyone who agrees the South Pole Village barge should be the home of the Academy of Kindness, please raise your hand – or wing," Birdie looked over at Squawk and then at Rio, "or fin as the case may be." Rio slapped her fin on the water.

"Seeing a unanimous response, the proposal has passed. Sandra, thank you and congratulations on providing a perfect place for what may be the best school ever," Birdie said as Sandra grinned. She added quickly, looking at Christina, "After St. Annalise Academy, of course." Christina smiled at her and rolled her eyes. Of course, she knew what Birdie had meant and had taken no offense. In her heart and mind, St. Annalise Academy would always be the best of the best.

". . . time for treats! . . . *squawk!*"

"You're right, Squawk," Birdie said, feeling happy. "Let's break out the banana cake I made and celebrate!"

CHAPTER 12

A Tempting Envelope

Location: St. Annalise

Things went along close to idyllic for almost two weeks on the tranquil island. Each morning, Sandra would spend several hours in the St. Annalise Academy library, researching possible places she could look for the elfin documents she needed. She hadn't determined anywhere specific but one or two of the books seemed to hold possible obscure clues, and she was painstakingly following up on every one. It was slow and tedious research but the time flew by, as the topic meant so much to her.

For fun, the three best friends met every day for surfing, and even Jason was able to join them for a couple of the days. The four had been friends for so long that having Jason join in was easy and natural. He and Sandra fell right back into their usual competiveness about catching and riding the biggest and best waves. Sandra wasn't sure when she had enjoyed the time surfing more. There were moments sitting, surfing, laughing on the beach, when she would look at Jason and believe they might indeed still have a future together. He was respectful but steady in his goal to win her back. She found whenever she looked over he was looking at her, and one evening at sunset he had hugged her. It sometimes seemed that things were progressing between them back to how they had been before Jason had smashed Sandra's heart into little pieces, but Jason would get called away for fairy business and the two would have to restart again. It was complicated between them, for sure, but neither was in a particular hurry. He was sure of what he wanted – nothing less than her heart – and would go at the speed she needed to get there. For Sandra, it wasn't out of the question. Jason had been her first love and she was opening to the idea that they still might be able to recapture what they once had.

After surfing, the academy board members met every day – still without Crow, though Birdie sent him the meeting minutes after every meeting – to work on details around the AOK, as they called the academy for short. The ideas were flowing with ease now and each of them were getting excited about how it was coming together. Sometimes, they planned for an hour-long meeting that would stretch into three or more hours because there was so much to talk on and they were so excited about the work they were doing. *It was the best kind of job*, Sandra thought.

Just like being Santa, to her, AOK planning never felt like it was work because it was so aligned with what she – and the rest of them – loved the most: making a difference in the world.

After the meetings, Sandra would usually spend some time by herself thinking on possible ways to finding her parents, ideas for the academy, plans for the elves when they woke up, and changes she wanted to make to the South Pole Village barge when construction started up again. She found, increasingly, as her plans were coming together, that the person she most wanted to share her ideas with wasn't there. She missed having Gunny on the island.

"It's more than that," she muttered to herself one afternoon. "I miss him." It was a big realization for her and the thought made her smile.

She was sitting on the deck of the *Mistletoe* processing her conflicted thoughts about Jason and about missing Gunny when on a puff of wind, an envelope blew into her lap. It was addressed to her formal full name, which told her immediately it wasn't a letter from Cappie or Gunny or Santa or one of her many other friends. And it was not addressed to South Pole Santa, so it wasn't from a child. No, this, she was sure, was from the saneers. She set it down on a table across the tug from where she sat as she considered what to do next.

She had actually tried to get a message to the two saneers since the night they had visited and had grilled Wistle and little Quisp on where she could send it but neither would share, if indeed they even knew, how to reach them. It was almost the end of January now and Sandra had dared to allow herself to feel like the whole thing with the saneers was over. She decided it had just been a bad experience that was better put behind them. Maybe Jason having been there had been more impactful than it had seemed that night. Now, she worried, that had not been the case.

Sandra sat there contemplating what to do next without opening or even touching the letter for longer than she realized until Squawk began squawking about what was for dinner and she went in to make the two of them something. After a quiet evening with just Squawk and a swim with Rio, Sandra finally returned to the back deck and the letter with a sense of foreboding that had replaced the happy place she had been in earlier.

Sandra desperately wanted to know where to find the documents she needed to free her parents. She knew she was now protected by Jason's shield so the saneers could not take her time as they had demanded as payment. So, part of her was strongly considering opening the envelope, reading the answer, and bargaining further for a payment they could agree on.

The other part of her she knew there was nothing they wanted that she would ever agree to pay. The saneers were as dangerous, maybe even more so, than Quisp and Wistle had warned her they were and she did not want them for her enemy. She doubted whether she really could offer them a

ENCHANTMENTS A SOUTH POLE SANTA ADVENTURE

payment they would feel was fair. Plus, Jason's words of staying away from them rang in her ears. He had given her his protection and now she could at least follow his royal order. She moved to put the envelope beneath a stack of books to keep it from blowing away. She would give it to Jason, unopened, to return somehow to the saneers and she would find another way to free her parents.

"Sorry, Mom and Dad," she whispered to the wind, closing her eyes and hoping for a response but heard nothing.

"What is it you have to be sorry for?" she heard, as her eyes flew open and her heart beat dangerously fast. The saneers had returned and were standing on her deck.

CHAPTER 13

A Return Visit

Location: *The Mistletoe*

"Kilt, Tambler, this is a surprise," Sandra stammered.

"A surprise?" said Kilt. "But surely you expected to meet with us again to receive what we promised and to pay what you promised?"

Sandra felt alone and unsure. It was late and, as safe as she always felt on the *Mistletoe,* she did not feel safe now. No one was around except Squawk and likely Rio but she would risk putting them in danger if she was too loud and woke them up. She took a deep breath to steady herself.

"Actually, I tried to send word to you that the agreement you believed we had struck was not as you believed," Sandra said as strongly as she could. She saw their insincere eyes grow darker but the smiles never left their faces. She pushed on.

JINGLEBELLE JACKSON

"I know you believed we had an agreement and I understand how that would seem possible but in actuality I had been saying to you that 'yes, I will need more time to consider my options' or something along that line. So, you see, this was just a simple misunderstanding. You heard 'yes I will' but I meant 'yes I will not.' I apologize for creating the confusion."

She stood there trying to smile and remain hopeful they would defy their reputations and prove to have an understanding nature. The fact that they were standing on her deck again, very likely, meant they did not.

They did not indeed.

"You are speaking nonsense," Kilt said, disregarding her explanation entirely. "We have delivered what you requested." He paused and pointed at the letter. "Now we are here to arrange for payment. Ten minutes of each day of your time for three human years we have decided will be fair pay. We are even willing to take that time while you sleep so you will barely notice."

Ten minutes of her life each day while she slept for the answer on how to release her parents didn't seem all that bad, Sandra found herself thinking. *Nonsense!* She heard her mother's voice in her head. *The price is far too great!*

Sandra snapped out of considering the trade off, picked the letter up, and handed it back to them.

"Thank you both very much," she said, trying to keep her hand and voice from shaking as neither one of the saneers reached out to take it from her. "I will not be reading this answer or paying for your services. Please accept my apologies for the misunderstanding and for wasting your time." Neither still took the letter so she turned and placed it on the side table again.

"Now it is very late and I'm in need of my sleep so I will bid you goodnight," she said shakily.

"Goodnight to you," Kilt said smiling. "We will begin the ten minutes tonight."

He had completely ignored what she had said!

"You will do no such thing!" Sandra exclaimed now less scared and more angry. "I have been kind to you and explained the misunderstanding, which frankly was as much on the two of you as it was on me. I haven't opened your envelope and read the answer despite wanting to very much. In return, I ask only that you take the envelope and go, and I ask, actually, no, at this point, I insist, you go now." She stood and pointed to the sky as the path for them to take.

Neither saneer budged.

"We had no misunderstanding and we provided our service to you. It was achieved with quite a great deal of effort on our part. You may read it or not, it makes no difference to us, but we will begin collecting our payment tonight as is due to us."

"Well, I didn't want to have to tell you this because I didn't want to get him involved but you will not take your payment from me because I am under the protective shield of your king, Jason Annalise. Now, goodbye to you both."

That, at last, seemed to get their attention and not in positive way. Tambler waved his hands at Sandra and sparks flew. Their eyes narrowed and for the first time, the smiles actually left their faces. It was Kilt who tried next with the same results and then both with simply more sparks as Sandra now was the one smiling in triumph.

"So, you see, despite your ways of trying to take what I did not agree to give you, that I am protected," Sandra said, trying hard not to gloat while the two stared at her with open hostility showing until Kilt seemed to regain his composure and his smile.

"I see," Kilt said at last. "This is very unfortunate for all concerned. We will depart now. Payment is still due, Cassandra Claus. With interest and penalties added. So unfortunate."

With that, before she could object or disagree, the two orbed away.

Sandra ran to the back of the big tug after them, envelope in hand. "You forgot your letter," she yelled out to the already empty sky.

CHAPTER 14

Wistle's Big Idea

Location: St. Annalise

Despite Jason and her friends assuring her that the unpleasantness with the saneers was behind her, Sandra was having a hard time shaking off the threat the saneers had made to her, despite Jason's protection over her. Wistle and Quisp both understood but that only made her feel worse. She was having trouble sleeping, and would wake up finding irony in the fact that, even if they didn't get to take her actual time, the saneers had been successful in taking time away from her sleep. Much more than just ten minutes a night, in fact. The restless nights were wearing and taking away from the fun days she and the others had been having. So much so that even Wistle had noticed and was concerned. One afternoon, she came buzzing by the big tug to find Birdie and Sandra.

JingleBelle Jackson

"Wistle, you seem excited about something. Is something wrong?" Birdie asked. It was very unusual for the fairy to seem anything but neutral or haughty.

"Actually, far from something wrong, I have a big idea that I think you both are going to like," said Wistle. "If we can't get the Holiday men to come here, then we need to take ourselves to the ranch," she stated in her matter-of-fact way, only this time with the hint of a sparkle in her eye and a rare smile on her lips. Like Wistle, Sandra thought it was a perfect suggestion. In the middle of worry and madness, adding in some Gunny fun was exactly what she needed.

"When do we leave?" she asked.

CHAPTER 15

A Texas Welcome

Location: The Holiday Ranch

Birdie wasn't quite as excited as the other two, which was understandable since Crow still wasn't talking to her much. She was reluctant about surprising them, but she too relented in the end. She didn't want to risk having Crow tell her not to come by calling ahead. She was missing the twin to Wistle's boyfriend too much to be left behind.

"Why, girls, look at you! What a nice surprise!" Josie Holiday, mom to all of the rambunctious Holiday boys, declared as they were dropped off by fairy transport. It wasn't Sandra's favorite way to travel — fairies had a way of making her feel somehow beholden to them — but the elves were still in slumber so the Reindeer Express was off-line. Sandra probably could have used her locket to get them there but she knew it wasn't really meant for that kind of convenience. So, that had left fairy transport.

Despite Josie Holiday's greeting, she had been expecting them. Sandra didn't mind surprising Gunny, as surprises often seemed to occur between the two of them with their busy lives, but she would never be so rude not to check with Mrs. Holiday first about them coming. She had asked Josie not to share their plans with the brothers since Birdie was afraid Crow would have asked her not to come and she wanted to see him so much.

"The boys are going to be so happy to see your beautiful faces," Josie said as if she was reading Sandra's mind right then about Crow and Birdie. "Come on in now out of this wind, and we'll get you settled while we wait on the boys. They're all out helping the Major this morning with ranch duties." Mr. Holiday was called the Major even by his children. Sandra found herself looking forward to seeing them all. The Holiday family always made her feel part of something special. "You picked a perfect time to be here. The annual Holiday Ranch Hoedown is in the barn tomorrow!"

"The Holiday Hoedown? What is that?" Birdie asked the question all three girls were thinking.

"You girls don't know what a hoedown is?" Josie asked as they all shook their heads feeling confused. "Well, you are in for the very best time ever then, because there is nothing more fun than your first hoedown!

"Basically a hoedown is a big dance, usually in a barn like ours with a bunch of hay spread around. You add in fiddle music and a caller telling you your next moves. The gentlemen all wear plaid shirts and string ties and you girls can look spectacular in some of Blue and Glory's hoedown dresses. I'm sure my girls can find something cute for each of you." Josie gave them all a long look like she was checking that she was right and seemed pleased with her assessments. Blue and Glory were the Holiday sisters and Sandra was just about as excited to see them as the boys.

"Yep, you'll be mighty cute in their dresses," Josie added, more to herself than to her guests.

This was a turn of events the girls hadn't considered, and Wistle, to put it mildly, was highly skeptical about. It sounded like way too much for a fairy girl like her or a gruff cowboy like Ghost.

"Are you saying that Ghost goes to these hoedowns?" Wistle asked of Josie to be sure she was clear on what she was hearing.

Josie broke out in a big smile. "Even the surliest of cowboys, of which I might add none of my boys are, and I know what I'm talking about, has a friendly side he brings out during a hoedown. Yes, even my Ghost, the quietest of my bunch until lately," she shot a quick glance over to Birdie that Sandra caught, "loves a chance to put work aside and get out his hoedown jig. You'll see! Now go on, you three, and drop your stuff in the bunk room while I get you out a pitcher of something cold to drink. Sandra, you know where the bunk room is. Take your friends on back."

Sandra smiled at the simple order. She loved that she knew where the bunk room was and how it made her feel. She passed on sharing with Wistle the spot where she had first met Ghost and he had kissed her. It was more than a year ago now and ancient history already.

As they finished setting out their things, they heard voices coming from the kitchen. The boys had clearly come in and were asking about the spread Josie was putting out. They could hear only that Josie was speaking and then, like a piece of dynamite that had been lit and exploded, came Gunny's voice.

"Sandra! Sandra, you here?" Gunny shouted as he strode down the long hall to the bunk house, and Sandra's smile changed to an ear-to-ear grin. Gunny Holiday had a way of making her happy.

"Sandra?" He stopped right outside the door. "You girls decent? I sure hope not because either way I'm coming in!" And in he strode, dirty clothes, unshaven, and eyes only for Sandra. Any girl would have melted to be looked at like that. He scooped her up and spun her around like she was weightless.

When he set her down, he just grinned at her as Ghost came striding in too, followed more slowly by Crow, who leaned up against the doorjamb while Birdie stood there awkwardly wishing she was anywhere but there. Until Gunny noticed and fixed it all right.

"What in the blue blazes are ya' doin' there in the doorway, little brother?" he said, swatting at Crow with his hat. "Ya' been moonin' over her for weeks and now she's right in front of you. Do something, Bro! Somethin' like that I'd suggest." He pointed over to Ghost and Wistle, who were lip-locked.

Crow stayed right where he was at but reached one long arm over to where he was just able to grab on to Birdie, who came sliding over at his tug.

"I missed you so much," he whispered to her as he pulled her close, and all of Birdie's worries about whether she should have come or not melted away.

Now it was Sandra who felt herself feeling funny about having come along. Technically, she and Gunny were not a couple like the others. In fact, she remained conflicted regarding her feelings about Gunny and Jason. She had things she was drawn to in both the fairy king and the cowboy and things that frustrated her about both of them. When she had tried to talk to Cappie about it once, Cappie had said that love was like that. Love was never perfect, she had said, and that, despite those conflicting feelings, she believed Sandra really did know the answer in her heart.

But if Sandra's heart knew the answer, it wasn't being clear with the rest of her. She was so used to pining away for Jason that her heart having tugs for Gunny confused her. She didn't want to mislead him but at the same time she knew, for sure, that she had been missing him. She felt happy just having him walk into the room and couldn't help but grin at him. Once again, she felt safe and welcome there on the ranch and, for now, she was going to let down her guard and go with it.

"Gunny Holiday," Sandra said. "I believe I owe you a New Year's Eve kiss." He had tried to get her to come out for the party on the island before he left for the ranch, and she had been almost rude to him. Not okay, she realized suddenly, seeing how kind he was to not just her but to all of them. She pulled his scruffy, dirty, handsome face down and planted the best kiss of her life on him. A "holy-smokes-did-the-room-just-start-on-fire" kind of kiss that stunned the both of them. It was a first between the two and sparks didn't just fly; it was more like a blowtorch had been lit! Awkwardly, it seemed to even be sensed by the other two couples, who were staring at them now.

Gunny didn't care. He stood there smiling smugly at the Santa he adored more than she had any idea. He loved her and had put those feelings completely into that kiss.

"I knew that was going to be good," he said. "I knew it. I've been trying to tell you but, no, you just ignored me on it but I knew —"

"Oh be quiet, you know-it-all-cowboy," Sandra said, shutting him up by planting another one on his still smiling lips.

CHAPTER 16

Gingham and Lace

Location: Holiday Ranch

It was a typical ranch dinner that evening with the whole family there except Chance, the older brother who was a big-time lawyer in the big-time city of Dallas. The rest of the family, including the two Holiday sisters, Glory and Blue, and a handful of cowboy ranch hands, all gathered at the long ranch-house table and dug into the platters of food that Josie and Blue seemed to just keep bringing out of the kitchen. It was a feast complete with raucous chatter going on everywhere. Everyone there, even the normally tempered Wistle, was laughing and happy. Sandra found herself thinking, over and over, how happy she was that they had come. The saneers and her responsibilities had all fallen away. It felt like a true vacation.

JingleBelle Jackson

After dinner, Glory and Blue pulled the girls away for fittings on the hoedown dresses for the next night. As Josie predicted, it was easy to fit the girls. On the other hand, it was not so easy to calm a fit. Like the one that Wistle was having.

"There is just NO way I'm going to be seen in one of these," Wistle declared after each hoedown dress was tried on and discarded. In fairness, there was something about the whole gingham and lace and ruffles that simply did not look right on the lithe fairy. Sandra and Birdie were hesitant about them as well, but for politeness' sake they each found one they felt made them feel "festive" which actually was girl code for "not as bad as the others." But on Wistle, each dress seemed to swallow her up, and she came out looking more like a Christmas ornament than a girl going to a dance – even if that dance was a hoedown.

After several disastrous try-ons, Wistle announced that she was sorry but she was just going to sit the evening out. She was fine with that and she believed that Ghost would understand – and even if he didn't, well, she still wasn't going.

Blue and Glory, though, were a lot like their brothers. They were raised on the same ranch, with the same parents and had the same stubborn streak in them. Blue kept digging through her closet until she pulled out a gold-colored dress that looked as flouncy as the others. In fact, maybe even more so, but it had no lace on it and just the tiniest bit of gingham.

"As much as I wanted this to, it just has never fit me. It's always been too tight around the waist to breathe comfortably.

But I think it would be perfect for you, Wistle. Can you try just one more?"

Wistle looked at it with as much skepticism as the others. It looked about the same when she stepped out to show it off. But Blue surprised them all when she stepped up and yanked off both sleeves. It instantly made the dress less all-encompassing like the others and gave it a slightly different personality – a little rebellious like Wistle's – and yet still kept the hoedown feel.

"What do you think?" Blue asked, pleased with herself as she stepped back and spun Wistle around to the mirror again.

They all held their breath, thinking Wistle looked magical. Sandra and Birdie wished they looked that good in their dresses but still knew it was totally up to Wistle whether she would or she wouldn't wear it.

"I think," Wistle said slowly. "That, unbelievably to me, this fairy is going to a hoedown." The happy, giggling girls all rushed in together for a big ole' girl group squeeze and squeal! Looking in the mirror, Sandra could see even Wistle was smiling.

CHAPTER 17

Ranching It!

Location: The Holiday Ranch

The next day the group split up so that each couple could get in some of their own catch-up time. Crow and Birdie especially had a lot of talking to do. Ghost was taking Wistle for a long tour of the ranch. Wistle seemed to be enjoying being there as much as Sandra did the first time, and every time since, for that matter. Sandra wanted to spend the day riding along with Gunny while he did his checks on the ranch outposts. She knew she could use the time to talk to him about the saneers.

He wasn't pleased with what she had to say. In fact, the only part of the whole story that he did like was the part where Jason helped her and that didn't make him happy either. He hated any time he found himself liking the guy. Especially, any time he knew Sandra liked the guy. Still, the saneers made his worry about Jason laughable.

JingleBelle Jackson

"Are you kidding me right now, Sandra? Nothing about this story is okay!" Gunny stormed. "I told you that I would be the one to contact those slimy fairies and now look what has happened. It's like they have you on their hit list. Why did you have to be in such a hurry?" He was stomping around the truck, scaring Sandra a little bit. He didn't care. Someone had to scare her into being sensible. Moving around helped him think while he fumed. The whole thing with the saneers completely freaked him out. He had spent much of his time the past month trying to temper his hopes and be realistic about his very low chances of landing the coolest girl in the whole of the world. That's how he thought of her. Then she goes and surprises him by showing up at the ranch out of the blue. Lays on the very best kiss anyone, anywhere, ever, could experience. Then she waits a day and tells him she's being threatened by some of the most clandestine and sinister of magical beings. To top it all off, he, once again, finds he is highly limited on ways he can help her by virtue of being just a human up against a very impressive fairy king who actually can help. Some days, loving a Santa was every level of frustrating.

"This just bites, blue girl." Sandra couldn't help but smile. He had called her blue girl or blue bird or some take on that since they had competed in the Santa competition and she had been pushed into a tub of blue paint. Gunny had literally saved her from drowning in it. He was finally resting on the back of the truck bed where she had been sitting while he stormed around. She reached over to hold his hand,

88

thinking fondly about the rescue. The hand-holding seemed to help calm him a bit. But he still didn't smile at her.

Thinking about the paint vat, she told him a theory she had recently developed.

"Gunny, I know this might sound weird, but I think it was a saneer that pushed me in the paint vat at the North Pole. After seeing them, they really only show in the dark as orbs but they have kind of a glow about them like a light bulb. The same kind of glow I saw in that room when I thought it was a light bulb."

Gunny took that idea in before asking. "Why do you think they would want to do that, Sand? It doesn't really make sense."

"It does if you remember they are really sort of fairies-for-hire. Maybe Calivon was trying to do me in even way back then?"

Neither of them had the answer but it did seem plausible.

"All the more reason for why I don't like the saneer threat on you one bit," Gunny said.

"I don't like it either, but not so much because I think they can hurt me. Thanks to Jason," Gunny tried not to flinch at the words, "they really can't hurt me now and they've never really tried again since that time. I don't like having them as enemies, though. Or anyone for that matter."

"Only crazy people would be an enemy of Santa Claus dot dot dot," Gunny said, trying to lighten up the mood. He was no less worried, he just didn't want her to worry

JINGLEBELLE JACKSON

more by seeing he was worried. "No gifts will be under their Christmas trees." Neither one of them laughed much at his quip. *Christmas gifts might actually help the saneers feel like being nicer,* Sandra thought, feeling sad that they'd probably never had a gift. Kind acts, like the gift of a Christmas present, almost always made hard times – and people – easier and nicer.

"What has Santa said about all of this?" Gunny asked.

"He doesn't know. I only saw him for a little bit right before he was going down for Slumber Month and I didn't want to worry him. Like all good elves, he's been sleeping ever since." As she mentioned the elves, Sandra's mood lightened up at last. "I miss them! Especially Em! They should all be waking up any day now. Oh, Jack Frost, it's February 5! They should have been awake this week. So, any minute, I'll talk to Santa on all of it as soon as I see him. I've found a few very weak possible clues in the research I've been doing about where the documents might be. You want to know the biggest surprise?" Gunny nodded and she went on. "I don't think they're in the magical realm. I think the papers are being kept in the human realm on the topside."

"Really? That surprises me, too," Gunny said, thinking on the implications of that. "Why would they hide them with humans instead of with their own magical kind?"

"From their view, I'm thinking that must seem like the safest place to hide them," Sandra said, having given the topic some thought herself. "Most magical beings prefer to ignore humans so I think whoever hid them might have realized that on the topside of Earth would be the best place to put something they didn't want found. Magical beings wouldn't think to look in such a 'boring' place, as they all tend to believe about the non-magical world, and human beings wouldn't know to look."

Gunny thought she sounded pretty smart. As usual.

"If you're right, that means we have an easier shot of finding them than if they had been hidden in one of the magical lands. That makes me hopeful."

What he didn't say but was thinking was that the topside of Earth meant he had as much of a chance of helping her find them – maybe even more – than Jason did. If they were hidden in the magical realm, he could be of very little assistance, but on Earth, well, he would settle for being second to none in that case.

"I'm really not sure but the evidence seems to be leaning that way," Sandra said, trying to temper his, and her own, expectations. "When we get back to St. Annalise, I'll share the little I've found with you and see if you come to the same conclusions."

Gunny nodded and Sandra chose that opportunity to change the subject.

"Now, do you want to hear about something way cooler?"

She knew he would and she plunged into her great ideas about the Academy of Kindness and all the changes that would need to be done to the barge. The day of talking and scheming got away from them, and they were the last two back to the ranch house with just enough time to get changed for the hoedown.

"Gunther Holiday! You are running late and you made our guest late," Josie admonished while still smiling to show she wasn't too terribly mad. "Get on with you two and get ready to help greet our guests!"

"Yes, ma'am!" Gunny said, grinning at her. "And Ma, you look great! The Major better watch out that none of the ranch hands try to run off with you."

"Why son-of-mine, such a true thing to say." His mother winked at Sandra, looking pleased with her son. She was very proud of the responsible, caring man he had grown up to be. She gave a full twirl in her pretty red dress, which got her son laughing.

Sandra stood there, grinning at them both happily. She loved watching their fun family dynamics in action.

"What are you doing still standing there, Sandra?" Josie said when her twirl was finished. "You may be one of the most popular women on the planet with your Santa job, but here on this ranch, I'm the top boss. Now go on with yourself!"

"Yes, ma'am!" Sandra said, echoing Gunny's words. "I don't want any kind of showdown before the hoedown." And off she ran grinning.

CHAPTER 18

Going to a Hoedown

Location: The Holiday Ranch

"Sandra, where have you been?" Birdie practically pounced on her friend as soon as she came into the bunkroom.

Sandra had to smile. "Birdie, you look like some kind of exotic flamingo in a tutu in that dress," she giggled.

Birdie frowned before she broke into a big smile, looking at herself in the mirror. She did look like a flamingo in a tutu. "We'll see if you're still laughing once you get your dress on. Hey, and at least my name is Birdie and I can talk to birds. Maybe I *should* look like a flamingo. You won't be able to say the same." They both laughed realizing it was true.

"First, the fastest shower ever," Sandra said, peeling off her clothes as she headed to the bunkroom showers. Birdie had Sandra's dress ready to slip into as soon as she was dried off.

JINGLEBELLE JACKSON

Sandra turned to have Birdie zip up her dress and laughed looking at herself in the big mirror. "I can't say for certain, but with this green color and the embroidered edges, I might be the first human Christmas tree." The girls both burst out loud laughing, looking at themselves and flouncing their layers.

Wistle walked in just then and both girls quit their giggling immediately as they stared at the fairy. "Not fair!" Birdie objected, saying what they both were thinking. "You look good in your hoedown dress! You're like Cinderella going to the ball and we're the wicked stepsisters."

Sandra and Birdie burst into laughter at how true that seemed as Wistle asked them, "Who?" That made them laugh even harder. It seemed super funny that fairies didn't know anything about the fairy tales told by humans.

Wistle ignored them and looked again in the mirror. Her dress had a smaller profile with fewer flounces. She had to agree with them. Compared to her friends, she was looking hot – and a lot slimmer.

"Oh c'mon, who cares? I'm glad one of us looks good," Sandra said, grabbing on to both of them. "We're here for a hoedown! Let's go flounce our ruffles and do-si-do with our toe-si-toes."

If they really did look silly in their hoedown dresses, you wouldn't have known it from the reaction of the Holiday boys or any other cowboy in the barn that evening. The threesome walked in and every eye looked their way. The dance

94

caller stuttered and the fiddler missed at least three notes. The Holiday boys just grinned with pride as they bowed low and swung their dates onto the dance floor. Hoedowns might have seemed like a little bit of hokey fun to the three girls from St. Annalise, but in the hands of the Holiday boys who had grown up swinging their partners around the floor, the hoedown was an art form. And it wasn't just Gunny and the twins who were good at the dances. It was all the cowboys, who cut in frequently and took their time swinging the beautiful girls all around the floor all night long. Wistle especially turned out to be the heart stealer of the hoedown as each cowboy came round time and again until Ghost just refused to let her go. His date, his dance.

"Gunny, the elves would love this," Sandra managed to say breathlessly while he was whirling her around the dance floor in a polka of some sort. "They would look adorable in these dresses and plaid shirts you all have on."

"They would," Gunny agreed, not even winded despite all their whirling and twirling. "None of them would look as cute as you, though." He smiled at her as she laughed out loud. She did look "cute," which was not her usual look. It suited her tonight, though she decided, as well as Birdie and Wistle and all the other women and girls gathered for the fun of the hoedown. The guys, too, for that matter.

By the end of the evening, they were all tired, with very sore feet, but they had had a blast! The boys walked them back to the bunk hall where the three were asleep almost

JingleBelle Jackson

as fast as they could crawl into bed. But not before Wistle mumbled some final words about the day.

"I swear I'll use my fairy powers to change you both into wood toads if you ever tell anyone I had fun at a hoedown."

Sandra could only smile in the dark. She and Birdie would never tell. Not because they were afraid of her toad threat but because they knew no one would ever believe them.

CHAPTER 19

Time to Wake-Up

Location: The Holiday Ranch

Morning came fast and it was already time to head back to St. Annalise. The travelers were waiting around for the fairy transport and thanking the Holiday family members again for their hospitality when, to their surprise, Barney, one of the North Pole elves, landed with a Reindeer Express Coach in front of them.

"Sandra! I found you!" he exclaimed, jumping down from the coach.

"Barney! Reindeer! What a great surprise!" Sandra proclaimed honestly. She was so pleased to see them. "I've missed you all and am so glad to see you're out of slumber month."

The reindeer kicked at the dirt to show they felt the same while Barney seemed to hesitate. Sandra was so excited to see them all she didn't notice that something might be wrong. Gunny did.

97

JingleBelle Jackson

"Barney," Gunny said. "Is everything all right?"

The little elf collected himself and then burst out with what he had not been saying. "No, nothing is all right." He looked directly at Sandra. "I'm the only elf who woke up. Everyone else is still asleep, Sandra. Everyone! Even Santa and Mrs. Claus! I can't wake them up!"

Sandra had a feeling of dread as soon as Barney spoke. It was the saneers. She felt it in her bones. She didn't know how or why but she knew it was them. And she knew it was her fault. Quisp and Wistle and Jason had all warned her, but she had stubbornly chose to move ahead thinking of no one but herself. Oh sure, it was to help her parents, but she wanted to help them for her own sake because she missed them so much. She could hardly stand thinking about the harm she had caused. Jason had helped her save herself, so the saneers had taken time instead from some of the people she loved most. They had said they would "take time from your life" and in some ways, this was exactly what they were doing. It wasn't her time, specifically, but it was definitely time from her life circle of friends and family. Now she had to worry for everyone she knew.

"It's the saneers," Sandra said at barely a whisper to no one in particular though they all heard her. "They said they would get their payment with penalties and this is how they are doing it. What have I done?"

# # #

The girls decided to spend another night at the ranch so the whole group could take on what to do next. Barney had shared that, like every year, he tucked in for Slumber Month in the barn with the reindeer and not with the elves in their bunk houses or village homes. He usually woke earlier than the rest, as did the reindeer, and he liked to be close-by his reindeer crew. Sandra's heart tugged when she realized that she had tucked in all the elves and not noticed Barney was missing. She was still getting to know many of them but Barney was one she knew well and she was sorry she hadn't noticed. Barney, on the other hand, didn't care at all. He knew she loved him.

Barney and the reindeer had all woken up on February 1, right on schedule. Typically the elves slept the whole month of January and woke up any day before the fourth of February. So Barney had waited patiently for the others, keeping busy with barn chores and grooming the reindeer until the rest were up.

When nobody woke up on the second or third day of the month, he thought it was peculiar. Every year, there were some early elves up and some late elves but never, that he could remember, was there a year when they all waited until the last day to awaken. Still, while he thought it was curious, he really wasn't worried, he just started to get bored and lonesome.

He had run down to the elf quarters on the fourth day unable to contain his excitement about everyone waking up and that's when worry kicked in. No one was awake. Not a single elf, or Santa, besides himself. Worse, no matter what he did, he could not get them to wake up. He shook them. He hollered. He played loud music. He even brought in big bowls of their favorite candy and rustled the wrappers, and not one elf so much as stirred. That's when he knew for sure something was wrong and had headed to St. Annalise to find Sandra. Christina had sent him to the ranch.

The group decided the first order of business, then, was for most of them to head to the North Pole and see for themselves. Maybe if enough of them made noise, they could get at least some of the elves to wake up.

Sandra was not going with them. She needed to find Jason and get his help to break any spell the saneers might have placed on the elves, Santa, and Mrs. Claus. She was also going to recruit Spencer and have him research possible solutions to breaking saneer spells. He was a genius at finding things online and in libraries that others wouldn't find. Lastly, she was going to open that envelope from the saneers. The two sinister fairies had taken time from those she loved – wake time that they could never get back and had not agreed to give. She was going to get the answer her friends had paid for and rescue her parents! First the elves, and then her parents.

CHAPTER 20

A Happy Return

Location: St. Annalise

Gunny didn't like her going alone at all and it had nothing to do with St. Annalise. He knew it was the safest place in the world for her and every other person there. Still, the saneers had found her there and threatened her there, and it simply didn't seem smart for her to be there on her own.

Sandra had been adamant, though, and not just because she didn't want any of them to know of her plans to open the envelope. She needed them, including Gunny, to get to the North Pole. Waking up the elves was critically important. Plus, as she told the worried cowboy, she wasn't staying at St. Annalise. She was passing through and then heading straight to the North Pole, too.

She also needed to make sure that Squawk and Rio were okay. She always felt fine leaving them on safe St. Annalise,

JingleBelle Jackson

but with Cappie and Thomas still gone she counted on the good nature of the islanders, in general, who all loved them both, but still were not direct family. Neither of them, especially Squawk, liked being away from her. She would take him with her this time when she left.

"Jason! Jason!" Sandra purposefully had her fairy transport drop her off at his home. Christina was the only one who answered her call.

"He's not on the island, Sandra," Christina said as she came to the door to let Sandra in. "He's been gone a few days now. You know how he goes back and forth. Can I help with anything?" She could see that Sandra looked distressed.

"I don't even know if Jason can help." Sandra lamented as she poured out the story. As she finished, Christina suggested, "Send word to Jason through the fairy transport and see if you can get him back to the island. This truly is an emergency!"

"Thanks, Christina. I'll do that. I've got to go."

"I'll send him your way if I see him first," Christina called after her.

Sandra found Spencer next and caught him up on what had happened and how he could help. He agreed to get researching and insisted she take him along to the North Pole to help wake the elves.

"I can do online research from there almost as easy as here," he argued. She was happy to have him go along. She headed to the *Mistletoe* next to check on Squawk and Rio.

102

"Squawk! Rio!" Sandra called out as she got close. The big bird came flying to her immediately.

". . . gone too long! . . . *squawk!* . . . stay home now!"

"Squawk! I missed you, my friend! You look good. Everything okay?"

" . . . *squawk!* . . . hungry!" Sandra could only laugh. Her fine macaw friend was as good as ever.

"*eeeeee eeeeeeeeeeeeeee*" came Rio's chatter from the water. Sandra didn't even stop to change into her swimsuit. She kicked off her sandals and dove into the water for a swim with her favorite dolphin.

The water felt fabulous, invigorating, and cleansing, and Rio loved the attention. Squawk flew along right above them as they played and swam until Sandra finally climbed out and lay for a minute flat on her back on the dock, feeling the beautiful tropical sun on her face and letting it dry out her clothes.

"We leave you for a few weeks and this is how we find you? Lazily sunning?"

"CAPPIE!" Sandra leapt to her feet in one swift movement, and though she was completely soaked, she reached over and hugged her favorite guardian so tight that Cappie was soaked. And then she reached over and hugged Thomas, too, who had been standing back letting the two of them have their moment. He was family now, though, and their moments were his moments, too.

103

JingleBelle Jackson

"Oh, Cappie, I'm so happy you're home! You have no idea!" Sandra couldn't believe how glad she felt to see them. Until that moment she hadn't fully realized how much she had missed them both. She'd wanted to talk to her guardian about her parents, of course, but it was more than that. It was having someone who loved you so completely that you could just be completely you and feel one hundred percent safe. Cappie stood back to look at her ward carefully, and Sandra broke into tears. The whole month had been challenging, but the wrath of the saneers on her treasured elves were proving to be almost too much for her to take.

Thomas graciously, or maybe with relief, said he would take their bags to the *Lullaby* leaving Cappie and Sandra to catch up on the *Mistletoe*.

It took hours. Thomas came over eventually and heard all of the story as well. Cappie chided herself for not having checked in, but Sandra assured her she wouldn't have shared any of what was happening anyway. She wanted the honeymooners to have their time together.

"Did you try using your locket to take you to your parents now that you know for sure they're alive?" Cappie asked.

"Over and over, Cap. Every day. I try it and, just like all the years apart when we didn't know if they were alive or not, it doesn't take me there. Somehow, Calivon and his "band of badees" have very successfully blocked me."

The news of her parents being alive didn't seem to shock Cappie much. Like Sandra, she had always wondered. But the

104

news of them having another daughter and why they were taken and hadn't returned shocked and angered her to her core. Calivon had robbed Sandra of her parents for no legitimate reason and had to be stopped! She didn't like what Sandra had done with the saneers, but more than anyone else she seemed to understand why. She agreed with Sandra that the saneers had taken what they didn't deserve and that since Sandra had ended up paying the price they had demanded by the saneers taking time from the elves, Sandra deserved the answer that the envelope contained. The two were so nervous about opening it but, truth be told, a little excited as well. The idea of being reunited with Sandra's parents was a dream they had never lost sight of, though it had dimmed as each year went by. Now it was glowing bright, not just as a dream, but a very real possibility.

Because they still didn't trust the saneers, and worried there could still be some way the villainous fairies could injure or enchant Sandra despite Jason's protective spell, they agreed Thomas should be the one to open the letter. He had no reason for the saneers to dislike him or want to harm him. He picked up the lilac envelope and without hesitation ripped it open, unfolded it, and read from it.

Or he would have if there had been any writing on it. Instead there was nothing. Not one word. The saneers had double-crossed Sandra — they had taken their payment and delivered no goods.

This was war.

CHAPTER 21

The Clue

Location: St. Annalise Island

Jason caught up with Sandra the next day and she shared the updates with him, including having a blank message, as she packed to head to the Pole. Spencer, Cappie, Thomas, and Squawk were all coming along and sitting with her as she packed. It was going to be a full reindeer coach.

"I'm going, too," Jason declared and Sandra didn't argue. She felt relieved in fact. Her heart told her that if anyone at all besides the saneers could lift the time-taking spell, it would be the king of fairies himself.

"You shouldn't have opened that," Jason said, looking over at the envelope delivered by the saneers.

Sandra was surprised. "Why not?" she asked, truly wondering his reasoning.

"What if the problem with the elves wasn't done by the saneers? What if it's something else or done by someone else?" he said, sharing his greatest concern.

"Done by someone else?" Sandra repeated. "Who would want to hurt the elves?!"

"I'm just saying that you don't know for sure, Sandra, and since you don't, you shouldn't have opened it. You could have been beholden to them if it had the answer you were looking for and they hadn't created the problem with the elves."

Sandra just looked at him incredulously. She was tired and her patience was worn thin. "It was them, Jason! I know it and I know you know it, too! You just hate the idea that a fairy, even such duplicitous ones as the saneers, could prove to be so bad."

Jason stayed calm. "Maybe, Sand, but I'm also right. I just care about you and don't want this to get any worse."

He picked up the blank letter. "Why did you say that they didn't give you an answer?" he asked, looking puzzled.

"What do you mean?" Sandra asked in return, looking equally puzzled but striding over to him on the deck to grab the paper. Had words mysteriously now appeared? She looked at it but it was still completely blank. She handed it back to him.

"Very funny, Jason," she said, not feeling very amused.

"Sandra, I'm not joking." Jason said, feeling truly confused. She could see by looking at him that he really was confused and her heart caught. Was he seeing something there that they could not? Could that be possible?

What Jason was seeing was clear as day to him. As the king of fairies, he had extraordinary eyesight. Seeing Sandra's sincerely puzzled look, it finally dawned on him that this was more duplicity on the part of the saneers. They had fulfilled their bargain but in such a way that most would not be able to see it!

"So, Jason, don't keep me in suspense! What does it say?" Sandra still saw nothing no matter how hard she looked at the page in his hand.

"The information you seek lies barely out of sight, we cannot tell you where but the clue hiding here might. There's a place in a canyon, the grandest of all. At a rock near a place where lava does fall. There may lie the answer you think that you need. We fulfilled your question and have given you this lead."

"What kind of answer is that?" Sandra said. Right or wrong, she really thought she was going to get a direct answer from the saneers, collect what she needed, and rescue her parents.

"Well, poetic," Thomas said, grinning and trying to lighten the mood. "A bad poem I grant you but it does rhyme."

"It's a riddle, Sandra, but also a real clue!" Cappie exclaimed, swatting at her new husband playfully. "It sounds like it's in the Grand Canyon! That's in America. Where's your atlas so we can figure this out?"

Jason felt excited, too. They had a lead. The saneers were cagey and dangerous and were most likely creating havoc for the elves right now, but they had kept their part of the bargain and given Sandra a lead.

"You think my parents are being held in the Grand Canyon?" Sandra asked with disbelief in her voice. She had never considered that not just the elfin documents but her parents might be being held somewhere on the topside of the world and not in the magical realm.

"Not really, but I do think that an answer to where they are being held lies in the canyon. I know we don't have time to think on this now since the elves need us but let's take your atlas with us and study it on the trip," Jason said.

"The little bit I had turned up through my hours of research on the elfin documents at the library also seemed to indicate they could be on the topside and not in the magical realm. This seems to agree!" Sandra couldn't keep the hope out of her voice.

"Just remember, this is from the saneers. I want to be excited, too, about this clue, but if we've learned one thing about the saneers, it's that they're not generous through words or actions. This could be true or nothing at all."

"But thanks to you we have their words in front of us and we are going to take action! That's at least something, Jason. Something good! Thank you!"

Jason wanted to feel excited but something kept him from it. Something nagging at him about the saneers that he couldn't quite remember or maybe he didn't even know yet.

He set the thought aside. As far as he was concerned, he had already learned more about them than he wanted to know.

CHAPTER 22

Santa in Charge

Location: North Pole Village

The whole way to the Pole, the small group split their time and looking for any hidden meanings in the clue, and studying a map of the United States with the Grand Canyon on it. It was frustrating for them all, especially Spencer, that there was no detail for the canyon area and they were too high up to use the Internet. On the press side, North Pole Village had a great shop that was full of maps, and Spencer planned to make it one of his first stops when they landed.

Truthfully, Spencer was feeling frustrated in general. He had spent the better part of eight hours searching online and through magic reference books in the St. Annalise library with maddeningly little to show for it. There was just very little about the saneers referenced anywhere. Sandra assured him that she had found the same thing in her hours of

JINGLEBELLE JACKSON

research. They were a clandestine group where the less you knew the better off you were. It was almost as if writers were fearful to mention them.

They all were quiet as the Reindeer Express landed at the village. It was strange to land at such a quiet North Pole. But hope came loping up the street in the form of a big golden retriever. "Dandy!" Sandra called out and the big guy came racing down the street, practically knocking her down. Dandy was Buddy, the town troubadour's, always nearby companion. When Buddy wasn't performing with Ellen and some of the others, he would ride Dandy through North Pole Village, strumming his guitar and adding music wherever he went.

"So, the elves are still asleep but the animals woke up like usual," said Spencer, clicking through all the things he knew so far in his big brain. Sandra always loved it when Spence was working on a problem because solutions tended to follow. Dandy took off back down the street to greet two more of their friends who were heading their way.

"Cappie!" Birdie called out as she increased her speed to a full run when she saw who Sandra had with her. "You're back! I'm so glad to see you . . . both." She added the 'both' on as she smiled at Thomas as well. He knew what she meant, and frankly loved seeing his new wife so loved on.

"Hey, how about a hello for the rest of us?" Jason joked. He reached out to shake the hand of the one Holiday brother who seemed to like him. Crow grinned. "Glad to see you, Jason," Crow said sincerely. "I think we need your help."

112

"I'm hoping I can be of help. No change then, so far?"

Both Crow and Birdie shook their heads.

"It's frustrating," Birdie said. "We've tried all the same things as Barney, but he's still the only one awake. North Pole Village feels lonely without them all bustling around."

"It does! It's not right," Sandra said, still petting Dandy.

" . . . *squawk! . . .* miss Santa! . . . let Em sleep . . . *squawk!*"

"Squawk! That's terrible!" Sandra admonished, but the big bird didn't seem to feel bad about it at all. Jason tried not to laugh. He would feel the same way if one of the people sleeping was Gunny.

"Everyone else is over in the elf quarters. Crow and I came to greet you and now we're working on making some lunch. Everyone is starved but no one wants to take a break from trying new things to wake them up. Even though there's really nothing that's working." Birdie said, as she and Crow crossed the street to the *Eat, Drink & Be Merry* diner.

"Well, let's see what we can do," Jason said as the new arrivals all headed off to the elf quarters with Dandy in the lead.

Not surprisingly, the greeting from the rest of the group there went similarly to how it had gone with Birdie and Crow — everyone was thrilled to see the newlyweds and barely acknowledged the rest. That went double between Gunny and Jason. Jason made the first move to establish how it was going to be while he was there.

"Sandra, you want to help me try some of the things we talked about on the ride here?"

"Actually, I have some things we need to go over first," Gunny countered.

Oh boy, Spencer thought, similar to the rest of those watching. *This is going to get awkward.* He wouldn't have missed it for the world. He wasn't big on relationships for himself presently but he wasn't above enjoying a bit of awkward drama when he wasn't the one involved.

Sandra wasn't going for any of the tussling between them. Yes, she was in the middle of it and yes, in some ways, she was responsible for much of it, but now wasn't the time for any personal issues. She was ready to be firm and in charge. She was the Santa on duty.

"The first thing I'm doing is checking on the elves and Santa and Mrs. Claus myself. Then I'd like a report from you, Gunny, and the rest of you who have been here. After that, I absolutely want to help you, Jason, in any way you need, to try to lift this horrible saneer spell. They have already taken way too much of the elves' time!"

Cappie couldn't help but smile. She was so proud of how Sandra was becoming a strong leader even if Sandra didn't always recognize the changes in herself.

"Everyone else, please think on ways we can help get things ready here at the Pole for when the elves finally wake up. For instance, I don't see Barney here so I suspect he is busy doing all the work in the barn of keeping the reindeer fed and the barn cleaned on his own. Could someone volunteer to help him?"

"On it!" said Thomas. "Someone just point the way. This is my first time up here."

"I'll take you and help, too," Ghost said. "A barn is where I'm most comfortable anyway. I'll give you a tour of the village on the way, Thomas. You're going to love it."

"We need someone to start baking cookies and getting some of the elves' favorite dishes ready too. They're going to be famished! Cappie, could you work with Birdie on that?"

"A perfect job for me," Cappie said. "I'll send Crow back here so you can use him where you need him."

"Thanks, Cap," Sandra said. "Gunny, can you and Crow be lead on seeing what we can do to get the factory fired up and ready to go? I hate to put the elves right to work after this trauma, but if I know them at all, they are going to want to make up for lost time."

Gunny paused before agreeing. He knew she was right, he just didn't like it. He would rather work with her.

"Yep," he said cryptically. "Makes sense. I'll get on it. Send Crow over when he gets here."

Sandra was pretty sure she knew what he was thinking but there wasn't time for hurt feelings right now. Time was of the essence.

"I'm going to check each elf individually. Jason, start thinking on what you want to try first because we're not stopping until they wake up!"

CHAPTER 23

Desperate Times, Desperate Measures

Location: North Pole Village

In the end, those were just big, hollow words. The elves continued to sleep.

Nothing any of them tried, including Jason, the king of the kind that had placed the spell on the elves in the first place, was working. He knew he had to try something different and he suspected there were only two people who might know the answer. Calivon was one of them and Reesa was the other.

"Are you sure those are the only two?" Sandra asked, hearing his suggestion on who to ask next. "Those are both horrible choices. Calivon is out of the question and Reesa can't be trusted not to tell him."

117

"Why not ask the two saneers who did this?" Gunny suggested as he came walking up to the table.

Why not indeed? Sandra thought. It was a good suggestion. She gave him a big smile and made room on the bench she was sitting on for him to join her. He didn't hesitate, sitting down closer than necessary as he looked at Jason across the table. "What do you think about the idea, Jason? Think it could work?" he asked him.

Like Sandra, Jason was evolving as a leader and was pleased that he could recognize a good idea no matter where it came from. "I like it," he said nodding. "I don't like the saneers or trust them, but they've taken a vow to not share that they are working with Sandra on with anyone else. And technically, through an unfortunate mix-up, they do believe they have only taken what was agreed on by Sandra." She went to protest but he held his hand up. "What they believe. I'm not saying it is accurate.

"So," he pushed himself away from the table. "I guess it's time I met a couple of saneers on my own." He looked at Sandra, as if willing her to understand, and then disappeared.

"Jason! NO!" Sandra leaped up. She alone at the table knew the true cunning of the saneers. She didn't want anyone to be in any danger because of her choices, not even their king.

"Wistle, can you take me to him? He shouldn't face them alone!" Sandra said, turning to Wistle forgetting how afraid the fairy was herself of the saneers.

ENCHANTMENTS A SOUTH POLE SANTA ADVENTURE

"I can," Wistle said, setting her own fears aside as she stood up and Sandra moved to stand with her while Gunny and the others began to object. Wistle paid no attention to any of them, including Sandra. "But he is my king and I will be the one to go." She looked briefly at Ghost, who realized her plan, and leapt for her as she disappeared as quickly as Jason had.

"Noooooo!" Both Sandra and Ghost cried out at the same time.

Sandra stomped around, kicking her feet into the air, beside herself with frustration. She just kept making this whole thing worse and worse.

CHAPTER 24

World Wide News Checks In

Location: North Pole Village

No word came for hours. Nothing. At all. Just hour after hour of no change. *Where were they?* Sandra thought over and over. The elves kept sleeping. Jason and Wistle were gone. And Sandra was inconsolable and unhappy. She had tried to use her locket to find them but it just sparked in her hand and she went nowhere.

Even though they were at merriest place on the planet, there was no real room for merriment. Besides the constant worry and wondering, there was so much to do. Each hour was long with work, the small group was getting very little sleep and exhaustion was playing on the moods of them all.

It was at this low time that Beatrice Carol, the reporter with the World Wide News out of London, called for Santa, looking to do a story on what to expect for the coming

Christmas season. Beatrice Carol loved to keep up on all things Santa and all things Christmas but this was not the time. If the story of Santa and the elves sleeping got out, it would worry children everywhere. The intrepid reporter was not one to be put off, however, and Sandra knew it was just a matter of time until Beatrice simply showed up at the North Pole Village as she had done several times in the past, despite Santa's frequent admonishments to call first.

"Hi again, Beatrice," Sandra said, trying to sound cheerier than she felt. "It's nice to hear your voice too." She had let the reporter's prior two calls go to voicemail but now, she knew she needed to take her call and help delay any visit Beatrice might be planning to make to the village.

"Oh yes, I'm just up here helping out Santa and the elves. You know how busy things are at this time of the year." Sandra smiled thinking about it. "Really, at all times of the year. Yes, you are right about that for sure.

"I thought you might be calling for an interview," Sandra said, nodding her head even though the reporter couldn't actually see her. "We're not quite ready with any announcements yet for the coming season or even have any travel plans determined. It's still pretty early, you know. Only still just February but you're right, March is coming up fast." She listened a little more.

"Yes, things are coming along with the Academy of Kindness. I absolutely promise to have you be one of my first calls about it when we have any news. You know how much Santa and I appreciate you helping us keep the children up-to-date on all of our special plans for them.

"Thank you for calling, Beatrice. Yes, a pleasure talking with you, too, and I will let Santa know you called. Oh Oh Oh." She managed to get out her signature greeting and sign off, but without much enthusiasm, and she hoped that Beatrice hadn't noticed.

She also hoped the reporter would now stay away for a while because if she did show up, things would only get worse.

"Oh Oh Ohhhhhhh," Sandra said and clunked her head down on the desk just thinking about it.

Thankfully, Beatrice Carol didn't show up later that day but Jason did. In the main hall, with someone that sort of looked like Wistle held gingerly in his arms. And a very big story to tell.

CHAPTER 25

A Retelling of a Meeting Gone Wrong

Location: The Dark Land of the Saneers

When he had disappeared from North Pole Village, Jason had taken himself to the dark place of the fairy lands. No one ever chose to visit, knowing they were the lands of the saneers. As the king of fairies, however, Jason had every right to travel to any part of the lands he ruled. He kept repeating that brave thought in his head as he looked around.

Wistle, like most every fairy, knew where the saneers lived as well. She found herself next to Jason as she had hoped when she had followed his lead.

"Wistle! Why are you here? It's dangerous!" Jason was instantly alarmed and dismayed to see her. It was no place for a king, let alone a regal but common fairy.

125

JingleBelle Jackson

"That's exactly why I'm here, sire." While she had grown more comfortable referring to him as Jason in their personal life, on fairy time and on fairy business, Wistle had no intention of being so informal. "None of us found it acceptable for you to face the saneers alone. Especially as a king they do not necessarily acknowledge. It seems important that you not be outnumbered and it made the most sense for me to accompany you."

Jason understood the logic but found no comfort in the words. It was too late to change the situation, however, as they could see two saneer orbs approaching. "You will stay behind me and not speak," Jason said, speaking quietly but sternly. "It is an order from your king."

Wistle only nodded. It was an order she was happy to oblige. She stepped back as the saneers changed to full-size.

"We heard that some kind of royalty was here. We would never have guessed it was our own king. Such an honor," the saneer Jason remembered as Kilt said. He wore the same fake smile Jason remembered without sincerity in his words.

"Thank you, Kilt, I'm here on follow-up to your transaction with Miss Claus," Jason said, getting right to the point.

"Excuse me, your royal highness," Tambler said, almost interrupting Jason, which was never done with royalty. "Who is the beauty you have brought with you?" He looked at Wistle, smiling. She stared at him in return in her high, haughty, fairy way with no smile, sincere or insincere, in return.

126

"It matters not to this issue, but this is Wistle of the Woods, my traveling companion for the day and, as you can fully see, a fairy, free to travel these lands as all are." *But never would*, he thought to himself but didn't say.

"Greetings to you, Wistle of the Woods," Kilt said, disregarding Jason's statement that she did not matter to the conversation. Wistle did not acknowledge him.

"Now, to the matter at hand," Jason said. "You have placed the elves at the North Pole, as well as Santa and Mrs. Claus, under a saneer spell. You had no right to take this time from them as they had made no agreement with you in any way. I direct you, as your king, that you release them at once."

"Your royal highness, with deep regret, you left us no choice and we had every right," Kilt said, trying to show shock in his insincere eyes as if the very request from his king was surprising. "You kept us from collecting directly from Cassandra so we had to take payment from other places – or people in this case – in her life. And penalties were due too, of course. You understand."

"I do not understand!" boomed Jason, sounding powerful and royal. "This is not acceptable! I placed her under my protection so that you could not collect on a manipulated agreement that, in truth, she did not make, which I believe you actually do know. You proceeded then to move ahead deceptively. I have witnessed the 'answer' you provided her, which actually appeared as nothing to her non-fairy eyes, and appears as only a clue perhaps leading to an answer, which

JingleBelle Jackson

is no answer at all. So you have taken what is not yours on many levels. Release them now! You cannot give them back this time you have taken but you will release them now! You tarnish the good name of all fairies with your actions."

"Your highness, such sputtering," Kilt said almost sneeringly. "If you do not want the elves to pay, who would you have pay?"

"There is nothing owed!" Jason boomed.

"We are willing to trade something for the time we are still owed. We collect many things. We do not insist just on time. For instance, you are a very good-looking man," Tambler said. "We love beauty."

Now Jason stared at them, trying to determine his next step. This was more confounding and more difficult than he had expected and he had expected it to be challenging. The two saneers had not actually threatened him directly – a crime in the fairy world – but just short of it. He could have them imprisoned for what they had done to the elves, but he feared that would just delay a solution further.

"You will not threaten our king!" It was Wistle who now spoke up, stepping around Jason. She was through with being quiet or intimidated. She had heard what they were saying and the underlying threat they had made to Jason – purposefully or not.

"He has asked of you, in a much kinder way than I would have were I your ruler, to undo the spell you have cast. Why

128

Enchantments A South Pole Santa Adventure

are you even chattering with him about it? You have no say in this matter. Our king has spoken, you must just act!"

The two turned and talked very quietly together as Jason and Wistle stood side-by-side. When the saneers turned, their smiles continued but their eyes burned with dislike for them both.

"Act, we will." The two swept their hands toward them and Wistle automatically stepped in front of her king out of a desire to protect him. Thankfully, nothing happened to either of them but a slight tingling, and she was relieved to know that the saneer's powers could not be used on them.

"It has been undone and we have accepted the trade," Kilt said. "Be gone now."

"Such disrespect —" Wistle sputtered.

"Never mind that," Jason said, stepping toward them. "What trade? Are the elves now awake?"

"Soon," said Kilt. "Though the full effects of the spell may take time to wear off, of course. We are satisfied."

And with that they orbed and were gone. When Jason turned, Wistle was crumpled on the ground. He whisked her up and returned to the North Pole where their friends were now crowded around hearing his update.

"That's exactly what happened," Jason said, agonizing over the outcome. Sandra felt even worse than she did before, if that was possible. Solving one part of the problem kept leading to another problem.

129

JingleBelle Jackson

"What are we going to do?" Sandra asked, talking low. "She'll be devastated."

"Maybe she'll just sleep?" Spencer suggested hopefully.

"I don't think so." Jason said. "I think she's just knocked out from their spell."

"What are we going to tell Ghost?" He hadn't joined the others yet.

"Don't let him see her like this. Not yet. She wouldn't like it. We need to think," said Crow.

"Are you sure this is Wistle?" Spencer asked, again, the question that would normally have sounded ludicrous but seemed perfectly acceptable to ask. They all were wondering.

"Yes, it's her!" Jason said, feeling very frustrated. How dare those saneers defy him and how dare they do this to Wistle.

"Where are they? Are they back? Did it work? Did my fireball fairy girlfriend straighten them out?" Ghost strolled toward them anxiously and took in the scene of Jason standing and the rest gathered around someone laid out on a table. The group automatically parted, knowing they couldn't keep Ghost from her. It looked like someone wearing Wistle's clothes but it wasn't Wistle.

"Wistle?" Ghost said as he got close, a lump forming in his throat. "Wistle?" he asked, looking for confirmation that it wasn't her from the faces of his friends and finding none.

130

"What did they do?" he said, directly to Jason, his dark eyes blazing with fury.

"They took her beauty."

# # #

"How is this even possible?" Ghost shouted and demanded. He was loud and unyielding and had no plans to be less. The brave, shriveled, unattractive fairy lying before him had literally gone to the middle of the Earth for him. He owed her his life and frankly, he loved her. He knew how hard this would be for her when she woke up. Fairies were vain and beautiful. It was part of being a fairy. He couldn't care less about all of that — though he did love having a hot girlfriend — but he knew how important it was to fairies, including his own, maybe especially to this one. He would have traded places with her in a flash.

"How could you let this happen?" he railed on Jason. "Why didn't you stop them?" And then in his frustration, "This is all your fault, Sandra! For what? Because you had to talk to the saneers even when Wistle told you they were dangerous!" He fought back tears. He knew his words were hurtful but he couldn't shut up.

Sandra and Jason said nothing to defend themselves. He was right. It was Gunny who stepped up on their behalf.

"Now wait a minute, little brother," Gunny said.

JingleBelle Jackson

"Don't even try, Gunny. It's not the time," Ghost said, wiping his eyes and picking up his fragile, emaciated girl-friend in one swoop. He looked at them all with enough defiance for two blazing in his eyes.

"I'm taking her to the ranch where she can be safe and away from others seeing her or her even seeing herself. By the time I'm done, there won't be a mirror anywhere within miles of the place. Jason, you're the ruler of fairies, spell cast her with some kind of fairy enchantment so she can't get away and disappear on me. I wouldn't trust her not to hurt herself." Jason nodded his agreement, and with a simple wave of his hand made it so.

Ghost stopped at the door. "I know this wasn't directly your fault," he said, speaking to Jason and Sandra. "I also know you are the only two who can fix it and you owe that to Wistle. She would take on anyone in the human world or the magical world who did this to either one of you or any one of the rest of us. I expect you to fix it."

He left with Wistle still unconscious in his arms. Sandra leaned against the wall to steady herself as Squawk flew in.

" . . . *squawk!* . . . the elves are waking up . . . *squawk!* . . . come quick!"

CHAPTER 26

Awake!

Location: North Pole Village

By the time the group got to the bunk quarters, most of the elves were sitting up and stretching. It was almost March, but Sandra was thankful it hadn't been more time. She clapped with joy and hugged Jason. The weight of what had happened to Wistle was still weighing heavily on him but he managed a weak smile. It was wonderful to see the elves awake, and in a way, it gave him hope that what had happened to Wistle would not last long either. He would do everything he could to see that it didn't.

No matter how many times he ran through what had happened in his head, Jason could not figure out how the saneers had manipulated things so fully. It was the same sort of sleight of hand and deliberate misunderstanding they had done with Sandra. They deliberately seemed to choose what

133

JingleBelle Jackson

they would hear or would not hear and what they would do or would not do. In this case, however, it was not with a human they had no regard for, it was with the king of their kind. That is what shook him the most. It was a deep insolence and his next step would need to be fully thought out if it was to be successful. And it had to be for Wistle's sake.

Meanwhile, like the rest, he found some joy in having success at getting the elves released from the spell. Sandra ran around hugging each one of them yet none seemed to be hugging her in return. The saneers had said the effects of the spell would linger and Jason guessed that this was one of those symptoms that would wear off.

Earlier the group had decided together that, at least for now, they would only share what had happened with Santa and Mrs. Claus. Elves hated to worry. The team would tell them only that they had overslept this year and not specifically why.

The waking up was not as joy-filled as the group had anticipated. None of the elves were their happy selves. They weren't happy to be awake like they usually were or to see Sandra and the others as they always were. Even Em was reserved about seeing Sandra.

"Em!" Sandra had exclaimed, hugging her little delgin. "I am so so *so* happy to have you awake!"

Em had just sat there being hugged. "You're hurting me, Sandra," was all she said and Sandra released her with a quizzical look.

ENCHANTMENTS A SOUTH POLE SANTA ADVENTURE

" . . . *squawk!* . . . you're awake . . . *squawk!* . . . good thing . . ."

"Be quiet, Squawk," Em said and swatted at the bird.

" . . . *squawk! squawk!*"

"Em! No swatting! Squawk was being nice," Sandra said, surprised. The two didn't get along at times but they never hit each other.

Sandra decided to let Em spend some time waking up on her own and went down the line to greet the other waking elves with similar results. No matter who she reached out to – Zinga, Breezy, Tack, Waldo, Violet, even Dear Lovey, who was always nice – the results were the same. Each of them seemed cranky and uninterested. A far different response than their normal wake-up from Slumber Month when they were always joyous and ready to be together and busy again.

One thing, though, was exactly the same.

"We're hungry!"

"I'm starved!"

"What's to eat?"

"I want cocoa!"

"Is there candy?"

They were all hungry. Sandra reasoned that they were likely extra hungry and that might be accounting for why they were also extra cranky. She knew she was less than kind when she was very hungry, too.

135

JINGLEBELLE JACKSON

"Okay, you're hungry! Now, that we have a cure for! Head over to the elf cafeteria, everyone. Cappie is there and has all your favorites ready!"

"Hooray!" a few of them called out but not with much enthusiasm.

"Cappie is there?" Em asked her. "That makes me happy." Sandra loved hearing the words but wished the tone of her voice matched them.

"Go on, Em," she said to one of her very best friends. "Cappie is going to be almost as happy to see you as I was."

" . . . *squawk!* . . . hungry too . . . *squawk!*"

"Of course you are, Squawk!" Sandra said, laughing. Her big bird was always hungry. "Fly on down there. You know Cappie will have something yummy for you, too."

Sandra was skipping the meal. She needed to see how the number one Santa was doing.

136

Chapter 27

Now Get Happy!

Location: North Pole Village

"Oh Oh Oh, Santa and Mrs. Claus!" Sandra called out as she knocked on the front door of their big home while letting herself in at the same time. "Anyone awake in here?"

"We're down the hall," called out Mrs. Claus.

Sandra walked down their long hall and found the pair sitting up in their favorite chairs in their cozy den.

"I'm so glad to see you both awake!" she exclaimed with joy. "You have no idea how happy this makes me."

"Why, how long did we sleep, dear?" Mrs. Claus asked. "Santa and I were just trying to figure out what day it is. The first? The second? Maybe even the third? It does feel like we've been asleep for quite a time."

Sandra hated to tell them the truth but it had to be done.

137

"It's actually February 27," she said. "You had an exceptionally long sleep this year."

"FEBRUARY 27!" Santa boomed. "Why did you let us slumber for so long? You know there is work to be done!"

Sandra scrambled for an answer. "Well, it's a little bit complicated, Santa, but we've been trying to wake you up all month. The elves have been asleep as well and are just waking up now, too. A spell was put on you all but Jason managed to get it lifted."

"A spell!" Santa boomed out again. "Who would do such a thing?"

"It's a long story. I will tell you all of it but first I would like to get you both to the cafeteria to get you fed and for the elves to see you."

"Fine," Santa responded. He had given her not so much as a smile since she had arrived.

At the cafeteria, Sandra was ready for the elf hug that always happened after time away from each other, but the elves gave the two Santas and Mrs. Claus barely a look. They were sitting at tables, eating without talking. Santa came in without calling out his usual "Ho Ho Ho" and only a few of the elves even looked their way.

What is going on? Sandra thought.

"Oh Oh Oh!" she called out jauntily, trying to get some excitement going. "Look who I found awake! The best and biggest elf of all!"

A couple elves managed to call out "Hi, Santa," and Goldie actually gave Mrs. Claus a quick squeeze when they walked by her table but that was it. Worse, after they ate they actually started complaining about being tired! Even Santa said he was going back to bed. That was enough for Sandra.

She jumped up on a chair to be sure they could all see and hear her. "Okay, that's enough from all of you. You have been asleep for *two months*. You're not tired! You might think you are, but you're not. You're elves! You have lots of energy and you are full of happy thoughts and kindness. You love to work hard, play hard, have fun, and build toys for children! So let's get busy like the busy elves you are! We are behind schedule! Tack, I expect you to get the factory going. Tonight. Right now, in fact. All of you who work there, you follow Tack. The rest of you all know what your jobs are here, and since it seems I need to, I will remind you that they are jobs you all love. Now, I want to see some happy faces and some smiles."

They all just stared at her. "Fine. Then Santa, since it seems I have to be bossy, you go first. Let me see your happy smile."

The man known for bringing joy around the world just sat there while Sandra waited. She was not going to waver. She had to stay strong for them all to work off whatever lingering symptoms this was from the spell they had been under. Finally, Santa relented with a quick smile that helped her to smile and turn to the others.

JingleBelle Jackson

"Okay, now it's your turn," she said to the room of elves and she tried to make eye contact with literally every one of them to coax out their smiles. Slowly, each gave something close to what could pass for a smile and she chose to call that good enough for a start.

"That's it," she exclaimed. "I knew you could do it! Now, everyone to your work stations and let's put the happy back into this merry place." The elves got up quietly and shuffled out. Sandra recognized the irony there was having to insist on people being happy, but as a Santa, you did what you had to do.

"Well, they're awake," she said to herself, wondering if the year was ever going to get back to normal.

CHAPTER 28

So Much to Do

Location: North Pole Village

"This is not a surprise!"

"Maybe not but I thought you would change your mind!"

"My mind never needed changing! This is not my idea if you remember!"

"Well it's sure not my idea!"

"It's only for a month. Then it's over."

"Oh, only a month."

"I'll call you!"

"I believe your mother said you couldn't."

"I'll try anyway!"

"Don't bother, Birdie. Just don't bother."

"Crow, don't be like that."

Crow Holiday stormed past Sandra who had been lingering in the hall.

JINGLEBELLE JACKSON

"Uh, sorry about that, Crow," Sandra said, feeling embarrassed. "I didn't mean to eavesdrop. I was just coming to tell her goodbye."

"What do I care?" Crow said in response. "She's not my girlfriend this month."

It was March First and Birdie's mother had sent a telegram to the Pole to remind her daughter she was due back at St. Annalise to fulfill her commitment of spending a month getting to know Sam, Birdie's fiancé, as her mother insisted on referring to him.

Uncharacteristically, Birdie had rebelled against the demand and the two had found themselves at odds – something that was unusual for the mother and daughter. Birdie usually complied with what her parents asked of her, but in this case they were talking about her life and happiness and she would not be forced into a marriage. Especially when she had a boyfriend who made her happy. Peace had only returned when Birdie agreed to a month-long visit by Sam so that she could make an informed choice regarding her future.

"This is horrible enough without him making it worse," Birdie said woefully, fighting back tears when Sandra found her. She knew who Birdie meant by "him."

"Well, not to take his side, Bird, but it is kind of awful. You have to let your girlfriend, whom you're over the moon about, go spend a month getting to know another guy. A guy who we hear is good-looking, clearly smart seeing how he's

142

ENCHANTMENTS A SOUTH POLE SANTA ADVENTURE

a medical intern, and obviously kind since he volunteers. I wouldn't like it either."

"You think Crow's mad about me?" Birdie said, smiling to break up the tension and show she did understand. Plus, she did like hearing her boyfriend that was crazy about her.

"Well, I do think he's mad *at* you," Sandra said in return, teasingly. "But okay, yes, he's mad about you, too." Sandra grinned. She knew Crow and Birdie could make it through this. It just wouldn't necessarily be easy or fun but then it would be over.

"Well, there's nothing to be done about it anyway," Birdie said practically. "I've got to head back and get this done. Have you seen Spencer by any chance? He's going back with me. The two of us and Christina and maybe even this Sam, I guess, are going to work on plans for the AOK. If that is a-okay with you?" She grinned at her little play on words.

"Yes, and thank you! We need to keep it moving forward. I've been so caught up in the drama here with the elves that I haven't even thought about it in days and we need to be thinking about it! Thank you!

"Cappie and Thomas are going with you. They offered to stay here but they haven't really been on St. Annalise at all since they got home from their honeymoon so they need some time there. Ask them to help if you need it."

"Will do," Birdie said, hugging her friend. "Here they all come. Take care of my guy for me please," she added.

JingleBelle Jackson

"I'll do my best," Sandra nodded.

After the Reindeer Express pulled away, Sandra took a few minutes of her own back in her office to list the big things that needed her attention. After she got it done, she read it out loud to herself while counting on her fingers.

"One, help Wistle.

Two, help my parents.

Three, follow the clue.

Four, help the elves.

Five, update barge plans.

Six, get Academy of Kindness going.

Seven, get caught up on Christmas planning.

Eight, throw elves a hoedown.

"That's a long enough list for four of me," she muttered, reviewing what she had written down. "Every one of these has twenty big things to do under it." She sighed thinking about it. She was feeling a little panicked.

"Number nine, spend time with Gunny. Ten, spend time with Gunny. Eleven thru infinity, spend time with Gunny. Here, just give me that pen and I'll fix the list myself."

Sandra smiled at the big cowboy as he came through the door.

"I knocked and I could have sworn I heard someone say 'come in,'" he said sheepishly. She believed he had knocked and she had missed it being so engrossed in her list-making but she knew he didn't really hear a "come in."

144

ENCHANTMENTS A SOUTH POLE SANTA ADVENTURE

"That's quite a list," he said, looking worried. "Where can I be the most help first?"

Sandra didn't argue with him. She knew she needed help.

"You can help with a lot of this, actually," she said, much to Gunny's relief. He didn't want to argue about helping. He just wanted to do it.

"We are down to just you and me and Crow and Squawk here at the North Pole," she said, strategizing out loud.

"Where'd Jason go?" he asked, genuinely surprised.

"To work on solutions to item number one," Sandra said. "We have to help Wistle and he's the only one who really has any chance of forcing the saneers to reverse their spell on her. "Meanwhile, I need to keep working on Santa and the elves. They aren't themselves at all yet."

"That's for sure," Gunny said. "For starters they're all grumpy! And they're not laughing. It feels really weird."

Sandra looked at him with worried eyes. "I agree," she said. "Which means I'm needed here the most until this spell wears off and they get back to their positive, happy selves loving the work the work they do."

Gunny nodded in agreement. "So where do you need me?" he asked.

"Back at St. Annalise," Sandra said. "I'm excited about the changes to the barge for the new academy but, more than ever, we need to get the barge completed so we have options for toy production in case of an emergency like the one we're

145

JINGLEBELLE JACKSON

experiencing right now. Getting the barge done is one of my top commitments. Birdie is working on how we're going to structure the Academy of Kindness, and if you can work on finishing the 'where' that we're going to offer it, we will be unstoppable." Sandra grinned just thinking about it. This was a happy topic.

"You already are unstoppable," Gunny said, meaning it completely.

"If that's true, it's because I have such a great team behind me," she grinned. He wanted to hug her but she was all business that morning so he stuck to business.

"Can I take a team of elves with me to St. Annalise?"

"Of course! They usually all want to go when asked but I'm not sure how helpful they'll be right now. You might have to remind them what they do and how to work."

"I'll bribe them with sno-cones! That should bring them around."

They both laughed thinking about it.

"Can you stand to do an assignment before you leave?" Sandra asked tentatively.

"Am I from the biggest ranch in Texas?" Gunny asked in response.

"Are you?" she asked. She really wasn't sure. He just rolled his eyes and nodded.

"Everything on this list matters to me fairly equally but, to be honest, the thing I'd like to do most right now, is investigate item number three: check out the clue. I think I finally found where it might be on a map."

She waved Gunny over to show him where on the map of the Grand Canyon she had been studying. "Are you willing to come with me? Like right now?"

"Grab your locket and my hand, I'll hold on to my hat, and let's go," he said without hesitation. "Try to set us down easy this time if you wouldn't mind."

CHAPTER 29

Making Reason From a Rhyme

Location: The Grand Canyon

The Grand Canyon was hot. That was Sandra's first thought as they landed, standing for a change, in a dusty part of what she was hoping was the Grand Canyon.

"I should have grabbed my water bottle," Gunny said, looking around. They were on a narrow rock shelf and it was a long way down to the bottom.

"Hopefully, we won't be here long enough to get thirsty," Sandra said, daring a quick peek over the edge from where they were.

"I don't know about you and your island ways, but in Texas we drink water whether we're thirsty or not. This kind of sun," he looked up, "can dehydrate you fast. And you don't even have a hat! Here, I insist." He plopped his on her head and smiled. He added, "Dang, Santa girl, you look good in

149

JingleBelle Jackson

that! You should change up that Santa suit once in a while."
She smiled at him.

"Such a charmer you are, Mr. Holiday. Okay, first, let's stay away from that edge, and second, let's get our clue and get out of here."

"So, read why we're here again to me," Gunny said, studying where they were as he listened to her.

"The information you seek lies barely out of sight, we cannot tell you where but the clue hiding here might. There's a place in a canyon the grandest of all. At a rock near a place where lava does fall. There may lie the answer you think that you need. We've answered your question and given you this lead."

"That's not much to go on but the locket says this is the place, right? This is 'lava flow falls'?"

"Yes and yes but I have no idea what we're looking for. A piece of paper seems unlikely but maybe it's kept in some kind of safe box or something. It could be something completely different, though. Look for writing on the rocks here – like a hieroglyphic kind of thing just in case it's not a document like we think of a document but something unusual."

"Yeah, and speaking as a guy from Texas, look out for snakes and scorpions, too."

Sandra shivered. She wouldn't put it past the saneers to have them find only snakes and scorpions.

The two carefully checked everywhere around the area the locket had brought them to – twice – without a single result. Nothing looked manmade or magical even. Just the beauty of the desert. Gunny knew how much it meant to her to get her parents back and didn't want to call the search off but one of them had to do it. They had been searching for almost two hours, the sun was beating down on them and they needed to get some water.

He went to speak up but Sandra beat him to it. "I know," she said resolutely. She grabbed his hand and the locket and they were back in her office.

"I have no idea where to look next."

CHAPTER 30

Sam

Location: St. Annalise

"Hello, Ambyrdena Snow. It is a great pleasure to meet again. I am Samuel Dalon. Please call me Sam." The dark and handsome man in front of her put his hand out to shake hers formally but friendly.

"Call me Birdie, please," Birdie stammered out, stunned by his eyes. He saw her staring and she blushed. He just laughed.

"Ah, but Ambyrdena is such a beautiful name. I shall save the nickname for others." He added, "Please don't be embarrassed about checking out my eyes. People do that quite often as you can imagine," he said graciously, still smiling. "I should come with a warning label or something. 'Man has hypnotic eyes.'"

153

That's for sure, Birdie thought, trying to look away but still not succeeding.

"I know this is rude," she said. "But exactly what color are they?"

"Well, as you noticed, they're not exactly one color. I've come to call them 'multi-layered.' They're layered like the lands we come from."

While it sounded poetic, she suspected he was being more factual then poetic. They were like no eyes she had ever seen. They had a layer of light green, dark green, brown, with a touch of blue. Was that even a spark of yellow at the top? Could eyes be yellow? They looked like a beautiful landscape at sunrise.

"Don't worry, you get used to them after a while. Sometimes they're not as dramatic as others. Like when I wear sunglasses," Sam joked as Birdie continued to stare at him. "I suspect this bright tropical light is bringing them out at their most strikingly best." He grinned and they sparked even more.

Look away, Birdie, she told herself. First order of business would be getting this guy some sunglasses. Not so much for him but for her! She shook her head to clear her mind and look away from those hypnotic eyes.

"You also have striking eyes, Ambyrdena," he said to Birdie graciously. Normally, that was true, but next to Sam's, they seemed plain.

ENCHANTMENTS A SOUTH POLE SANTA ADVENTURE

"Excuse me, Sam," Birdie sputtered, reaching for and taking Spencer's hand to pull him over closer. "This is one of my very best friends in the world, Spencer Mantle. Spence, meet Sam."

"It's a pleasure to meet you, Spencer," Sam said graciously. "And kind of you to come greet me today."

Spence felt guilty hearing the words. He hadn't really wanted to be there at all, but Birdie had insisted he come along to support her. Now he was glad he had. The guy seemed cool.

"Good to meet you, Sam," Spence said. "Welcome to St. Annalise."

"It looks to be a beautiful place. Would it be okay to have one of you show me around?" Sam asked while both Birdie and Spence stared at him now.

"Yes. Yes, of course," Birdie managed to sputter out. "That's exactly what Spence and I planned to do. We have lots to show you actually. We'll start at the home of Christina Annalise, the headmistress of the St. Annalise Academy and owner of this island. She has graciously offered to host you in her home if that's all right with you, and we can drop off your bag there."

"Very generous!" Sam said. "I am honored to be hosted there."

"From there, we'll show you everything else around the island and get some lunch, too, right, Bird?" Spence said,

155

JINGLEBELLE JACKSON

nudging his friend to try and shake her out of her weird staring.

"Yes, right, lunch," Birdie said, trying to concentrate. *What was the matter with her?* She had seen many handsome men before. *Get hold of yourself, Ambyrdena.*

"This way, Sam," Birdie said, sweeping her hand toward the beach. "We'll take the beach trail." She stepped in front of him to lead the way and looked straight ahead. Sam had incredibly enchanting eyes but she had a boyfriend. A great one with perfectly lovely, albeit normal, eyes. Eyes that she loved actually. The thought helped clear her head and she picked up the pace.

156

CHAPTER 31

Elves in Turmoil

Location: North Pole Village

"Em! Here you are! I've been looking all over the village for you," Sandra said, sitting down next to the little green delgin where she was sipping on a hot chocolate with a small group of elves. "Hi, Northern Lights elves! How's the cocoa?"

"Pretty good," Goldie said. The others said nothing as they sipped on theirs. Sipped, not gulped, Sandra noticed with dismay. Elves never sipped cocoa. They were all gulpers.

"Em, we need to get in the air today," Sandra said enthusiastically. Em loved to fly in her full delgin size. "Let's do some practice runs around the village and give elves a chance to ride along. They always love that. Right, everybody?"

In response, the group just shrugged their shoulders at her. "It's okay," Violet said.

JingleBelle Jackson

"Okay?" Sandra tried hard not to shout. "Since when is riding a delgin just okay? Every time we practice, there's always a long line of you waiting to ride because it's so much fun. Em loves it, too."

"It's okay," Em mumbled as she sipped on her cocoa. "I don't really want to fly today."

"Emaralda! You ALWAYS want to fly!" Sandra said, pushing back from her seat and pacing. "There is something really wrong around here when none of you want to go flying. In fact, not an elf at the whole of the Pole wants to fly or work or sing or do anything fun. All you all want to do is sleep and you've had plenty of sleeping. I want to hear some talking and laughing and joke- telling and Christmas carols being sung."

"Sorry, Sandra," Perriwinkle said. "Time for us to get back to work." The group got up without a word and trudged off, single file, to the toy factory. Not one of them looked back.

Sandra stared after them. This was not okay. The saneers had ruined her happy elves and she wanted them back. She headed to the barn to find Gunny.

# # #

"I can't figure it out either," Gunny said, shaking his head as Sandra finished telling him what had just happened. "Maybe the worst part is we don't really know if this is a permanent situation or something that's going to wear off. So far, there's been no sign that it's going to wear off at all." He was as worried as Sandra about it.

"I asked for volunteers to head back to St. Annalise to help me with the barge and I got none," Gunny continued.

"None?" Sandra knew she shouldn't be so surprised at this point.

"Only Redwood volunteered later. He doesn't seem quite as affected by the spell as the others. Maybe because he's from Iceland or maybe because he's just bigger than most of the others. Although, Santa and Mrs. Claus still aren't back to their cheery old selves either, so the bigger theory probably doesn't hold up."

"Well, if they won't volunteer, then we are just going to have to assign them. The way it is right now, I don't think they will care where they are as long as they get to nap in the afternoon and sleep at night. That seems to be the only two things that get them excited."

"Well, they may like that schedule, but there'll be no elf-napping on my watch," Gunny said.

"Or mine," Sandra replied. She just didn't necessarily believe her words.

CHAPTER 32

Trying Again

Location: Back at the Grand Canyon

In the end, Sandra and Gunny decided to wait before Gunny headed for St. Annalise. They were hoping that, with more time, the elves would come out of their haze and want to volunteer. In the meantime, there was plenty for Gunny and Crow to be doing, staying there at the Pole.

North Pole Village was considered by many to be the happiest place to be anywhere on the planet but none of that was true right now. No one at the whole of the Pole was happy. The elves and Santa were all glum, Sandra and Gunny were worried, and Crow moped around, going back and forth between missing his girlfriend and being mad at her.

Sandra had never felt like she wished she could be somewhere else, anywhere else but at the Pole, but she did now. Every day that went by was full of sadness. That made it a perfect time

JingleBelle Jackson

to pursue the clue the saneers had given her if she could just figure out where to go next. Nowhere else seemed to match the clues and she was frustrated with her lack of new ideas. The elves and Wistle had paid a large price for something worth nothing if she couldn't figure it out. There was also no way to help her parents and sister if she couldn't find what she was seeking.

Fortunately, while Sandra may have had no place she could think of to look next for the documents, Gunny did.

When they were on the narrow canyon ledge that the locket had taken them to the first time, Gunny had spent part of the time looking around at where they were. From the perilous, rocky outcropping, it had been a straight drop down to the bottom of the grandest of canyons. But looking closer at the rocky canyon walls close to them Gunny had noted there were several other outcroppings near the one they were on. Most of them looked no more promising than the one they had landed on but one had held a little more promise. That one looked as though it had a cave carved out in the rock wall behind it. That's where he suggested to Sandra that they try next.

"It's still in the area known as Lava Falls on the map and it makes sense that someone would hide a document in a cave," Gunny said.

"It does," Sandra agreed. Gunny's suggestion made sense even though the idea of going into a cave held no appeal to her at all. The last cave she had gone in had swallowed up two of her friends for weeks and Jason for much longer than that. "Why does it have to be a cave?"

Enchantments A South Pole Santa Adventure

Gunny squeezed her hand, knowing exactly what she was thinking about. "We won't go in if there is any sign of a drag around or if it feels dangerous at all."

Drags were gatekeepers at portals to inner earth. Sandra was pretty sure that after rescuing Jason out from under their noses, she had been labeled an enemy of the species. She definitely had no interest in seeing any drag ever again, but, on the other hand, they were a lot less frightening than a saneer. Plus, she knew that if a drag was posted there, it would surely indicate they were in the right spot since portals to inner earth were always places of magic. Sandra could totally believe that kind of cave would be exactly the kind of place Calivon, or his duplicitous supporters, would choose to hide something so important.

"Drag or not, dangerous or not, I'm willing," Sandra said. "But I'm glad you're going with me," she added, smiling. She was brave, not crazy.

"Okay then, grab your jewelry and let's go spelunking," Gunny said. "And this time, take a hat and water – and some sunscreen lotion would be a good idea, too. Nobody wants to be seeing a sunburned Santa. You have red hair, you don't need skin that color to match it."

Sandra ran off to collect what she needed and was back faster than Gunny thought was possible without the use of magic.

"Okay, let's go," Sandra said, reaching for Gunny's hand and the locket with her other. She had barely finished her words when the two found themselves again standing on a

163

dangerously narrow ledge on the side of the Grand Canyon right next to the one they had been on the first time. The view was unique and spectacular but very hard to appreciate under the circumstances. At that moment, looking at the rock wall behind them seemed like the better view. It at least was something solid. They carefully turned themselves around to hug the wall while they inched their way slowly down the ledge to a wider spot – and realized they were on the wrong ledge. They could see the ledge and cave they really wanted across from them with the entry on an outcropping of the canyon wall.

"This is frustrating," Sandra said. "I try to be specific but sometimes the locket has a will of its own. Or, more likely, I'm just not giving it good enough directions. Ready to try again?" she asked, reaching for Gunny's hand.

"Hold on, hold on," Gunny said. "That ledge doesn't look big enough for one of us let alone both of us." Sandra could see his point. "Any chance I could borrow that locket for a few minutes and make it work just for me?" It was frustrating to him that he was totally dependent on Sandra for this kind of getting around and it was out of the question to let her go alone.

Sandra just shook her head. Even if she was willing, she knew it only worked for her. She wouldn't chance taking the necklace off in such a place anyway where it could be dropped and gone for good. Sandra didn't like the truth any more than Gunny did but, it seemed this was an assignment she was going to have to do on her own in the end.

"I'll be careful," she said as the big cowboy started to shake his head, feeling more frustrated with his limitations than he had ever been.

"No, Sandra, no. Absolutely not. We will figure something else out. Just give me a minute to think."

"Gunny, there's no other way! The ledge is half the width of this one and this one is barely wide enough for us to stand on – even in the widest part of it where we are now. And the cave is too small to land standing up and looks too small for two of us. That means one can go and one has to stay."

Before he could object anymore, Sandra continued. "Besides, it looks totally quiet over there. The cave part looks small and shallow. There's no way that's a portal, which means there will be no drags over there. I'm starting to doubt it's even the place we're looking for but we have to check it out."

Gunny hated it but everything she said was true. She would have to go alone.

"Alright, but here's the deal. You get over there and if it's any different than it looks from here, you come right back." She nodded. "And when I call out, you answer back." She nodded again. "Okay, then, let's get this done." She turned slowly around and gravel on the ledge went flying off the edge. "And come back and get me," Gunny added.

"I'll try to remember that part," Sandra grinned, trying not to feel so nervous. She grabbed her locket and landed on the ledge across from Gunny. As they had guessed, it was way too small for two and barely big enough for her. The ledge

165

felt more fragile than the one she had come from. It felt like there was a very real chance of it giving way and she would go crashing to the canyon floor. Even breathing felt dangerous as she crawled into the cave. Finally she got turned around and was able to call out to Gunny.

"I'm okay," she called over, waving. Gunny waved back. "Going to look around now." She sat there waiting for her eyes to acclimate and dug the small flashlight out that she had shoved into her front pants pocket. They had been right. The cave was bigger than it looked from their view across the way but not large. The ceiling on it was low. She would be able to stand straight in most of it but it would have been too low for Gunny to stand up in. She felt relief, knowing how unlikely it was that anything but an occasional bird had been there before. And maybe devious bad-doers trying to hide something they had no right to hide.

"No one here," she called and could almost see the relief on Gunny's face. The cave actually felt both safe and much cooler compared to where she had been standing with Gunny. She needed to find what she had come for and get him off that cliff he was on before he burned up or fell off from heat exhaustion.

She decided to be methodical with her search so she wouldn't have to return again and wouldn't miss an inch of the space. Slowly, she worked her way around, looking high and low and periodically popping her head out to assure Gunny she was okay. She knew she needed to hurry for his sake, but she also knew she had to go slow for her parents' sake. When she arrived back at the opening from having searched the entire cave, she wanted to sit and cry. There was nothing there.

"All of this effort for nothing," she said to herself. She was sure she hadn't missed anything and made her way out of the cave back to the perilous ledge.

"Come back," Gunny was saying and waving at her.

Did he really think I would leave him? Sandra thought. She knew that wasn't it. He didn't like her going from the start and was likely ready to drop from heat. She held her locket and was back by his side.

"Sorry I took so long," she said glumly. "I went slow to be thorough but I still found nothing."

"I'm not surprised," the burnt cowboy said. "Because I did." He grinned really big as Sandra resisted the temptation to throw her arms around him for a hug, which would send them both off the edge and straight to the bottom of the very deep canyon.

# # #

"Show me! Show me!" Sandra said, almost too impatient to see what he had found. She didn't see anything in his hands and started looking toward his pockets. *Where did he put it?*

In the end, it seemed the locket had known best and taken them exactly to where they needed to be. While Sandra had been looking around inside the cave, Gunny had taken the time to look around the cliff he was stuck on. At first, like the previous place they had visited, it seemed there was

JINGLEBELLE JACKSON

nothing there. But just as he was about to give up, he noticed a large rock unlike any of the others placed at eye level on a flat spot of the canyon wall. He checked to be sure there were no snakes or scorpions hiding away from the heat of the sun before he moved it and spotted something unusual. It wasn't some kind of box or hieroglyphics as they had theorized. Instead, almost too small for anyone not looking for it, were a set of numbers and letters that were definitely not put there by Mother Nature.

Gunny carefully pulled Sandra over to the spot and pointed his discovery out to her. Sandra looked at the writing with skepticism and defeat.

"Is this it?" she asked. "This is what the saneers have given me? Not the papers I seek but a number of some sort? Another clue?" Even as she expressed her skepticism, she knew it was true. This is exactly what they would do. Send her someplace where a clue could be found but not what she was seeking.

"I think it's a longitude and latitude address for a location," Gunny said. "I wrote it down here on my hand." He held it up. "I remembered a pen but forgot paper," he said as an explanation.

Sandra didn't care. It wasn't what she had hoped for but it was a next step. She grabbed Gunny's hand. "Let's get out of here" and she wished them home to the Pole.

CHAPTER 33

Fight! Fight!

Location: North Pole Village

They arrived just in time. There was no chance for the two of them to talk about what they found. Instead they landed to shouting coming from the elf dorms and found themselves in the middle of a fight. A big fight. With what looked like every elf at the North Pole involved.

Feathers from what had been pillows were flying everywhere. Paper "snowballs" were being thrown at each other – and now at Gunny and Sandra – along with marshmallows – and the whole room smelled like burnt popcorn. A bucketful of the popcorn was thrown their way. Gunny managed to duck but Sandra wasn't as quick, and most of it landed in her long, already-messy-from-being- blown-around-in-the-canyon hair.

169

JingleBelle Jackson

Sandra stood there stunned while Gunny suppressed an overwhelming urge to laugh. It really wasn't funny or okay, it was just Sandra looked so shocked and, wham, Gunny got hit with his own full bucket of popcorn. His urge to laugh changed to shock at being the target.

"WHAT IS HAPPENING?" Sandra hollered to be heard over the elves, while Gunny spit out popcorn kernels. "Quit this nonsense! Quit this right now! RIGHT NOW!" The room just got louder.

A shrill whistle came from next to Sandra that she realized had come out of Gunny, which got everybody's attention. Sandra looked at Gunny, surprised by the noise. "It's one of my secret talents," he said, shrugging. The elves paused, looked at Gunny, and then went right back to hitting each other with pillows, throwing popcorn, and yelling.

"THIS WILL END NOW!" It was Santa now who stood at the door, eyes wide as though he couldn't be seeing what he was seeing. Immediately, the chaos ended. The sound of Santa's voice seemed to shake them out of their fighting.

Santa stood there looking at the elves, who refused to look right at him. "I don't think I've been this disappointed in years," he said loudly out to the room, his voice full of emotion that matched his words. "Sandra, have them clean up every feather of this mess." He turned and left.

Sandra was a little stunned; Santa wasn't going to stay to help her keep order. She turned back to the room. "You heard Santa, you will clean up every single feather of this mess,"

170

she was mad at them and she sounded stern. If it seemed like they had been having fun that had just got out of hand, that would have been one thing, but this simply seemed to be a fight. Not any kind of a fun fight, just a fight. "First, though, I want to know what happened."

"Rollo burnt the popcorn."

"All the popcorn."

"Yeah, and we were hungry."

"And then he wouldn't make more."

"So you're telling me that all of this," Sandra paused for effect and waved her hand to the disastrous mess in front of her, "is the result of a little burnt popcorn?" She had to ask because she was sure that couldn't be the only reason.

"Not a little burnt popcorn, a lot of burnt popcorn," one elf close to her managed to mutter. None of the elves said anything more. None of them were even looking at her. It seemed they were coming back to their senses and realizing what they had done.

Sandra wasn't even sure what to do next. Every day she kept expecting, hoping, that the elves would show some signs they were coming back to being themselves, and every day they seemed the same or even a little worse. This minute was an all-time low in her time with them. They had made messes before – they had spilled glitter all over the council members at one of their visits – but there had always been an underlying hint of joy and fun. There was none of those feelings here this afternoon. Just anger from the elves – tinged now with

JingleBelle Jackson

a bit of remorse – and sadness from her. Well, and a touch of amusement thrown in from Gunny. He still felt they would shake off their blahs that the saneer spell had created and get back to normal soon. This was just a glitch along the way.

"Well," Sandra said sternly. "Each and every one of you in this room will do exactly what Santa said and return this room to the clean order it is usually in. You will pick up every feather, every marshmallow, every snowball, and every single piece of burnt popcorn without exception." She pulled a piece out of her hair and threw it on to the floor to add emphasis to her words before continuing. "Then you will determine who will sew new pillows and who will stuff new pillows."

The elves began to mutter and Sandra held up her hand. "I'm not done," she said loudly as Gunny silently cheered her on.

"In addition, there will be no treats for two full days. No candy, no cocoa, and no popcorn for sure." The room burst out in wails and protest.

"Not fair!"

"No candy? No cocoa? Waaahhhh."

"You're mean, Sandra!"

The last comment cut her to the core, because she recognized the voice. It came from Em. Still, she knew she could not relent.

"Fine, since you feel that way," Sandra said. "I will add on no sugar in general and no play time. Please don't continue to object or I'll make these restrictions last for even more days."

Mercifully, the room stayed quiet this time. Sandra hated doing this and didn't want to make the punishment more severe. She was pretty sure none of the elves would ever love her again and felt Santa should have taken care of this part, but she was the Santa in charge and it fell to her. Not every part of any job, even the best job in the whole world, was always fun.

"Now, get to it! No exceptions on this. Gunny will be back to inspect in three hours." The tall cowboy jumped to attention at this assignment but he was willing. She needed reinforcements and he was her man. He liked thinking that in his head and smiled despite needing to look stern. Sandra gave him a look with raised eyebrows and a cock of her head, and he wiped the smile away. She squelched her own smile at him as she turned to go.

"And elves, please be happy. Please," Sandra practically pleaded. "You're elves. You're always happy. Even when you're at work or doing chores you're happy."

She looked at the room and didn't see a single smile. Not so much as a happy glint in a single set of eyes.

CHAPTER 34

So Much Confusion

Location: St. Annalise

The month of March lived up to its name as each day marched somberly by. At the Pole, the elves, as long as they were closely managed, went through all the motions of getting toys made but without any of the usual joy added that made each toy special. Toys could be made by anyone. What set apart a gift from Santa each year is that elf-made toys, delivered by a Santa, came with an extra dose of joy and love.

Gunny had stayed on at the village to oversee the toy production while Sandra tried to keep up on everything else. Santa spent most of his time reading through the letters arriving daily from children. He seemed to enjoy reading them but answered none of them, which left Sandra to stay up late each night getting responses back to children. All of the rest of them, Santa and the elves, went to bed

175

JINGLEBELLE JACKSON

early each night and only got up in the morning with prod-
ding from Sandra or Gunny.

While all of this malaise was going on at the North Pole,
it seemed that Birdie had caught it, too. She was in a funk
being away from Crow. Or maybe it was more about Sam
and the fact that she found herself liking him much more
than she had intended. He made her laugh. He was helpful.
He was nice and kind and always polite. Everyone on the
island who had met him had liked him immediately. He was
also very attentive to her and seemed to like her company.
Thinking about their time together made her smile. And
that smile put her back in her funk.

Sam was set to leave in just a few days and her feelings
were mixed about it. For whatever reason, the two of them
had barely talked about the looming deadline and what would
come next. She had approached the time he would be there as
something to get through and now she felt his departure was
coming too fast. Her feelings were so confused.

"Why did he have to be so likeable?" she asked herself
out loud.

"I assume, by likeable, you are talking about Sam?" Spence
said as he came and sat down next to Birdie at the table where
she was writing out more plans for the Academy of Kindness.

"Yes," she replied glumly, knowing she could always be
honest with her best friends. "I just never expected to like
him. I mean at all. I didn't even want to because my mother
practically forced him on me, and then he turns out to be a

176

good guy. And I already have a boyfriend I'm crazy about! I miss Crow. But I know when Sam leaves this week, I'll miss him, too. It's just too much."

Spence really had no idea what to say in response. This was a conversation for Sandra and Birdie to have. He usually read something when they got talking about this kind of thing. But Sandra wasn't there so he tried to do his best.

"Have you tried talking to Sam about how you feel?" he suggested.

Birdie shook her head. "What should I say? 'Gee, I like you more than I thought I would?' I don't even know how he feels about me. For all I know, he came here under protest too and doesn't even like me. He's never said anything about how he feels about being here. He's just been polite the whole time. He hasn't so much as tried to hold my hand while he's been here! Does that sound like a guy set on courting me? Or proposing?" The thought made her laugh. "No. He's not once been pushy or demanding or even down that I can tell. He's simply been nice and positive and helpful and curious about everything every day. Pretty much just perfect." She sighed dramatically, crossed her arms, and put her head down on them on the table.

Spencer was way out of his comfort zone now but he tried.

"If it means anything at all, I understand. They're great guys. I like them both too."

"Well, don't be thinking you can have one," Birdie now teased, sitting up, grinning and trying to lighten the mood

177

JingleBelle Jackson

as Spence rolled his eyes. He knew he should have left this kind of conversation for Sandra. Birdie smiled at her best guy friend knowing he hated this kind of topic and that it was time to move on to other things. "In all seriousness, it means a lot to hear it from you. It's especially great that you listen to me," she said. "I couldn't have a better friend than you are."

"That is true," Spencer said, smiling broadly too. "Now, share with me the latest and greatest on the academy plans. It looks like you've been making progress without me."

"I have! I took all we talked about with Christina last week, brushed it up, and sent it off to Sandra. She and Crow and Gunny have been reviewing the ideas and added in some cool additions. After lots of back and forth, I am very pleased to say that I think we have an agenda set for our first AOK camp session! Spence, I am super excited about it!"

Spencer was too, if for no other reason than the academy planning seemed to be the one thing that consistently kicked Birdie out of her funk. Truth be told, the past several weeks since Sam had arrived had been like an emotional amusement park for Spence. Not just one ride but all sorts of rides. Birdie was up, then down. Happy, then sad. Confused, then clear. Sometimes all within the course of one short meeting with her! He worked to stay calm and centered because he knew that, more than ever, she needed that from him. And that was part of being best friends. Birdie and Sandra added excitement to his calm and pretty routine life, and he added sensibility and reason to theirs. He smiled, knowing that thought was a little bit overstated.

Birdie took his smile as being pleased with her plans too and, in truth, he really was. The academy was one of the coolest things he expected he would ever get the good fortune to be involved in helping to launch in his entire life. He was not just interested, he was as committed as the others to making it the best it could be.

"Hey, anyone in here? What's a guy gotta do to get a good greeting around here?"

"Gunny?" the two said at the same time as they heard a voice they thought they recognized but didn't expect. "Gunny!" they now exclaimed as he came into full view. Birdie went in for a big hug and Spence gave him a nod from the other side of the table.

"Why didn't you tell us you were coming?" Birdie asked. "Anyone else come along with you?" she added, looking past him in hopes of glimpsing his handsome brother. These were confusing times for her.

Gunny knew who she meant by "anyone" and cleared that up as kindly as he could. "No one this trip," he said softly, "but I know he misses you something awful." He was trying to help. It did and didn't all at the same time.

"We really planned on me being here weeks ago but it's taken this long to get the elves back to full production at the factory. It was too much for just Sandra and Crow, and there

179

was no way we could bring some of them down here to help with the barge until we had that straightened out."

"So does this mean it's getting better up there?" Spence asked hopefully.

Gunny shook his head woefully. "Not much," he said. "Yes, the elves are more productive but no, they still aren't very happy. Maybe a little bit but nowhere near their normal. We couldn't put off work on completing the South Pole Village barge any longer, though, if we want it to be ready this year so, here I am." He smiled and bowed with a tip of his hat to be silly. "And there's a bunch of reluctant and sour elves joining me in the morning."

"Hooray!" Birdie said, clapping her hands as the guys looked at her with skepticism. She knew how they felt but she felt differently. Even dour and down elves sounded good to her. She loved being around elves. Sooner or later they, like her, would snap out of their confusion and malaise, and life would go back to its normal, happy ways.

It would. She knew it. She had to believe.

CHAPTER 35

The Look of Despair

Location: Holiday Ranch

It wasn't just the elves and Birdie who were suffering from the dark malaise. In fact, their funk was child's play in comparison to the deep, very dark hole where Wistle spent her days and nights since her meeting with the saneers. It was such a deep, deep place that Ghost worried she would never come out.

He was completely out of ideas on ways to soothe her. True to his word, he had worked with his family to remove every mirror and reflective object from the ranch. With a single glance at Wistle so tenderly held in Ghost's arms, and the tears in his normally dry eyes, the Holiday family had immediately gone into protection mode. At Ghost's direction, no one but family was allowed to come into the ranch house and even family was not allowed in the bunk room where she was

JingleBelle Jackson

staying. He had protectively located her in a far corner of the room. Ghost had moved his things to the bunk room as well and located himself across the room and close to the door.

For days, Wistle had been in the sleep the saneers had enforced on her. The spell had placed her in a hold of some kind where she could exist without food or water. While Ghost had worried whether she would ever awake, he was thankful she wasn't at the same time. Each day asleep and unconscious to the world meant a day closer to Jason getting the saneers to undo the wicked spell they had cast and restore to her what they had outrageously and wrongly stolen.

He knew why they had taken her beauty. Wistle had the kind of looks that others envied. She was stunning, more so even than most fairies and all shan fairies were generally described as stunning. Their beauty was part of who they were and how they defined themselves. Unlike shan fairies, shanelle fairies could be stunning or plain and didn't particularly care either way. But Wistle was a full shan. She cared very much. The saneers obviously cared, too. Owning that kind of beauty for their own, to keep or trade for something else, must have been one of their greatest prizes.

They hadn't just taken her beauty, in fact. They had also taken at least some of her time as her days unconscious ticked on as she slept and slept. Ghost barely could rest at all, however. Sleep eluded him most nights. He wouldn't be calmed in any way until Wistle got back what was taken from her.

182

He was angry and outraged on Wistle's behalf. His girlfriend couldn't protest, but he paced the floor day and night, planning and plotting, and still coming up with nothing. The frustration of it all kept him from sleep and kept him quietly pacing. *Why Wistle?* he pleaded to the full moon one night as he gazed out the window. *Why couldn't it have been Jason?* He knew that wasn't a fair way to think but Wistle was, by far, the most innocent of victims ever in this saneer travesty of injustice as far as he was concerned.

"Ghost?"

He whirled around at the whisper of his name, and in just a few strides was by Wistle's side as she sat there on the side of her bed in the dim moonlight.

"Wistle!" He felt relief flood through him. She was awake! He knelt down and folded her in his arms. The feelings of relief left him quickly, knowing he had hard explanations ahead of him.

"I'm at the ranch?" Wistle asked, understandably confused. Ghost nodded his head.

"How'd I get here?"

"I brought you here," he said, slowly looking at her with eyes full of love and concern, willing her to see that and believe in him through this conversation.

"Why?"

"What's the last thing you remember, Wist?"

She sat quietly thinking. "I was with Jason meeting those awful saneers." She shuddered as she spoke and faced him with alarm in her eyes. "Ghost, they were even worse than I imagined and I imagined pretty bad."

He hugged her again. Holding her close so he wouldn't have to see the look in her eyes when she heard the truth. "You were so brave to go with Jason to face them. They were more devious than any of us could have imagined, Wist. True monsters!" Despite his misgivings about looking at her, she deserved to have the truth told to her directly, and not by some coward hiding in a hug. He pulled back and looked at her confused eyes, struggling to remember and understand what he was saying. He started with the good news.

"Wist, you and Jason were successful! The saneers lifted the spell from the elves and they're awake! Not entirely back to normal yet, but awake. All thanks to you and Jason!" He smiled stronger than he felt, willing her to find strength in the achievement. She nodded her head, feeling pleased about the news but she wasn't just a normally beautiful fairy, she was also a smart fairy and she knew there was more.

"But?" she asked, looking at Ghost directly and seeing in his eyes now that something big and horrible was coming next. His eyes were begging for understanding and full of compassion. She felt herself afraid before she even heard his answer. She pulled away to get some space. Ghost stepped forward and she stepped back again with a shake of her head, which he honored by giving her the space he understood she needed. He struggled to find the right words and she pushed.

184

"Ghost! C'mon! What is it? Did they cast the spell on me? Is that it? How long have I been sleeping? Is that why I'm here? What year is it? You don't look any different to me so it can't have been long – or maybe you just age really well." She cast a quick hopeful grin his way. He didn't look too different so she couldn't have been asleep that long. She'd be mad they took any of her time but she was awake now and could handle it. Getting even would become her quest.

Ghost was glad to see her feisty, fighter personality coming back. He knew that it would serve her well as they worked through this challenge.

"You haven't been sleeping that long," he said as he formed his words carefully. She was staring down, trying to think about what happened and looked at her hands for the first time. Her hands? Those couldn't be her hands? They looked old and withered. She looked up at him and he realized what she was thinking. The words now tumbled out.

"The saneers gave the elves back their time but demanded something instead. They were going to take it from Jason but you, being the loyal and brave fighter that you are, stepped in front of him to save him and they took it from you instead."

She was catching on now, vaguely remembering. She took the hands that she didn't recognize and put them up to feel a face she didn't recognize and ran them through thin hair that didn't feel like her own and she knew. She knew what Ghost wasn't saying and looked at him with the despair that he knew he would see when she realized the truth. He wished with everything in him he wasn't the guy who had put it there. He wasn't the cause but he was the messenger. She covered her face with her hands and flew to the bathroom.

"Wistle, wait! We have to talk about this," he called after her as she slammed the door and then immediately reopened it.

"Where are the mirrors? What did you do with the mirrors?" She was accusing and demanding.

"Wistle, trust me, you don't want to see a mirror right now," he said. "Come sit down with me so I can fill you in —"

"Get out." She whirled around not facing him and pointed to the bunk room door.

"What?"

"I said, 'GET OUT!' Now, Ghost! GET OUT! Quit looking at me!"

"Wistle, it's not like that. Of course I'm going to —"

"NOW! Now, now, now!"

"Please, Wistle —"

"Please, Ghost," she said, now quieter, her voice full of a sadness he had never heard before. "Please. I need to be alone. I understand what happened. Please go."

Reluctantly, as slowly as he could remember ever moving in hopes she would reach out to him and change her mind, he moved to the door.

"Ghost?" His heart soared as he turned with love in his eyes that she couldn't see because she was still turned away from him.

"Yes?" he said, hoping she was going to let him stay after all.

"Never look at me again."

He closed the door quietly, stepped out, and slid down the door to the floor overcome with exhaustion and grief.

Wistle climbed back into the bed, facing the wall, and slid down the sheets into a very dark, dark hole where only she lived and where she allowed no visitors.

CHAPTER 36

An Unexpected Elf Cure

Location: St. Annalise

Miraculously, within hours of the elves arriving on St. Annalise, things did begin to change. It was the most unlikely person of all who brought it about.

Right on schedule, Reindeer Express coaches landed at St. Annalise, full of elves assigned to "Equator Pole" and working on the barge with Gunny. One by one, elves would slowly emerge from the coaches, rubbing their eyes after having slept most of the way. For Birdie and Spencer, it was easy to see why Gunny had felt the need to caution them about the changes in the little toymakers. Gone were the talkative, giggling, energetic, and happy elves they all knew and loved, and in their place were somber, zombie-like replacements that seemed almost to be sleep-walking through their days. They were quiet and methodical. They responded to direction but took no

189

JINGLEBELLE JACKSON

initiative on their own. Where before they had taken great delight in getting their tropical shirts and dresses, flip flops, and especially their glittery sunglasses, now they accepted them from Birdie with barely a thank you. Only the mention of sno-cones brought any kind of true joy to their faces.

Sam had been anxious to help too, and Birdie had given him a task fitting of his experience and one that could provide some real insight to all of them. He would be leaving the day after next and so time was of the essence.

As the elves sat at the big tables centered in the eating area of Equator Village, slurping down their rainbow-colored sno-cones before noon in the hot island sun, Birdie stood with Gunny for announcements. She loved seeing them all together and especially in their bright, sparkly, over-sized sunglasses.

"Attention, bargers," Gunny said with a clap of his hands, a smile on his face and more enthusiasm than he felt for the task at hand in his voice. "Welcome back to St. Annalise Island! I want to thank our always gracious and exceptionally generous host, Christina Annalise, for allowing us this very private place in the world to build such an important gift for the world." He turned to face the headmistress of the island who had come down to greet the elves. From her place on the sidelines, Christina gave them all a wave and felt the sting of the post-spell elves when none waved back. Gunny shrugged an apology to her, which she waved off. She had heard from Jason what had happened and wasn't at all insulted by their lack of interest. Only worried. Gunny plunged on.

190

ENCHANTMENTS A SOUTH POLE SANTA ADVENTURE

"We have a great deal to accomplish here in a short time and I'll be making work assignments for you starting this afternoon. This morning you will be checking into your bunks – without a nap," he had to add that and heard groans that made him glad he did. "You will also check in with Birdie who has a very special person for you to meet with a very important assignment for each of you. Birdie, will you explain?"

Birdie smiled and stepped up to the front of the group. "My beloved elves," she said warmly. "It is so wonderful to have you back here sharing the place I love the most and the place I consider home." Perhaps the person listening to her most intently was the man she was about to introduce. "This year, I am so pleased to introduce you to a special friend of mine. Sam has come to join us all the way from Africa and is studying to be a highly regarded doctor who is going to give you all check-ups!" She tried to make it sound very exciting as Sam smiled and waved from his spot on the sidelines.

"Check-ups!"

"Noooooo!"

"We're not sick!"

"I hate shots!"

"Shots! I don't want a shot either!"

And with the mention of shots, the whole group started crying.

"Elves, elves!" Birdie called out, trying to get them calm again. In their new joyless state, she and the others had

191

JingleBelle Jackson

forgotten how sensitive they were and how easily they could become criers. She was upset that the news had upset them.

"I'm not actually that kind of doctor," Sam now said, giving a glance at Birdie to be sure it was okay he spoke. "I'm a doctor with a highly unique specialty. I'm here to check your funny bone."

"Our funny bone!"

"He's going to check our funny bone!"

"That's funny!"

For the first time in weeks, there were genuine smiles and curiosity showing on the faces of the elves.

Elf hands went in the air.

"Yes, you there, in the back, with the gorgeous pink sunglasses and perfect hair. Please state your name and your question."

The group parted a bit to see who he was talking to as the elf selected spoke up smiling.

"Why thank you, Sam from Africa. I'm Diva and I'm wondering where my funny bone is? And also thank you for noticing my hair."

How did he know Diva loved to be complimented? Birdie wondered, so pleased with Sam and the unexpected turn of temperament the elves were showing.

"Excellent question, Diva! Who else had that question?" Sam asked, as every elf raised a hand. "I thought so. Well, that is part of why I must give each of you a thorough check-up to determine where your funny bone is and to make sure it's not missing or in need of some kind of attention since I

Enchantments A South Pole Santa Adventure

understand many of you haven't felt very happy lately. That makes me think your funny bones might be out of order. It can happen to all of us from time to time but is generally quite easy to fix." The elves all came a buzz about this news and started talking, even giggling, with each other.

Gunny stared at this clever guy that he had just met. He was genius! Out of a self-decided loyalty to his brother, Gunny hadn't wanted to meet Sam. In fact, he had tried to wait to return to the island until Sam had left but when Sandra had listed all the pressing reasons that were waiting for attention, he had set his qualms aside and headed back. Still, he had had no intention of meeting Sam if at all possible. Now Gunny realized he had been shortsighted to prejudge the guy.

If Gunny had looked over at Birdie on the other side of him, he might not have been so happy with Sam, however. Birdie was beaming at him. With a look that was quite different than she likely would have given Spencer, for instance, if Spence had just come up with this clever approach. It was less a look of friendship affection and more a look of, well, flirtatious affection.

"Now, are there any other questions?" Sam asked, keeping his serious doctor look on. Two hands went up.

"Yes, you first, in the sparkly green glasses."

"I'm Dervish and this is my girlfriend Periwinkle," Dervish said, introducing the little elf next to him. "We were wondering how you fix a funny bone."

"Well, it's not painful, really, and quite simple. When we find a funny bone is out of order, you are prescribed an oil to rub on it and a daily medication."

"Blech."

"Blech."

"Yuck."

The elves all started sticking their tongues out like they had tasted something bad.

"But we don't like medicine," Periwinkle said sadly, speaking for them all.

"Do you like peppermints?" Sam asked.

"Yes," came the answer from the group.

"Well then, you will like the prescription for fixing your funny bones. You must take one peppermint candy in the morning and one at night without fail. As well as rubbing a tiny bit of peppermint oil into the broken spot. That is all. Anyone willing to do that?" Sam asked, suspecting he knew the answer.

"YES!" they all yelled back, now smiling.

"Okay, time for one more question. You in the pretty purple glasses."

"Hi, Peppermint Sam, I'm Violet." Violet beamed a smile at the doctor that Gunny and the rest hadn't seen the likes of since before Slumber Month.

"She called him 'Peppermint Sam'," came the buzz from around the group with giggles attached.

"Hi, Violet," Sam said, actually appreciating his new nickname. "What would you like to ask me?"

Enchantments A South Pole Santa Adventure

"Can I go first?" she said, smiling while all the elves broke into protest.

"Nooooo!"

"I want to be first!"

"No fair!"

"My funny bone really hurts. I should go first!"

"Because someone has to go first and Violet thought to raise her hand and ask, Violet goes first," Sam answered, talking loud now to be heard above the elf protests. "Whether you go first or last, I have plenty of time for all of you and won't quit until we find, and fix, each of your funny bones. Okay?"

"Okay!" the group called out, now acting more like themselves than they had in months.

Gunny stood there with Birdie and Spence and Christina, all stunned by what had just happened. He wasted no time taking advantage of the momentum.

"Well, what are you all doing here? Run and get your stuff put away on your bunks so you can get in line for Peppermint Sam, the Funny Bone Man!" He smiled at own cleverness, everyone laughed, and away the elves went. Not stoically walking in a reluctant single line dragging their feet in the sand, but running in flip flops, hanging on to sunhats, bags in hand, and smiles on their faces.

Birdie wasted not a single minute but boldly walked over to her forced fiancé from Africa and kissed him full on the lips, putting a big smile on his face as big as the one on hers.

195

CHAPTER 37

Fixing the Funny Bones

Location: St. Annalise

"Next, please," Birdie called out solemnly to the line-up of elves.

Sam had successfully banished reluctance for a check-up out of the elves but, despite that, this was truly meant to be a real check-up to be sure there wasn't some kind of malice lingering on them all from the spell.

Thanks to looking for their funny bone, Sam was able to listen to their heart rates; check their pulses; check ears, eyes and throats; get a look for cavities; feel for fevers, and ask them general questions about how they felt. In the end, he was successfully able to determine that each of them was in perfect health, as elves most generally are all through their long lives, but that each had a funny bone out of order. This was, he said, likely due to not laughing enough and sleeping

197

JingleBelle Jackson

too much. They also needed to sweeten up and have a daily reminder of Christmas. Each elf was given a large bottle of peppermint candies with their name on them and a recommended "dosage" to "take two a day and always with laughter." They also each received a bottle of peppermint oil to "rub sparingly on the funny bone and/or smell regularly out of the bottle whenever you need to feel a dose of Christmas magic." Finally, they were admonished not to sleep more than eight hours a night, preferably less, since they were all well rested and could convert back to elf sleeping patterns of little sleep needed.

For most of the elves, Peppermint Sam had found their funny bones located in the area of one of their elbows. A few had their funny bone hidden behind their knee, three had it hidden in a little finger and one had insisted his funny bone was behind his ear. When Doctor Sam looked close, he had indeed found it there and applied some peppermint oil immediately.

"Okay, Hot Rod, thank you for very graciously going last. I'd like to treat you to a sno-cone tomorrow on me to say thank you," Sam said as he handed Hot Rod his bottle of peppermint oil.

"Thank you, Doctor Peppermint Sam! My funny bone is feeling much better already!"

"You are welcome," Sam said, smiling. He smiled even bigger when he saw Birdie leaning against the doorjamb smiling at him.

198

"This was the greatest day, all thanks to you, Peppermint Sam," Birdie said.

"I don't know if I agree with you," Sam said in return, continuing on as he saw her go to protest. "I mean, I think it went well, even better than expected, but from my view at least one smile," he pointed to his own, "was all thanks to you and that surprise 'remedy' you laid on me back at the picnic tables."

Birdie felt her face flush. It had been impulsive and forward, two words that were normally not generally used to describe her. It had also been a sincere kiss that expressed fully the affection she had been feeling for him at that moment.

Now, though, she found herself feeling shy and not sure what to say next. Sam understood and started a conversation the two needed to have.

"I leave the day after tomorrow, Ambyrdena," he said.

"No one's leaving the day after tomorrow," Gunny said, striding into the room excitedly. "Are you kidding? We can't have you going now! You're Peppermint Sam the Funny Bone Man! The elves love you! Maybe more than they love Santa! How did you know that was what they needed anyway?" Gunny asked. Birdie had wondered as well.

"It just didn't make sense to me that there could be anything physically wrong with them from the spell, which meant it was some kind of lingering suggestion of woe, so to speak. Maybe even a little bit of hypnosis had been used on them," Sam said. "It seemed like they needed to have someone tell them that what had been ailing them could be and was

JingleBelle Jackson

fixed and they were free to be funny and have fun again. I caution, however, that we still don't know for sure it has worked. It may take several days to know, for sure. That means I'll be gone. I hope one of you will let me know if it was a success."

"No, Sam, I'm serious. You really can't go. We need you. The elves need you. Sandra and Santa need you. The children of the world need you." Gunny was imploring him. This guy – using no magic but good humor, smarts, and kindness – had managed to do in a matter of hours what none of the rest of them had cracked through in weeks. Gunny couldn't let him leave them.

"I'm willing to stay longer," Sam said quietly, nodding his head. "But I have a condition."

"Name it! Anything! We can make it happen!" Gunny said, caught up in his goal of keeping Sam there.

"My condition is that Birdie says she needs me," Sam said, standing and talking now just to Birdie as Gunny found himself in an extremely awkward position. Birdie was blushing furiously at this point and embarrassed to have this playing out in front of the brother of her boyfriend.

"What do you say, Birdie?" Sam said intently.

"I say 'yes,'," she said, giving a glance at Gunny, who was missing from the door now, and then giving her full attention to the man with the striking eyes standing right in front of her. "Yes, I need you too. Stay." This time it was Sam who did the kissing.

200

CHAPTER 38

Hugs of the Best Kind

Location: St. Annalise

Like his younger brothers, Gunny paced when he was worried. And worry seemed to have taken up residence with him since the day he met Miss Cassandra Penelope Clausmonetsiamlydelaterra "dot dot dot" he said out loud.

He had always had such a carefree life on the ranch growing up. Sure, he'd had the occasional runaway cow, a horse that bucked him off, some broken bones even from time to time, but nothing worth pacing the floor for. But with Sandra in his life and the elves and new friends and the kids of the world to worry on, well, he paced more than he liked. In this case, he was pacing the floors of Mistletoe Hall on the barge, worrying for his brother and what he saw as a broken heart headed Crow's way.

JINGLEBELLE JACKSON

Even if they were just realizing it, he could see that Birdie and Sam were well suited. And that was big coming from Gunny because he saw that only begrudgingly. It wasn't a match-up he wanted to hear about or wanted to see for that matter. Up to a few hours ago, when he had landed on St. Annalise, he had felt Birdie and his brother were the two that were well suited to each other. And they were, no doubt, but this match seemed to have a pull that was almost tangible, almost inevitable, really.

So now what was he supposed to do? Tell Crow? Not tell him? What would he want if he was in that place? To know for sure, that was the answer. Unless it wasn't. Why would he want to know exactly the worse thing he would ever want to know? He wouldn't. Oh buckin' buck-a-roos, what if this happened to him in the end? What if Sandra chose Jason? He would never want to know that. So, that settled it then. He wouldn't tell Crow. Or maybe he would. He went back to pacing the big, open floor, which seemed to be doing nothing for him.

" . . . *squawk!* . . . here he is! . . . *squawk!*

"Squawk! What are you doing here?" Gunny asked, surprised to see the big bird, then quickly realized who Squawk was likely talking to. He stopped pacing and replaced it with an almost full-out run to the ballroom door where he slowed himself down and tried to look cool and not too excited to see her. *Get a hold of yourself, Holiday,* his head shouted at him. *You just saw her two days ago. Yeah, for a few minutes,* his heart

ENCHANTMENTS A SOUTH POLE SANTA ADVENTURE

hollered back. *Every minute of every day would still not be enough.* His heart won in the end as Sandra came in view on the barge deck, wearing a big smile, and he impulsively gathered her up in his arms for a twirl in the wide space.

"What was that for?" Sandra asked, holding onto the sun hat she wore with one hand and onto him with the other.

"That," Gunny said. "Was just because I love surprises." He wanted to say "because I love you" but somehow he just couldn't. Call it Holiday pride. Call it watching Crow's relationship imploding. Call it listening to his head and telling his heart to ratchet it down a few notches. Call it flat-out fear that she didn't feel the same and never would. Whatever it was, he just couldn't do it. He felt it. He knew it. He doubted the feelings would ever change but it was enough right now to keep it to himself.

"And you are the best surprise of all," he added.

"And this is the best welcome home ever," Sandra said, setting her feet back down solidly on the deck but not moving out of his arms.

"Sandra!"

Sandra turned at the call of her name and at what sounded like elf voices – except that they were too happy sounding to be the new version of elves.

But they were! She couldn't believe her eyes when she looked across Equator Village and saw the elves running up the ramp her way as fast as their elf legs would run. She turned to look at Gunny with delight and question in her eyes,

203

which he loved seeing. Those were happy eyes, he thought, and nothing made him happier than seeing her happy.

"Yeah, I don't know what brought you back right now but your timing couldn't be better. We have some huge things going on and I'm not even talking about this barge we're standing on, which is, by far, the biggest thing on this island."

Sandra clapped her hands in delight as the elves reached her and caught her up in the best elf hug she could remember ever having. First a crazy good hug from Gunny and now an impossibly perfect hug from the elves. *Could life be better in that moment?* she wondered.

She had loads of questions and it sounded like Gunny had answers. That was good enough. She could wait for them just like she had waited weeks for this. She looked over at Gunny from inside the elf pile and smiled from her heart.

CHAPTER 39

Say No to Saneers

Location: Somewhere in Fairy Land

Jason was getting nowhere. The saneers had used some kind of powerful and vexing force-field on their part of the realm that was completely effective at keeping Jason out. He was king of the fairies with access to every part of the fairy kingdom but someone needed to tell that to the saneers it seemed!

The saneers knew, they just didn't care. They took direction from no one but themselves. They had no problem, however, taking priceless valuables from whomever they chose. Most often for their own amusement. They had no loyalty to or interest in speaking to Jason. He was simply a bother to them. Without that meeting, Jason had no way of reversing the spell they had placed on Wistle.

It was appalling to him that such vile individuals as the saneers could possibly be part of his own kind. Yes,

205

JingleBelle Jackson

fairies, especially the shans, could be haughty and feel superior to others but his shan side understood those feelings. They *were* superior! *Ah, such a fairy way to think*, Jason thought wryly. He was truly embracing who he had discovered he was.

He wasn't just a shan fairy, however. His mother, he was told, was shanelle and he felt equally attached to that side of his heritage. The shanelle fairies were approachable and helpful. Often bullied by the shans, they found their joy in being of service to others. Humans lucky enough to know a fairy usually had met a shanelle. Shans wanted very little to do with the "very limited human species."

Jason, like all students at St. Annalise Academy, had learned there were two sorts of fairies, but not once, that he could recall, had the saneers ever been mentioned. Even now, all fairies, no matter their background, seemed to avoid speaking of the saneers in any way as if the conversation alone would cause the saneers to seek them out. Having seen the saneers in action, he understood the extreme avoidance. He also knew to avoid them was to allow them to flourish, take, and torment. They hurt their own kind and they hurt others. They presented an untenable example of fairies to all the world. Their reign of terrorizing would end with him. When they had struck such a blow to Wistle, meant for him no less, and refused to undo the spell, they released a commitment deep inside Jason that would find no relief until justice prevailed. Surprisingly to him, this pledge for change was not

ENCHANTMENTS A SOUTH POLE SANTA ADVENTURE

welcomed by others, including the council members of the Supreme Council of Fairies of who he ruled over.

"No!" Reesa shouted as the rest of the council members joined in with the same outcry. "You ask for too much." With a nudge from the fairy sitting next to her, she added, "Your Highness." Reesa, who had been heir apparent as the reigning ruler of the fairies, now begrudgingly recognized Jason as her king but she knew she would have been a far superior ruler. Probably every shan fairy at the table felt the same about themselves. Jason knew that, of course. His shan side rather enjoyed their discomfort and his shanelle side was determined to provide them leadership they could be proud of in their king.

"Too much?" Jason boomed out "It is asking too much that we seek out the saneers – our own kind – and insist they face their Council, our system for justice, on charges that have been brought against them?"

"Your highness," said a council fairy assigned with administrative duties at the meetings. "There are no outstanding charges against them."

"How can that be possible? I personally know of several cases where the price the saneers have charged for their supposed 'services' has far exceeded the value they provided. Often, their methods have been plainly misrepresented and payment has still been taken. Not paid voluntarily but taken without consent. You mean to tell me no one has ever complained to this board and asked for justice?"

207

JingleBelle Jackson

"Complaints regarding the saneers are not allowed to be brought forth," Reesa said flatly. "For obvious reasons."

"And what are those reasons? Please do tell," Jason said, trying to keep sarcasm out of his voice. He doubted the reasons had merit but wanted to hear their thinking.

Reesa chose to stand to present the reasons.

"One, fairies who have been wronged by the saneers sought out the saneer's services and knew the risks of such interactions.

"Two, saneers do not recognize the power of this council or your position of king.

"Three, saneers are the most powerful magic-makers and magic-takers in the fairy realm.

"Four, there is no remedy that we can enforce to make them change.

"Five, to that end, any futile action we would take would risk their wrath directed at any or all of us.

"Six, it is believed that the saneers were involved in the loss of the last two fairy rulers, several council members and, with due respect to your highness, even your own parents."

Reesa sat down as Jason reeled with this news. *The saneers were involved in why he likely ended up in a dingy that had floated to St. Annalise and he was raised by Christina Annalise, who he loved as his mother, and not by his own kind?*

Any other ruler likely would have turned from this pursuit after hearing the reasons that Reesa had listed. He was not any other ruler, however, and he would not be turned

208

away. Her list flamed the ember inside him into a full-on four-alarm fire of vengeance. *No, not vengeance, Jason*, he thought only to himself. *You're the king. Justice.* That is what he would pursue. Justice for all who had been wronged. He would need the Council's help and, fortunately being half shan, he knew the words that might get that for him.

"So you all are afraid of them then, is that what I understand?" Jason asked as calmly and as innocently as he could, knowing the words would be seen as an attack on their individual and collective pride. *Target hit,* he thought, as the majority of the members jumped to their feet in protest.

Now he had a formidable group to back him as they pursued the saneers.

# # #

None of this processing was helping Wistle, however. Day after day, she slept. She never left the bunk room. Only Ghost's mom Josie was allowed in to see her. Wistle hadn't looked in a mirror. She hadn't wanted to or needed to. She had seen the truth reflected in her boyfriend's eyes the day she awoke.

CHAPTER 40

Time for a Beach Party

Location: St. Annalise Island

It had taken Sandra more than an hour to get all the answers she needed on how Sam had "cured" the elves. After that, her goal was to catch up with her friends and family. She had managed to get a big group, including Christina, Cappie and Thomas, gathered down at the beach for an evening bonfire. Everyone was kicking back enjoying some of the great perks of living on an island: great views, great sunsets, great beaches, great bonfires and, in this case, great friends to throw into the mix. Even Jason's dog Mango was there playing fetch with Spence on the beach in the very last light of the day.

Just like Gunny, Sandra had found herself instantly "in like" with Sam and could see that there were sparks going on between Birdie and her dreaded fiancé. Apparently, the month had not gone as bad as Birdie had projected it would.

211

JINGLEBELLE JACKSON

One look at Sam's eyes – made even more striking, if possible, in the bonfire light – and Sandra understood what Crow was up against from the minute Sam arrived on the island. He was mesmerizing and hard to turn away from!

Sandra wanted to catch up with Birdie on all the details of how it had been going, but right now, things seemed like any alone time Birdie had would not be spent with Sandra. Though they were being surreptitious about it, as the sun went down on the beach, Sandra could see her best friend and Sam touching their fingertips together in the sand. She stretched out one of her hands to copy the couple and touched her fingertips to Gunny's hand as he talked with Thomas, who was sitting on the other side of him. Without so much as looking at her, or missing a word in his conversation with Thomas, Gunny interlocked his fingers in hers like it was a normal thing that happened all the time. His hand around hers made her feel safe and happy.

"I'm sorry, Cassandra," Sam was saying to Sandra now, bringing her out of her friendly finger flirting. It was rare to hear her full name said. She found it to be another of Sam's charming traits. "I didn't catch what brought you back to St. Annalise? Ambyrdena had said she didn't think I would get to meet you."

"I needed a break, to be honest," Sandra said. "I've been gone for most of two months now and I get lonesome for home. Once, when Santa seemed like he was doing well enough to oversee the elves and Crow volunteered to check

ENCHANTMENTS A SOUTH POLE SANTA ADVENTURE

on them, I decided I could get home for a few days." She paused, feeling awkward about having mentioned Crow to Sam. Gunny gave her hand a quick squeeze of understanding and she pushed forward, but she noticed that Birdie had moved her hand away from Sam's and was sitting with her arms wrapped around her knees now.

"There's so much happening with the barge and even more happening with the Academy of Kindness, thanks to Birdie, Christina, and Spence, that I didn't want to stay away. Plus, I also hoped to meet you. So, here I am!" She threw her hands in the air for emphasis, thinking Gunny would let go. When he didn't, she could see the surprised look on Birdie and Spence's faces that she was holding hands with Gunny. Cappie smiled when she saw it and Sandra smiled back. So what if people knew? She kept her hand where it was, although, as tight as Gunny was holding it, she doubted she could have let go anyway. She smiled a ridiculous silly grin of happiness that would have been embarrassing if it was broad daylight but it was dimmed down and not quite as crazy big in the flickering shadows of the fire.

"I have a question for you, Sam," Sandra said. "Well, first a giant thank you from me and Santa and every child on the planet who loves Santa Claus for taking such kind care of the elves. I don't know if we can ever thank you enough."

"It's been so much fun, helping them find their funny bones, that I feel the honor was completely mine. I think

213

JINGLEBELLE JACKSON

the elves made me happier than I made them," Sam said graciously in return.

"I completely understand that. For me, being Santa is no work at all compared to the joy it brings me – especially getting to work with the elves. I'm glad to hear you feel that way too," Sandra said slyly. "I'm also pleased to hear you are staying on for a while since I would like to ask a huge favor of you." She paused, and then rushed on with her question. "Would you be willing to visit North Pole Village with me and help the rest of the elves too?

"Before you say yes, you should know that there are several hundred of them still in need of your magic doctoring. It would likely take a week or more to get it all done."

"Of course my answer is yes," Sam said without hesitation. "I believe in going where I am needed whether that is to a village in Africa to help children or a village at the North Pole to help elves."

"That makes me so happy!" Sandra said, releasing her hand from Gunny's so she could reach over and hug on her new friend.

"Well, actually, Sand, I'm not so sure that will work with Sam's schedule. We have quite a bit to do here for the AOK that I was counting on getting his help with," Birdie said.

"Bird, I promise we'll get it all done. When Sam helps the elves, we might even be able to get some of them to help us and catch up that –"

She cut herself off mid-sentence seeing Birdie behind Sam shaking her head no and making a slicing motion with her hand at her neck, indicating to Sandra to knock it off. *Why on earth is she doing that?* Sandra thought until finally it hit her. Crow! Of course Birdie wouldn't want Sam at the North Pole, Crow was at the North Pole. What had she done?

But it was too late. Sam was outright excited about going and, truth be told, even Birdie would agree, they needed him to go.

"I cannot believe I will get to visit the North Pole, meet Santa Claus and the elves and serve the world in such a humble way. Of course, all of this depends on Ambyrdena going with me and approving of the trip," Sam said, reaching out and taking Birdie's hand in his own.

"Well, uh, that is to say," Birdie stumbled all over her words. She wanted to say no and knew she couldn't. "Of course," she spit out at last. "I'll help you and we'll stay with it Sandra until every elf has their funny bone fixed."

Or I get mine broken by a certain Holiday brother, she thought. *Oh, Birdie, what a mess you've made!*

CHAPTER 41

Tug on a Tug

Location: The Mistletoe

Sandra always slept great to the gentle rocking of the *Mistletoe* and she had been in desperate need of a good night's rest. With the worry over the elves, she hadn't slept more than a few hours every night, but on this night, back on her beloved tug, she slept solidly with barely a stir until the smell of bacon grilling in her galley woke her up.

Bacon? Who was cooking in her kitchen?

" . . . *squawk!* . . . wake up! . . . *squawk!* . . . elf in the kitchen! . . ."

"An elf? What elf?"

" . . . don't know him . . . *squawk!*"

An elf that Squawk didn't know was cooking bacon in her kitchen and making a lot of noise doing it. Every day brought something new and interesting, Sandra thought as she ran her fingers through her messy morning hair and headed down the hall.

"Good morning," she said to the elf facing away from her.

"AHHH!" the elf exclaimed, throwing his hands up, apparently startled by getting a greeting from the person who lived on the tugboat he was cooking on. "Oh excuse me, your Royal Highness. You scared me! I thought you were still sleeping!" The elf coughed out the words as he patted at his shirt. He was covered from head to toe in a light layer of flour that had flown out of the container in his hands when Sandra scared him with her greeting. He swatted at the air to clear the floating flour dust as he turned to speak to her directly. "What a terrible way to meet you, your Highness, in this flour-covered state."

Sandra smiled. "You just look a little dusty," she said, reaching out to try and dust some flour off of him and instead sending more flying in the air. She realized she wasn't helping and stepped back. "I'm sorry, but I don't believe we've met. I'm Sandra Claus dot dot dot, South Pole Santa and owner of this wonderful boat."

"Oh yes, your Royal Highness, I know who you are! I'm Toby, the elf, assigned to help you here on this tug. Please call me Tug from now on."

"Assigned to the *Mistletoe* huh, Tug, you say?" Sandra said, holding back a smile.

"Yes, ma'am, Tug. Self-assigned, your Highness. My specialty is clean-up and if you don't mind me saying so, you could use a little help."

Enchantments A South Pole Santa Adventure

Sandra didn't even look around to know it was true. She and Cappie and Squawk had many wonderful attributes but housekeeping, or in this case, tugboat-keeping, was not necessarily one of them. It was usually clean enough but not super clean.

"Self-assigned to be my own personal tug boat elf?" Sandra repeated, pondering the idea. She had never considered anything of the sort. It might be wonderful having such a service provided but she doubted how much they really needed it and wondered how Em would feel about having another elf on board.

"Well, Toby," Sandra started.

"Tug, please, your Highness."

"Well, Tug, for starters, please do not call me 'your Highness.' I'm not royalty." Never mind that she was. She knew this little elf couldn't possibly know that. "I go by 'Sandra' to everyone."

"You are royalty!" Tug protested. "Being South Pole Santa is the most royal job anyone in the world could have. You should wear a crown instead of a hat, in fact."

Sandra laughed out loud, now understanding his reasoning for calling her royal, and thinking how silly she would look wearing a crown with her Santa suit.

"And you're so beautiful, too," Tug adding shyly. "Like a princess beautiful, your Highness."

"Now, Tug, I promise to work on calling you Tug instead of Toby if you promise to work on calling me Sandra." The

219

JingleBelle Jackson

flour-covered pancake-maker said nothing and just looked at her dubiously. "Ack, my bacon is burning!" he said at last, as smoke joined the floating flour dust in filling the galley air.

"What do you usually do at the North Pole, Tug?" Sandra asked, suppressing a laugh.

"Housecleaning, your Highness," he said without a pause. "I find it very satisfying. I wanted to try something new, though. When I heard they needed elves to work on the South Pole barge and there weren't enough volunteers, I hung up my North Pole feather duster and jumped on a reindeer coach before Cleaner, the boss elf of housekeeping, could stop me. Unfortunately, it turns out, I'm better with a broom than I am with a hammer. But that turned out to be your good luck because now, here I am! Serving on your ship to keep it ship-shape!"

He was so chipper and enthusiastic, Sandra hated to turn him down.

"Well, Squawk and I are the only ones here most of the time, although Birdie usually stays when she's on the island and sometimes a few other guests, but there's never very many of us here. We really just don't need a full-time elf, you see."

"No, your Highness!" Tug said politely while flipping a pancake. "With complete respect, I have to disagree." He took his finger and wiped it across the windowsill, held it up, and showed her it was covered with dust.

"Okay, I know we could use a little help with cleaning around here but we're used to our mess. Squawk and I don't mind things a little messy. Do we, Squawk?"

220

ENCHANTMENTS A SOUTH POLE SANTA ADVENTURE

" . . . another pancake please. . . *squawk!*"

Sandra laughed at the happy big bird.

"I see that you've won Squawk over. I hope you've left some for me, Squawk," Sandra said, sliding into a seat for some breakfast.

"Who's cooking over here?" Thomas asked, popping his head through the galley window. "Got enough for two more?"

"Yes, sir, Mr. Jackson, sir," said Tug, pouring more pancake batter on the griddle.

"Ahoy!" called out Cappie.

"Good morning, Mrs. Jackson, ma'am!" Tug said as Cappie gave Sandra a quizzical look.

"Thomas, Cappie, please meet Tug, who wants to be my new tugboat elf. Tug has self-assigned himself to the *Mistletoe* for care, upkeep, and cleaning."

"I'm very good and won't let you down," Tug said seriously. "My friends call me Er as in clean*er*, shini*er*, bright*er*." He emphasized the "er" part of each word as he said them. "I know they meant it as teasing but I didn't mind. I pride myself on my cleaning talents." He said that as he rubbed on a dark spot on the front of one of the kitchen cabinets that had been there for years. "Hmmmm, I'll have to bring my high-powered, super-secret cleaning mix for that," he said, talking to himself.

"Well, if he can clean as well as he makes pancakes," Thomas said, cutting into his third one. "Then I vote he stays."

Cappie bit into her short stack. "Mmmmmm, Sandra. These are better than mine."

Tug smiled. The whole group of them turned and looked at Sandra.

"Okay, okay, you win, Tug. Welcome aboard! We'll give it a try. Perhaps we can use a little 'er' around here."

Tug put his heels together and saluted Sandra, pancake spatula still in hand and covered head to toe in flour dust. *This is my new super cleaner?* Sandra thought smiling.

"You won't regret it, your Royal Highness!"

She knew she wouldn't.

CHAPTER 42

A Happy Day

Location: St. Annalise

In the two full days Sandra had at home, she spent most of it working with Gunny and the elves on the barge and putting final touches on the Academy of Kindness plans.

Both projects were so exciting! The barge was being slightly redesigned so it could accommodate the academy, and work had begun now on finishing the lower levels. Elf quarters and living areas were getting painted with touches of sparkles and glitter that she brought into the academy rooms as well since the effect was so positive and inviting. In each academy room, she had one full wall outfitted with whiteboards to encourage the creativity that was a top goal of the camp. Now, as they finished, she realized she was ready to speak with Beatrice Carol, the reporter with World Wide News, and share the exciting news with the world. Once they

JINGLEBELLE JACKSON

were back at the North Pole and Sam had treated Santa's and the elves' funny bones, she would call the reporter with the news. The idea made her excited, which was a nice change from her usual bit of dread that came with talking with the overly exuberant reporter.

She realized, too, that it had been weeks since she had heard from Jason. While that wasn't particularly unusual, she felt certain that, in this case, no news meant there was nothing good to report. Why was a fix for Wistle taking so long?

She missed the king of fairies but noticed her feelings for him were definitely changing. Her thoughts drifted more often now to Gunny, who seemed to always be there when she needed him and added so much fun to her life. She still had some trust issues with the cowboy but her heart was healing these days and she was willing to be open again to love. She smiled over at the Texan hunk and he came wandering over, hammer in hand. It was hot out on the island that day and the normal ocean breeze was missing. Sandra had brought the work party a bucket of cool drinks. Gunny reached for one and emptied it in what seemed like one big gulp.

"Exactly what I needed," he said, reaching for another.

"I thought so," Sandra said.

"I mean that smile on your face," he said, flirting outrageously with her. "This is nice though, too," he added, indicating his bottle of water.

Sandra was pleased with the attention. "I've come for a favor," she said. "Can you take a break?"

224

"Yep," Gunny said, setting the hammer down. When Sandra asked, his answer was always yes. She was the light in his life – and also his boss. "Where we going? Maybe to check out that clue?"

"Gunny! You are getting to know me too well," Sandra said, surprised he could figure that out so fast. "Yes, I had time to do some research in the library and found that the latest clue looks like it is to a coordinate on an island not far away from where we are. Willing to go with me?"

In response, he got serious, "Sandra, never go without me. You understand that, right?" It panicked him a little that she was so independent and could choose to pursue these clues on her own. "Even the canyon was dangerous."

Sandra nodded her head and looked at him steadfastly so he could see she meant what she was saying. "I promise not to go alone." That wasn't exactly the answer Gunny wanted but it would have to do. He wanted to be there every time but as long as she agreed to take someone and never go alone, he could live with it. Anything associated with the saneers warranted caution.

"Give me ten minutes to shower and change while you check in on the elves and we'll go. Deal?"

"Perfect," Sandra said as three thirsty elves came running up beside her. They all showed no signs of going back to the sullen ways that had plagued them after the saneer spell. Each day they were taking their peppermint candies, rubbing and smelling their oils, and reducing their sleep – exactly what Peppermint Sam had ordered. He kindly came to check on

225

them each day as well. She thought it was sweet, but a little weird, that they seemed to like him as much or more than they liked Santa or her. In fact, everyone he met seemed to respond in a similar way. *Of course Birdie was crazy about him*, Sandra thought again.

The two best friends had barely seen each other the past two days except at Kindness Academy board meetings, which were so full of planning there hadn't been any time for girl talk. They had agreed to catch up on the Reindeer Express ride back to the North Pole. The boys could ride together and the girls would catch their own coach.

"Do you know what, Sandra?" Redwood asked her.

"Nope," Sandra said. "Tell me what, Redwood."

"I feel happy today," Redwood said.

"Me too!" said Breezy.

"And me!" said Goldie.

"Do you know what, you three?" Sandra asked back.

"What?" they all asked.

"That makes me super happy to hear! Happier than you can know," she grinned.

"I know a lot," Redwood said. Sandra grinned at the words.

"Me too," said Breezy giggling. *Was she flirting with Redwood?* Sandra wondered. That was new!

"See you, Sandra," Goldie said as the three went flying from the picnic table area she was at, back to the barge for more work. She could hear them laughing the whole way.

Enchantments A South Pole Santa Adventure

"One cleaned-up cowboy reporting for detective duty, South Pole Santa," Gunny said, coming up to stand next to her.

"Looking good, Mr. Holiday," Sandra said. "Hope we're not going somewhere messy."

"Hand me some water for both of us please, and I'll stuff it in my backpack." He held up an already overstuffed and heavy-looking bag. "Can't go if we're not prepared," he said when he saw her dubious look about the bag.

"You're right!" Sandra said. She reached out for his hand, held her locket and off they went.

CHAPTER 43

A Treasure Hunt

Location

Off they went to where? That was the question they were both wondering when they landed on a small cay that looked like most of the cays in that part of the Caribbean Sea – small and nondescript with lots of sand and just a little bit of vegetation.

"Do you recognize this place?" Gunny asked Sandra, knowing she had been to many of the local area cays while she was growing up at St. Annalise.

"Not that I can tell," Sandra said still looking around. "It doesn't look like anyone has ever been here. Like most of the cays. There's no real reason to visit the cays which makes them a perfect place to hide the document we're seeking." There was excitement in her voice as she thought about it.

"Where should we start looking?"

JINGLEBELLE JACKSON

"How about right here?" Gunny suggested, pointing down to a spot next to them where something was sticking out of the sand. He reached down and pulled out an old amber-colored bottle that they could see held a rolled up piece of paper. "Looks like your locket brought us to the exact spot."

"The last message in a bottle I received turned out to be from my mom and brought Cappie and me to St. Annalise Island so I'm a big fan of them," Sandra said as Gunny worked with a knife from his backpack to get the cork open and remove the document. He unrolled it and held it high out of Sandra's reach to examine.

"Let me see! Let me see!" she exclaimed, jumping for it, too excited to wait. Gunny gave it a last good look before giving in and handing it to her. He watched to see what her reaction would be as she read it.

"What is this?" she asked, looking at him puzzled.

"I think it's something like a treasure map but without the map part and just the directions."

"Those saneers are something else!" Sandra said, frustrated.

"I don't want to defend them, Sand, but in this case of hiding the elfin papers I don't think it was them. I think this was set-up by Calivon and his band of baddies."

Sandra nodded, agreeing. "Okay, well, the first line says to take 103 paces from where we stand perpendicular across the island."

"So, let's do it."

Enchantments A South Pole Santa Adventure

"Wait, your strides or mine?" Gunny had much longer legs than Sandra did.

"Fair point," he said. "Let's use yours. You stride and I'll count. Go!"

Off the two went, unsure but determined. The 103 paces seemed to land them nowhere but they didn't want to start over. Gunny read the next step.

"Sixteen steps sideways to the east."

Sandra took off. "Done!"

"Fifty-seven hops forward."

"Hops! C'mon!"

"It says hops. Do you want to find your parents or not?"

Sandra took off hopping, happy she was in good shape since 57 hops was quite a few actually. Gunny tried not to grin but he couldn't help himself. "This actually is fun," he said.

"Because you're not the one hopping," Sandra replied, trying not to laugh herself.

"Hippity hoppity, little rabbit."

Sandra was too busy counting to even groan or grin at Gunny's comment. "There. Fifty-five, fifty-six, fifty-SEVEN! Now what?"

"Thirty-eight steps backward," Gunny answered, sounding puzzled by what he was reading.

"The elves would love this, Gunny," Sandra said, ideas forming in her head. "Kids would love this! We need to add a treasure hunt to some of the Kindness Camp sessions!" She was more excited by that idea than by what she was doing.

231

JingleBelle Jackson

"Okay, thirty-eight backward steps," she said as she finished.

"Now turn around and walk eight," Gunny said, reading the directions.

"Walk eight?" Sandra replied as she turned around. "But that takes us right back to where we started.

"Imagine that," Gunny said, feeling wronged again on Sandra's behalf by Calivon and his pals. This wasn't supposed to be a game. Elfins had a right to their own historical documents!

"That's it, this is the spot? Are we supposed to dig here or what?"

"I think there's one more clue. It looks like it's the border to this message but when you turn it you see it's actually very small, hard-to-read writing.

"'*If instructions followed correctly, dip paper in sea water to see what you will see.*' They obviously thought that was very clever," Gunny noted before reading on as he turned the paper to read the margins. "*Beware! If steps not followed correctly, no clues will be revealed, for seven years information will be sealed. Seeker, replace document in bottle and rebury. Ignore this at your own peril.*"

"That's it," he said, handing the document to Sandra. "Double-check me to be sure."

Sandra read through it out loud to be sure and it read the same to her. "Real warm and fuzzy ending to it there," she said, feeling frustrated. Should they dip it in sea water or not? Did they do the steps correctly enough to risk it? Gunny knew what she was thinking and decided to shift the decision to him. If it went wrong, she could blame him and not herself.

Enchantments A South Pole Santa Adventure

"I say we go for it," he said. "Calivon is a bully and is likely just trying to be intimidating and discourage people. Or maybe there is no clue and, no matter what, it won't make a difference. If it really does seal up on us for seven years, we look for the papers another way. Like shaking it forcibly out of Calivon." He added the last, thinking how much he would like to do it.

Sandra slowly nodded her head. There was no real option except to move forward.

"My hands are shaking too much, Gunny," she said, handing the paper back to him. "You'll have to do it."

Gunny took it and strode the few paces to the water. He placed it in the sand, and holding on, he let a wave wash over it. He picked it up and took it back to Sandra so they could both see it. To their relief, writing appeared where there had been none. Sandra smiled with relief.

"Quick, right it down!"

Gunny grabbed a stick and wrote the new message in the sand. It wasn't an answer but new coordinates to the next place but they were both happy to get them. Sandra dug through the backpack for paper and pen and wrote them down as the message disappeared again.

The two carefully rolled the document back up, placed it in the bottle with the cork and reburied it. They knew better than to ignore a warning from the elfin ruler of the magical world. Besides, they had what they had come for.

"Locket, take us home!"

233

Chapter 44

Two is Too Many

Location: St. Annalise

The two landed smack in the middle of the *Mistletoe* deck, much to the complete surprise of Sandra's new housekeeper elf, Tug.

"AAAAHHHH!" Tug cried out, throwing his hands up in the air like before, but this time spilling a large glass of ice water all over himself.

"Your, your, Royal High-Highness," Tug sputtered, snapping to attention on seeing Sandra. "You surprised me again."

"I'm so sorry, Tug! You're right but truly I haven't meant to have such an effect on you." Sandra felt bad about surprising the little guy but had to work hard not to laugh at how wet, and, well, messy, he looked again now.

235

JINGLEBELLE JACKSON

"Excuse my manners, Tug. I'd like to introduce you to Gunny Holiday. Gunny, have you met Tug before? He was an elf in housekeeping at the North Pole and has self-assigned himself to being a cleaner extraordinaire here on the *Mistletoe*." She dared not look over at Gunny for fear she would laugh. She loved how much personality each elf had and Tug was no exception.

"I don't think we've had the pleasure of meeting before," Gunny said politely, reaching out and shaking Tug's wet hand. "I'm pleased to hear Sandra is getting a little help around here, Tug." He looked around the deck. "It already looks better," he added graciously.

"Thank you, sir!" Tug said, smiling. He loved for Sandra to hear the praise so she knew she had made a good choice having him stay. Sandra couldn't really see any difference, if anything the deck seemed a little messier than usual with ice water dripping all over, but Tug knew it was cleaner. He had spent all morning cleaning and polishing the two Adirondack chairs located on the back deck. He took pride in how thorough he was and liked Gunny already for noticing.

"*eeeeeeeeeee*" came the greeting for Gunny – right before the big splash followed. Gunny and Sandra knew to brace for it and move away if they didn't want to get soaked but Tug hadn't yet met Rio. Sea water joined ice water in making sure the new house cleaner was completely soaked.

"Wha-wha-what was that?" The expression on Tug's face was so priceless that both Gunny and Sandra burst out laughing as Sandra grabbed a towel from the pile they kept

Enchantments A South Pole Santa Adventure

on deck. A wet deck was common when one of your family members was a dolphin.

"That, Tug, is Rio. Family member and the most beautiful, smartest, bravest dolphin in all of the seven seas," Sandra said with pride and affection in her voice. "Rio, say hello to Tug – without splashing him again, please."

Rio obliged and instead of splashing chose to dance around on her tail on top of the water, smiling in the big way that happy dolphins do.

"*eeeeeeeeeeee eeeeee*" she shouted over to Tug.

"A fine eeeeee to you too, my lady," the polite and kind elf said in return, bowing to Rio who splashed him with a fin playfully. He sputtered and then smiled back. Elves, after all, love having fun.

"Rio, we're coming in," Sandra said, peeling off clothes down to her swimsuit underneath as Gunny too slipped out of his shirt and kicked off his shoes. Gunny dove in first. Sandra stopped just long enough to ask Tug to put the backpack in the kitchen for safe keeping and then joined the two for an afternoon swim.

"Tug, you wanna join us?" Gunny called out.

"Oh no, sir, Mr. Gunny. I'm not sure elves can float. It's best if I stay *on* the boat, not *under* the boat." He waved and took the backpack down the long deck into the kitchen.

"Elves can't float? Where did you get him from again, Sandra?" Gunny asked, feeling amused with the newest family member aboard the *Mistletoe*.

237

"Self-assigned elf," Sandra responded, smiling. He was growing on her. "Kind of like how you are my self-assigned escort." She grinned and he splashed at her. He went to dunk her under just as Rio came by and Sandra caught a ride on a well-timed dolphin fin and was quickly out of his reach.

From the dock, Jason had caught just enough of the flirting fun the two were having to know he likely had been gone too long. It would sting to lose Sandra but he knew he was the one who had actually broken her trust originally. He wanted her back but so much had changed between them. There were such big responsibilities assigned to each of them that he wasn't sure they could make it work even if they tried again. Still, reason set aside, if Sandra's choice really was Gunny, Jason couldn't let the guy have the win that easy. He was, after all, half shan fairy. He sat and waited patiently on the dock slightly out of sight till the trio returned from swimming around. As Sandra came up the ladder, he was there smiling. "Sand, there you are!" he said. "Let me help you up. Even all wet, you look beautiful." He meant that. She did.

Sandra was shocked to see him. Once again, no warning, no notice, he was just there. "Jason? What a surprise," she stammered as he wrapped a big towel around her and pulled her too close, and too tight, for a hug on the premise he was drying her off, just as Gunny came up the ladder. Gunny debated for the slightest moment on whether to go ahead and get out or grab a dolphin tail and dump out in the sand beyond the docks. Ultimately, there was no way he was going to look the other way and let the fairy ball boy make headway with his Santa. He grabbed the last rung of the ladder and climbed out, dripping all over the dock, until Tug came running with a towel.

"Tug," Gunny said. "Do me a favor and spill some of that ice water all over that fairy king sitting too close to Sandra."

"SIR! Lower your voice," Tug urged. "He's a royal guest!"

"No, Tug, that's where you're wrong. He's a royal pest."

# # #

In the end, once the two contenders for Sandra's attention and affections got their egos back in check, even Gunny had to agree it had ended up being an important meeting with Jason. They had talked over ideas about the saneers. While all of the ideas seemed unlikely to have much effect, it felt good to make plans to help Wistle. Maybe, Gunny thought, just maybe, some far off day when he was happily settled with Sandra and Jason had his own main squeeze, he could see the two of them being friends. They had things in common like righting wrongs, speaking up for those who were wronged, and not caring much what other people thought of them. Oh, and the small detail of both being crazy about Santa – the one with the dots at the end of her name. *Yeah, who was he kidding*, Gunny thought, *they would never be friends.*

JINGLEBELLE JACKSON

But they could be allies, and in this case they would have to be. Sandra had called the gang together so they all could get Jason's report on progress with the saneers first-hand. Not a single word of what he had to tell them was good news, however, and they were all distressed to hear that Wistle still had not been released from the saneer spell. Worst of all, none of them had a single idea on what to do next.

CHAPTER 45

Next Stop: North Pole Village

Location: A Reindeer Express

"Everybody in?" Barney called out.

"Yes, Barney, we're all on board and ready for liftoff," Sandra called out. She and Birdie had selected the back row of the new three-row coach Barney was driving. The other two rows were packed with elves returning with them to help encourage the rest of the elves to get their funny bones checked by Sam. Zoomer was also driving a three-row coach, and it, too, was packed with elves along with Gunny, Spence, and Sam. Spence actually had wanted to stay at St. Annalise to continue his research on the elfin doctrines Sandra was searching for but Gunny really wanted him to go along. It was too awkward to hang out with the guy who had seemingly stolen his brother's girlfriend away from him. Gunny didn't want to like Sam and yet, weirdly, it was impossible not to. Still, he didn't want to spend any guy bonding time with him and he sure didn't want Crow to see him get out of the same coach. In fact, he needed to get to Crow fast once they landed at the Pole. His plan was to send him back to the ranch for a while. Heartbreak was hard enough, but heartbreak playing out right in front of him for all the world to see, especially Crow, would be too much.

It was too much for Birdie, too. She was pretty much a wreck. When she was around Sam, she felt she knew her mother was right and Sam was indeed the guy she was meant to marry. But when she was away from him, the feelings she had for Crow would come flooding back. She found herself feeling almost an animosity for Sam at those times for stealing Crow away from her. She knew it wasn't really a rational way of thinking, but love sometimes did not make sense.

"Sand, a big part of me can hardly wait to see Crow," Birdie said as the elves talked busily away in the front two seats. "Another part knows I'll just break his heart or he'll break mine or me breaking his heart will break mine. Do you see how awful this is?" She looked to her friend miserably.

Sandra understood those feelings. Getting her heart broken by Jason had been the hardest thing, besides losing her parents, she had ever been through at the time. There was no doubt that he still tugged at part of her heart and that probably, with work and commitment, the two could be a couple again. But in the meantime, through the break-up and the heartbreak, Gunny had been there with her. Always picking up the pieces. Always cheering her on. Patiently waiting for her, even when the odds seemed so compellingly against him that he could ever win her heart. She was still figuring it all out but she gave her best friend the only tip she personally had on how to sort it out.

"Give it time," Sandra said, reaching out and holding both of Birdie's hands in her own. "Don't make any commitments to either of them while you sort through your own feelings. Yes, you might lose one in the meantime, but then it wasn't meant to be anyway and you'll know your answer."

"But that's just it, Sandra, I don't have time!" Birdie said. "Sam has already stayed past his deadline. Not surprisingly, my mother believes this means good news for her and is pressuring me for an answer so she can make an announcement of betrothal to her kingdom." Sandra noted Birdie said "her" kingdom, not "our" kingdom. Like Sandra, Birdie thought of St. Annalise as her home. "Once a betrothal is declared, it cannot be broken, and while I admit I am strongly drawn to Sam, I don't feel ready to make that commitment. We're both so young!"

"Is Sam ready?" Sandra asked, surprised to think that he might be after having known Birdie for so short of a time. He was smart, though. Birdie would be the catch of the decade for any man in his right mind. Even a man as striking and successful as Sam Dalon.

"That's one of the strange things about all of this. We never talk about it. It's like he goes out of his way not to discuss my mother or our childhood engagement or our royal obligation. We don't ever talk about anything uncomfortable like that."

243

"What do you talk about?"

"Work! A lot! We both love what we do and being of service. We love it like you being South Pole Santa. That is one thing we both have in common."

"That's it? No romantic or practical stuff like where you would live, how many kids you would have, how much you love each other?" Sandra smiled knowing she was being pretty nosy but knowing, as a best friend, she could be.

Birdie knew it too and didn't care that Sandra was asking such personal questions. There just wasn't much to tell. "Not really. I mean there's been some hand-holding and a few very nice kissing sessions but all of that has only been recently. And truthfully, they feel right and wrong, all at the same time.

"Oh, Sandra! You're my best friend. Just tell me what to do!"

"I wish I could and I wish it was easy. I guess it comes down to which one you would miss the most – Crow or Sam – if he wasn't in your life. Look there for the answer, I think.

"Meanwhile, you better think fast on what you are going to say to Crow because this is going to be super awkward real soon. We're getting ready to land."

Sandra looked out the coach window and could see the village below complete with Santa and a small group of elves, which might be a good sign, she thought. Maybe the spell had naturally worn off.

Even before Zoomer's coach had completely set down, Sandra saw Gunny jump out and stride down the village street. She knew where he was headed and was thankful that Crow had such a caring brother.

As their coach landed, the elves all scrambled out to elf hug those that were waiting. The differences between the two elf groups was striking, and Sandra found herself being thankful again that Sam had been willing to travel all this way to assist where he was desperately needed. With a bit of good fortune, Sandra felt sure that, by the month of May, they could have every elf back in ship-shape and things back to a normal level of happy elf chaos at the North Pole. Although, by the sounds of Birdie's conversation with her mother on a call that came through by satellite phone the minute they landed, Sandra would be lucky to keep Sam that long.

"Mother, we just landed here!" Birdie was saying. "Of course we're not going to head back already. "You are treating me like someone who works for you. I'm your daughter! You can't just order the two of us back and you can't make us declare our intentions! Mother! I really am trying. I seriously like him. More than I thought I would, and even more than I really want to, but we haven't had that much time together and –" Sandra saw her friend roll her eyes as her mother apparently was talking.

"I don't get it, Mother, I really don't. I don't understand the pressure you are putting on us around time. We're young. I know you keep saying we don't have time but we do."

Again a pause followed by an outburst.

"Yes, we do! I will not simply agree to telling you within ten days. Maybe we will know and probably we will not. Our courtship right now is not our top concern, the elves are."

She paused for more listening, followed by more apparent frustration.

"Believe me, I know how you feel. You've told me every day since Sam arrived. I've gotta go.

The faster Sam can work to meet with every elf, the faster we can return to St. Annalise and the more likely we will have an answer for you.

"Tweet Tweet, Mama!" She put the phone down and turned to Sandra.

"Seriously, what am I supposed to do?" Birdie said, feeling numb from having the same conversation with her mother that she had had every day for the last six weeks.

Sandra squished up her lips to one side and cocked her head in a look of puzzlement before saying lightheartedly, "Don't pick up the phone?"

Birdie laughed and linked her arm in Sandra's. "Come on, let's show Sam around the village and you can buy us both a cocoa to show your appreciation."

"The tallest cup they have coming up!" said Sandra. "First, though, I gotta find my Em."

CHAPTER 46

Brother to Brother

Location: North Pole Village

Gunny had found Crow in the barn, hard at work cleaning out reindeer stalls. The conversation he had imagined in his head the whole trip to the pole wasn't playing out as he had hoped.

"More than anyone I know, Gunny, I would think you would understand this. I'm not going. I'm a Holiday. We don't run from hard even when hard means heartache." As frustrated as Gunny was with his little brother, he couldn't remember ever having more respect for him than he did right then.

"They need me here. It's been just Santa and me running things this past week and, frankly, Santa is still not his old self yet either. Most days, the jolly old elf isn't so jolly. Just old acting, to be honest, with lots of naps and lots of sleep. That has left just me and while, at times, it has been a little overwhelming, most of the time I have been thankful for the work because it keeps me from thinking about her. And him."

Gunny still had to try. He just hated to see his brother hurt. "The ranch needs you too, little brother. And Ghost could use a check in, you know he could."

"Seriously, Gunny, tell me the truth. You think I need to be at the ranch or you want me to be at the ranch so I'm not here?"

Gunny kicked around some hay out of frustration before he answered. "Some of both, I guess." He kicked around some more before finally stopping and speaking again.

"I'm going to give this tough news to you because you're my brother and I love you deep down in here," pointing to his heart. "But I'm your big brother. I'm supposed to be your protector so I hate telling you. The fact is, it's not just Birdie who is here, brother, it's the fiancé guy, too, Sam." Gunny saw Crow flinch at the news but he pressed on.

"Sandra had to bring him back with us because he figured out a 'cure' for the elves. It's a long story and a surprising solution but it worked fast and remarkably well and the elves are crazy about this guy."

Gunny continued speaking very low as if a quieter tone could soften the pain. "And, Crow, Birdie seems a little crazy about him, too. Truth is, the guy is hard not to like. If things were different, you might even like him."

Enchantments A South Pole Santa Adventure

Those words were too much and Crow grabbed the pitchfork and started moving hay around again like he was when Gunny had found him in the barn. He said nothing, just moved hay. Gunny pressed on.

"I don't think anyone would think you were running if you headed back to the ranch for a while. Everyone would understand and no one would judge you for it."

"Well everyone can just keep their understanding in some kind of very special place because I don't want it and I don't need it," Crow said, speaking stronger than Gunny had expected. He threw down the pitchfork and turned to Gunny with tears in his eyes. He wiped them away on his sleeve and shook his head.

"I'm not embarrassed by these tears. Losing Birdie is worth some tears. She's the best person I've ever known. But you don't think I have anticipated this might be the outcome?" There was less sorrow in his voice now and more anger. "From the minute her mom touched down, I was pretty sure I was on borrowed time.

"I'm not running, brother. If it's awkward for Birdie, too bad. If it's hard for me, that's on me. If it's hard for you and the others, you'll have to deal with it. And if it's hard for this Sam guy, then I'm glad I didn't run."

Gunny said nothing. He stood there wondering how and when Crow had gained such wisdom and courage. *Maybe he was born with it,* Gunny thought. He really couldn't remember

JingleBelle Jackson

a time his brother hadn't come from a place of huge integrity. Like he was now.

"Well c'mon then. Let's have the Holiday brothers walk down the middle of the street at the North Pole Village like we own the place because, frankly, after all you've done lately, you deserve to walk that way. I'll introduce you to the guy and get that out of the way. Where's your hat? Let's show how intimidating a couple of cowboys from Texas with big boots, big hats, and big hearts can be."

CHAPTER 47

Talking the Cure

Location: North Pole Village

The duo had found Sam, Birdie, and the rest drinking cocoa at everyone's favorite village stand and, as expected, the meeting was awkward. Crow was cordial and polite. Sam was Sam – exceedingly nice and hard not to like. Birdie was miserable. Crow had tipped his hat to her, "Birdie" he had said, and then moved on. Sandra wanted to follow the two Holiday men as they left but her top priority was not them at the moment. It was Em.

"Em, I'm so glad you're here, because it means you get to go first!" Sandra was pulling out all the stops to get back her Em. She needed Em to agree to let Sam give her a check-up.

"First at what, Sandra?" Em asked flatly, slurping her cocoa.

"First to get your funny bone fixed," Sam said, jumping in to help Sandra.

251

JINGLEBELLE JACKSON

"Hooray!" said two of the elves who had come with them from St. Annalise, giggling over having whip cream sticking to their noses.

"You're going to love it, Em," Breezy said. "You get to eat peppermints every day."

"You *have* to eat them," Goldie said, correcting her.

"That's true, Em," Sam said. "If you all don't mind, Em and I will just move over here – "

"No thanks," said Em. "I'll see you guys. I need a nap."

"No, Em," Sandra said, hating to speak sternly but having to be the leader now. "There'll be no more napping. Part of Doctor Sam the Peppermint Man's remedy includes not sleeping so much. Elves don't need that much sleep."

"I'm not an elf," Em said in retort.

"Fine, delgins don't need that much sleep. You know that, Em!" Sandra implored, willing her little delgin to remember. "Usually you need less sleep than the rest."

"Not anymore," Em said.

"Well Peppermint Sam can change that for you – and for the rest of you, too," Sandra now said loudly to the other elves who were slurping down cocoas round them. All but Em seemed willing and interested. The idea of free peppermints was a big enticement.

"It's simple really, Emaralda," Sam said to her. "I'll give you a quick check-up to see where your funny bone is and we'll get it back into working order. Okay?"

252

Em sat there. She looked at Sandra looking at her with so much hope in her eyes. "Okay," she finally said. "For her." She pointed to Sandra who put her hands over heart to say thank you to her favorite elf of them all.

"I want my funny bone fixed, too," said Alexander.

"And peppermints," said Hotshot. Sandra was glad to see Hotshot getting out more again in social settings. They had gotten off to a rough start during the competition to be South Pole Santa but she had long ago forgiven his part in undermining her chances to win.

"Me too!" said Lulu.

"Everybody will get a chance," Birdie said, relishing the distraction of work that eased the worries that had been weighing on her. "Em, you're first, then Alexander, Hotshot, and Lulu. Everyone else, line up single file behind them, please. It looks like we have twelve total here. We can get through all of you today and start in on twice that many tomorrow."

"Ho Ho Ho! How about me?"

"Santa!" The elves all shouted out his name, even the ones who Sam had not seen yet, so Sandra knew they were improving a little even without Sam's "cure."

"You go first, Santa," Em generously offered, either to put off going or out of genuine care. It was kind either way.

"Why thank you, Em, I would be happy to be first. I have genuinely missed my funny bone and getting in some really

JINGLEBELLE JACKSON

big laughs with you all. Once we all find our funny bones again, let's plan another Big Laugh party, okay, Zinga?"

"Of course, Santa," Zinga replied, writing it down in her always-with-her-notebook. Sandra was happy to see Zinga in this first line because she knew she would be so much help with the others in the days to come. Zinga was an expert in her role as chief assistant to Santa and very charming in her many ways of getting others to adapt and think it was their idea. Sandra felt she learned things from Zinga every time she got to spend time with her.

"Alright then, Sam, Sam the Peppermint Man," Santa said, rolling up his sleeve. "Let's find and fix my funny bone so I can get some ha has back into my ho hos."

CHAPTER 48

Making Sense of it All

Location: North Pole Village

Like most of Sam's patients, Santa's funny bone had been in his elbow and, like the others, Santa had responded well to the "treatment." Sandra didn't have an answer for why such a preposterous course of treatment worked. She suspected it had something to do with replacing one strong suggestion from the saneers with a stronger, more positive suggestion from Doctor Sam, but she didn't really dwell on the why. She didn't care about why. She was too busy feeling thankful that it worked and had given her, and the world, Santa and the elves back.

It had taken several weeks as suspected, but thanks to Sam's patience and creativity, all the elves had received a true, overdue check-up on all the basics. Every single one had come

JingleBelle Jackson

through with high marks, and they all were getting quickly back to being their normal happy selves.

All but Em. The little delgin was coming back around slowly but much slower than the others. Surprisingly, it seemed to be Squawk who was having the most effect on bringing her out of her lingering lethargy. Bickering with the big bird was almost a sport and Em didn't like to lose. The more Squawk bragged about Sandra loving him most and that sort of thing, the more Sandra was seeing sparks of Em's little delgin-self come back out. Sandra missed her little sassy "shadow" and was more than ready to have her fully back.

Thinking about Em and her recovery got Sandra's mind drifting to some of the other events of the past month. *Thank goodness it was May,* she thought. She wasn't sure she could get through another month like April.

The "exams" for the elves had gone smoothly but, as they had suspected might happen, not quite as fast as they had hoped. The longer the month dragged on, the more often Birdie's mother called. And the longer things dragged on, the less the elves seemed to be intrigued with Sam. The whole process was proving to be taxing on all of them.

And then there was Crow. Sandra would forever be grateful to him for all he had done at the Pole when they needed him most, but this month she couldn't help but think it would have been easier if he'd been gone. Sam had been his congenial self at every turn whenever he met Crow in

256

whatever situation. Perhaps that was the easier role when you were the guy with the girl on your arm.

Crow was having none of it, though. Unlike the rest, he didn't seem taken by the charming African at all. He was polite to Sam and cold to Birdie. To Birdie's credit, she had tried to talk with the Holiday twin several times but he would have none of it. Sandra knew Birdie had mixed feelings and felt like if Crow would just talk to her, some of it could be sorted through. Yes, Birdie had an infatuation with Sam but honestly everyone seemed to have one. Sandra thought it was his eyes but it turned out to be something very different than that.

It was little Quisp who cleared it all up.

"Sandra, I've missed you!"

"Not as much as I've missed you, Quisp! Where've you been?"

"I went home to see my mom. I wanted to know if she could tell me anything more about the saneers to help Wistle. Then I went and shared what she told me with our king and now here I am back with you! My favorite place to be." The tiny fairy buzzed into Sandra's hair where she loved to safely hang out – especially whenever there were other people around. That's where she was during one of Sandra's daily, routine meetings.

It had been a meeting with Birdie and Sam providing an update on the elf exams. The three had gone over charts and filled bottles with peppermints for the next day's appointments and lamented about Birdie's mom calling several times

JINGLEBELLE JACKSON

every day that week. When they finally left, Quisp had come buzzing out again.

"Quisp, you didn't have to hide that whole time," Sandra said. "You know Birdie. And that's her new boyfriend. Or fiancé. Or friend. I'm still not sure." Sandra waved her hand in the air to indicate her confusion and frustration with it all.

"He's enchanted, Sandra," Quisp said quietly. "Do you know that?"

"What?!" Sandra had exclaimed, knowing well enough by now that often the tiniest fairy anywhere knew a great deal more than the rest of everyone else put together. She turned to face the little fairy who had landed on a shelf to be eye level with Sandra.

"It's true. It's plain as day to a fairy. He has a green spell glow around him that is easily seen if you're a fairy. Has no other fairy met him?"

Sandra thought through the many people that Sam had met and realized the one fairy he would have met was Jason. Sam had sent his regrets the afternoon that they had all gathered for an update on the *Mistletoe* by saying he needed some time to contact home. That was reasonable for sure but now Sandra had to wonder if it was deliberate.

"You're the first one, Quisp, and I wonder if you would have seen him if he had known you were here." The little fairy amazed her time and again. "Could you tell what kind of spell it is?" Sandra suspected she knew but wanted confirmation.

258

ENCHANTMENTS A SOUTH POLE SANTA ADVENTURE

"A charm spell, Sandra. He probably doesn't even know he has it. Often they're cast without the recipient's knowledge. Charm spells play up the recipient's naturally charming qualities. If he's already charming, for instance, he'll seem more charming. If he's good looking, he'll seem better looking. Both of those seem true of Sam. Charm spells are meant to make the person who is cast charming and irresistible to all those he, or she, comes in contact with to some degree or another. It's unusual, in fact, if someone they meet is not taken by them. Sometimes people use them for job interviews. People have sought them out to become celebrities and, of course, they have been used by many for romance. All charm spells are time-limited, though. Maybe that's why Birdie's mom is calling so often."

Maybe indeed. A charm spell! It explained everything!

With Quisp in tow, Sandra had hurried off to see Birdie who was still with Sam processing the last of the elves. *Thank goodness*, Sandra thought, *because this might be his last day here when Birdie hears this.*

Birdie listened to everything Sandra and Quisp had to report as she watched the kind and good-looking Sam from across the room. She agreed all of it made sense and she felt surprisingly calm hearing the news. Like Quisp, she didn't think Sam knew either, and, like Quisp, she thought he was, by his nature, a generally good guy. She also knew the spell had affected her, and others, and the way they felt about Sam. They would have undoubtedly enjoyed him as himself but

259

JINGLEBELLE JACKSON

the spell – put there, she was sure, by her mother's direction – had accelerated feelings and manipulated the outcomes. That made her blood boil.

They all could tell the spell was beginning to wear off. Everyone felt calmer about Sam in general – not quite as enthusiastic and jubilant after every interaction with him. They all still liked him, they just had lost their infatuation for him. Quisp could actually see it was fading. Added to that were the many, many calls from Birdie's mother. That was the biggest clue.

Birdie wasted no time now that she knew. She turned and left the room and headed straight to a phone for a call with her mother, leaving Sam to handle the exams and write-ups on his own. Dear Lovey was nearby and wheeled over to help him.

The perfect elf for the role, Sandra thought, smiling with love for the physically challenged elf. The talented elf accepted no bounds to what she could do and was loved by all elves for her kind ways and great advice in the Dear Lovey *North Pole Times* newspaper column.

"While we wait, Dear Lovey," said an elf named Giggles, "could I just get your advice on a problem I've been having with my bunk mates?"

"Well, of course," Dear Lovey said as she leaned in to listen.

How I love every single elf, Sandra thought, smiling as she went dashing off to find Gunny and share the news.

260

CHAPTER 49

From Bad to Worse

Location: North Pole Village

The call had been worse than even Birdie had imagined with shouting and crying and name-calling. Birdie wondered if she and her mother would ever be able to repair the relationship between them based on some of what had been said, and she found herself sobbing for the loss.

She sobbed for the loss of her mother and likely her father, too, as Zeentar always stood loyal to his wife. For the loss of her innocence in believing her life was her own to decide and that whatever she chose would be supported by her parents who loved and cared about her. She sobbed for the loss of Sam, whom she would miss and who might have really become someone special if her mother had just allowed it to happen. And for the loss of Crow, the man she believed really

261

could have been the one, but that her mother, and herself, had pushed away.

It was in that state that Crow came upon her. Sobbing and unbearably sad. He wanted to keep on walking but his heart hadn't hardened yet that much around her and he reluctantly stopped to see if he could offer her some comfort.

Birdie reveled in the feel of his safe arms around her. She said nothing, didn't try to explain, and he didn't ask. Seeing the phone next to her, he suspected it had something to do with her mother and he dared to think perhaps she had declined the demand to marry Sam – it was the outcome the Birdie he knew and loved would have made – but he said nothing. There was nothing really to say. It wouldn't have mattered. Their time had passed. The intrusion of Sam had set them on different paths. For Crow, loyalty was one of the things he valued most in the world and Birdie had proven she possessed less than he had believed.

As her sobs finally diminished and she regained her composure, Birdie wanted to take the time to tell him what had happened, how her mother had manipulated the situation and bewitched them all. All but Crow, anyway, who never saw the charm in Sam. Crow, however, had not come to her aid for talk. His heart was raw and his feelings of betrayal too close to the surface. He knew to hear her speak or to engage in conversation around this topic right now would be to risk words he could never take back. He pushed away, stood, looked at her with eyes that made her reach for him and he walked away without saying a single word. He heard her crying again but he knew she was strong enough to overcome whatever she was sobbing about. He needed to guard the same strength in himself.

Less than twenty-four hours later, Crow had to draw on that strength when, out of the blue, members of the Esteemed High Council of Magical Beings had shown up at the Pole.

Both Santa and Sandra hated the Council's surprise visits. They were never about something joyous. They both felt tremendous relief that all the elves were back to their old selves – except perhaps Em – so they would not have to explain what had happened. The last thing Sandra wanted was to have to talk with Calivon about her dealings with the saneers.

As usual, the council representatives were led by Calivon and included Laile of the moonrakers, Grosson of the granites, Reesa of the fairies, and Zeentar of the water wizards, who also happened to be Birdie's father. Immediately on seeing Zeentar there looking stern, Sandra suspected she knew what this unannounced visit was about and she knew it wasn't going to be good.

Santa greeted each council member warmly, trying to assume the best. Sandra noticed that somehow, every single elf had found something else to do and even Squawk had flown off. *Maybe he's part chicken*, she thought, which helped her to smile and look happy to see their guests. She kept her hands behind her so Calivon, particularly, could not see them shake. More with anger than with nerves. It was the first time the two had met since Sandra had learned he was the one

JingleBelle Jackson

responsible for her parents being locked away and her growing up without them. Facing him now, she was shocked by the level of dislike that she felt.

And he must not know. Sandra heard the words and knew it was her mother speaking again only to her. She was glad to feel her strength and she willed her hands to quit shaking. She would not give him power over her in any way. She directed her genuine feel-good welcome to Laile who she liked the most of those before her.

"Laile! It is such a rare treat to see you," Sandra said. "May I inquire as to how the moonrakers are faring of late?" She added politely. Moonrakers were a nighttime species who gathered their vitality from the energy of the moon and nighttime stars. They were generally shy and unknown to most. Sandra felt honored to know a moonraker and such a kind one as Laile.

"We are fine and thriving, Sandra. Thank you for asking," Laile responded. "The full moon has been long and large of late and we have welcomed its gifts."

"Hello to you all!" Santa was saying. "To what do we owe the honor of this visit? Are you here for an off-schedule check on production? If so, I would be happy to begin the tour if you follow me this way." Santa started to the factory.

"Thank you, Santa Claus," Calivon said while looking at Sandra as he always seemed to. Sandra refused to turn from his gaze. Let him look. He would find nothing of interest with her. "So nice to see you again, Sandra," he finally said.

ENCHANTMENTS A SOUTH POLE SANTA ADVENTURE

"You, and all of the Council members, as well," Sandra said, bowing her head politely at them all, as was the expected gesture.

"Right this way, Council members," Santa said again as he swept his hand to indicate the nearest door. He really had every reason to assume they were there for a surprise check.

"We will not be staying," Calivon said. "We are here at Zeentar's request to meet with Ambyrdena Snow and Sam Dason. Please fetch them for us."

I knew it, Sandra said in her head, trying to think how to help her best friend.

This news caught Santa off-guard. "Well I'm actually unsure where they might be," he said honestly. "Sam has been so kind to offer his medical services to us for an annual check-up on the elves and the two were planning to travel back to St. Annalise today."

"I see," said Calivon. "You are being honest with us, of course, Santa?"

"Why, I am surprised by the question, Calivon!" Santa said with outrage tinging his voice. "Perhaps if the Council had thought to notify us of your visit, we could have had them with us here to greet you."

Calivon had to concede there was some truth in that. "We will accompany you to your main square while you locate where the two may be. Lead the way." *There was never any "please" or "thank you" with this guy,* Sandra thought, as she followed behind Santa, a fake smile pasted on her face.

265

JingleBelle Jackson

Unfortunately, as bad luck would have it, they arrived at the square just as Sam and Birdie were boarding a Reindeer Express for St. Annalise where Sam would gather his things and depart for his return to Africa. Birdie had explained to him what they had learned about him being spelled. As they all had guessed, he had no idea and was appalled to have been subjected to such manipulation, even from his country's ruling queen. Maybe especially from her. Unlike Birdie, he had not run from the obligation placed on him from childhood despite any hesitations he might have personally felt. He understood the expectation that his service to his country and queen could be served in that way and had found Birdie to be engaging and stunningly beautiful inside and out. The situation was acceptable to him with the one caveat, he had told Birdie's mother, Selena, being that Birdie must want it too. Or at least agree without protest. He had committed to doing his very best to reach that outcome and felt he had stayed true to that commitment. To now find out how little Selena had believed in him was disheartening. In the ruler's zeal to force them together, she had likely blown them apart forever. Sam had accepted Birdie's decision without question.

"Ambyrdena, please know, there is no one else for me right now and will not be for years. If you find your heart tugging or even your head with the obligation, do not hesitate to reach out to me," he had graciously said. "I believe our time together, our interest in serving those less fortunate than we

Enchantments A South Pole Santa Adventure

are, and those kisses that we shared, prove that we could be quite compatible together." He grinned at her shamelessly when he mentioned the kisses.

All of those things had been great for Birdie too. She knew he was right. They were compatible and could likely be happy together but she was going for nothing less than crazy-in-love when she got married. They might even have gotten to that point if her mother had given them the time and let the relationship unfold at its own pace.

Birdie's face showed the shock of understanding immediately when she heard her name called by the voice she recognized as her father. *Of course her mother would send her dad,* she thought, Selena knew he would be harder to disappoint for Birdie personally than her mother.

"Father," Birdie said, walking away from the coach and giving him a kiss on both of his cheeks while whispering quietly, "Please do not do this."

Zeentar responded only with a shake of his head and, "You have made it impossible not to be here."

Sam now walked over and bowed to Zeentar. He made no movement to any of the rest of the Council, having no sense of who any of them were, but Birdie bowed quickly to all.

"Zeentar, this is a surprise," Sam said honestly. He too knew it wasn't likely a surprise he was going to like.

"A surprise?" said Zeentar. "You and my willful daughter, beloved by her mother and me, send us word that you have broken your betrothal and you are surprised?"

267

"Broke our betrothal? We never agreed to be engaged!" Birdie burst out. "We broke only that which you and mother and Sam's parents arranged, not something we arranged. And Father, even if we had agreed to it, we would still have the right to change our minds. That is the way of our world and our rights as individuals!"

"Zeentar, if I might," Santa started.

"SILENCE!" Zeentar boomed and his voice echoed all around the empty square. Elves with their excellent hearing heard it even in their hiding places in the factory and slinked further back. It was scary!

"Ambyrdena Snow, we have clearly given you too much independence. On this issue, the matter was decided years ago. You and Samuel will be married by noon tomorrow in our country where you will stay. This will be done voluntarily or under protest."

"I will not," Birdie said this quietly. "I'm sorry, Father, but this is not something you and mother get to decide. She tricked me! She tricked Sam! She tricked every person he met since he arrived! I do not trust her."

"You will not speak ill of your mother!"

"I am only speaking the truth," she responded.

"I, too, am speaking the truth when I say to you both now, this has been decided," Zeentar said. "Sam take her hand and we will be on our way."

"NO!" The protest was loud but it hadn't come from Sam. It was Crow. "With all due respect, sir, to you and the rest of the Council, Birdie and Sam have given you their answer." Crow had been standing out of sight, listening, and had heard enough to understand what had happened. He didn't like being manipulated either.

"And you are?" asked Calivon.

"Crowder Holiday," Crow said, using his full name. "Past boyfriend of Ambyrdena."

"And the man I love," Birdie said looking over at him. Crow gave her no response. He wasn't at the forgiveness point yet.

"Well, this is certainly a more interesting trip than I expected it was going to be," Calivon said with amusement in his voice that none of them appreciated, except the other council members who quietly felt the same.

"Love is not a factor in this decision," Zeentar said, ignoring Crow completely. "Now, come along, you two. We are done here."

"You are not done, sir!" Crow started toward Zeentar and then went flying through the air and crashed against the barn.

"Father! How dare you!" Birdie cried out, finding it impossible to believe her father capable of such cruelty. She went to run to Crow but was locked in place.

"It wasn't your Father, young woman, it was me," Calivon said. "This has grown from amusing to tiresome and, frankly, these humans that hang around take too much of our time."

Sandra had to run to Crow to keep from completely attacking Calivon. Even the other Council members seemed to

JINGLEBELLE JACKSON

gasp with outrage at what he had done. And he wasn't done. In the blink of an eye, Birdie and Sam were gone.

"Birdie!" Sandra cried out as she caught the brief glimpse of her best friend's frightened eyes as she left.

"Zeentar, I have sent them to Selena. You can thank me later," Calivon said matter-of-factly. "Santa, please see us to our transport portal. Good day to you, Sandra. I look forward to when we meet again."

She did too, she thought as she reached Crow and saw he was managing to stand up. *She did too.*

CHAPTER 50

Beatrice Carol

Location: North Pole Village

One good thing came from losing Birdie that day. Sandra had called Cappie in her grief to tell her what had happened, and Cappie had hurried to the Pole to console Sandra and the others who were missing their friend.

The moment Cappie stepped out of the coach and Em saw her, she, at last, shook free of the residual effects of the saneer spell. In Em's case, it wasn't her funny bone that needed fixing apparently, but a missing piece of her heart that needed to be filled. Whatever it was, Cappie was the cure. Sandra marveled at it, felt a little jealous about it, but, ultimately, was grateful for it. Besides, she felt exactly the same about Cappie – she always made her feel better.

For Cappie, it was just what she needed, too. She was loving her new life as a wife and newlywed with Thomas, but

JingleBelle Jackson

she found herself missing her favorite Santa and welcomed the chance for some time together. Having such a warm welcome from both Sandra and Em helped her feel immediately needed and glad she was there.

"How can I help? Where should we start?" Cappie said.

"Well, Cappie, I think we should start with knitting," Em said seriously, as Sandra and Cappie burst out with quick laughs.

"Now, Em," Sandra said carefully, not wanting to suppress the enthusiasm of the finally rejuvenated delgin but having some very pressing things to discuss. "How about if I promise Cappie can do some knitting with you in the evenings and we all concentrate on our work and chores during the day?"

"Okay," Em replied. "See you later then, Cappie!" She dashed off just as Squawk arrived.

" . . . *squawk!* . . . sorry I'm late . . . *squawk!* . . . helping Gunny!"

"Hello, Squawk," Cappie said, as the big bird swooped in low for a fly-by. "You look handsome in this Arctic light."

" . . . *squawk!* . . . thank you! . . ."

"Cappie, in just a couple hours, Beatrice Carol with World Wide News is going to be here. Birdie usually helps me get ready. Would you mind helping me with this mop of hair and a dash of make-up? I think I look a little pale lately."

Cappie had been thinking the same. She even saw some dark rings under Sandra's eyes. "We will make you look bright and shining for the children so they don't worry about you for a minute," Cappie said, knowing that was what Sandra was worried about.

By the time the reporter and her production crew arrived, there was no sign of the tired, sad and worried Santa girl who had greeted Cappie but instead stood a bright and beautiful, smiling Santa transformed simply by having Cappie there and by putting her Santa suit on. Sandra honestly felt the best she had in weeks as she stood with Santa waiting to talk with Beatrice Carol. The interview had been lined up for several weeks. She had intended to have Birdie join her on it but, now, she was determined to do her kind, best friend in the world proud.

Beatrice Carol spoke animatedly to the camera – and, consequently, to the world. "I'm here on this beautiful May Day, reporting live from the North Pole with breaking news for the children of the world. Parents, gather your children around your television sets, because this is a report you will not want to miss!"

Sandra and Santa stood to one side letting Beatrice work her magic at reporting the news. Both Santas appreciated the reporter's enthusiasm for all things Christmas no matter what time of the year it was, though they sometimes winced at her dramatic questions and frequent use of exclamation marks in her tone.

Sandra reached over and squeezed on Santa's gloved hand. They were both dressed in their full Santa suits as that was how they liked children to see and remember them. As she always did at times like this, Sandra found herself feeling overwhelmed with gratitude that Santa had selected her for the best job in the world. It might come with challenges but they were nothing at all compared to the opportunities and joy that being South Pole Santa brought to her.

Santa squeezed her hand back. "This really is your interview, Sandra," he said graciously. "I'm here for support and back-up if you need it but, honestly, I prefer to be in the background. I fear I'm still coming out of the effects of that saneer spell."

"So, children, are you ready?" The two Santas heard the reporter starting up her introduction. "You know who I have here! North Pole Santa and South Pole Santa – come on out!" The two Santas walked toward her across the square, waving the whole way at the camera covering them.

"Santa, Sandra, you both look marvelous! The year must be treating you right!" Beatrice said as both the Santas suppressed the urge to guffaw at the irony. Still, the truth was, while it had been rough at times, it also had been wonderful in many ways as well. That was life. They both chose to concentrate on those good moments.

"Why thank you, Beatrice, thank you!" Santa boomed out. "Ho Ho Ho! We will accept that compliment and return it. You are looking fabulous as well." Then he got up real close to the TV camera as he liked to do to add, "And children, you all look great! Such happy faces I see out there! Why, I don't think I see a single naughty face in the whole of the world right now!"

Oh that Santa, he was such a natural charmer when it came to children, Sandra thought, smiling bigger and bigger as she watched her greatest mentor in action.

"Sandra, what do you think?" Santa asked. "Don't you think they all look better than ever?" Sandra happily played along and got up close to the camera panning her face back and forth.

"I have to say, Santa, just like every time I look, every single child, everywhere, always seems beautiful to me," she said honestly.

"Well, you two Santas, let's step back from that and talk about some of what is in store for this next Christmas season. Santa, anything special being built by the elves this year?" Beatrice asked.

"Ho Ho Ho, Beatrice!" Santa boomed. "You know, truly, every single toy the elves make is special. They're each put together by elf hands and lovingly designed and produced. As something a little different this year, they're currently working on a method where they may be able to personalize more toys with the name of the child they're being produced for, making it even more special on Christmas morning. I have to say, however, this is a very big factory change and we may not have it ready for this year specifically."

"More personalized gifts! Done by the elves themselves! How wonderful! Now, Sandra, I know you have been teasing me with bits and pieces of an announcement you are ready to

JingleBelle Jackson

make. Please don't make me and the children wait a single moment longer. Catch us up on what you have to tell us."

"I can't wait to share it with you all!" Sandra exclaimed, meaning it and clapping her hands together. "As you know, a project I'm so fond of has been in the works called the Academy of Kindness. I've been fortunate to have my very best friends in the world lead this effort on my behalf, Birdie Snow and Spencer Mantle. Birdie is away today but Spencer is here. Give a wave to the world please, Spence." He never sought attention, but Spencer was as excited about this as Sandra and Birdie and the rest of the board members, so he gamely gave a wave with a big smile to the camera.

"I'm excited to share with you all that we have completed our plans around the Academy and have three important updates to share."

"We are anxious to hear each one," Beatrice said, pointing the microphone even closer to Sandra if that was possible.

Sandra smiled. "First, we held a trial session last year and we will begin next year with 'AOK Camp' sessions! Each session will run three days across weekends. We hope to have those sessions running almost year-round in the future and accommodate thousands of children. It's all part of our quest to change the world through kindness. We're starting with a few sessions this year as we fine-tune all the pieces that go into running a camp for children."

"Kindness Camps!" repeated Beatrice. "This is already soooo exciting!"

"Second, and I am especially excited about this part, the academy is going to be going worldwide and by that I mean, it will be coming to you, children! As we increase the number of sessions, we will be bringing the South Pole Village barge to ports around the world so children can attend without traveling far from home! Some children may choose to stay on board the barge, but others can come for the day and return home each night — wherever they are most comfortable. Additionally, we're working on being able to offer the academy in many languages. All of this makes me very excited!"

"Never mind about the *children* and the academy, Sandra. What I want to know is, if the South Pole Village barge is coming to foreign ports, will the local *adults* get a chance to tour it and meet you and the elves?" Beatrice asked.

Sandra laughed. She did love Beatrice's enthusiasm. "They will. We know that adults are all just grown-up kids, really. We plan to have tour times set up in each port. There may not be as many hours as some would like," Sandra warned, suspecting this could be an issue, so she wanted to let people know ahead of time. "After all, we are a working factory, and the elves, while they love to play, also love to work and must get a lot done to ensure children have toys each Christmas. I'm sure people everywhere will understand."

"I might fly in and cover you at each port," Beatrice said in response. Both Santas worked to keep smiling at the thought.

"Finally, and my favorite news because I think it is so important," Sandra continued. "We will be offering our camp sessions on kindness to randomly selected children who have their names drawn from the acts of kindness lists they send in to us year-round. Santa and I both appreciate them so much and love nothing more than a day spent reviewing those long lists. It is truly magnificent how many kind children we have in the world.

"It's easy to believe that kindness is simple and natural and that we don't really need training. For most children that is certainly true. They're kind and loving from the start and have supportive and loving people around them, helping those actions and natural tendencies to develop and flourish. For many, however, that is not necessarily the case. There are children in the world who grow up afraid, who grow up hungry, who don't get enough love or the other support that we all need to feel safe and secure. For those children, fear can be the primary driver in their lives and love and kindness something that, perhaps, they haven't had many examples of. They may even live too fearful to try being kind or even receive a kind act. We understand that, and we want to help those children most especially. So, the kindness camp will also welcome children who land repeatedly on the naughty list. Or those who live in fear or lack and want to change but might need a little more support. We will include them in hopes of showing them a different way and giving them a new chance to shine their own bright lights."

Enchantments A South Pole Santa Adventure

Sandra knew she had been talking too long but it just meant so much to her. She was humbled when the people around her at the Pole, including Santa and Beatrice all applauded and cheered when she was done. Unbeknownst to her, people all over the world, in their living rooms and even offices, were doing the same thing.

"Bravo! Bravo, Sandra!" Beatrice said, now with tears in her eyes. "You never fail to surprise and delight us. I know the whole world feels closer to our original Santa Claus for his brilliance and bravery in selecting you to be his equal. Santa, how kind you were to bring this gift of Sandra Claus dot dot dot to the world."

"Every single day, I am thankful she accepted," Santa said kindly, reaching out to hold Sandra's hand up high.

"Well, as you always do, you two, once again, gave us more than we expected and made this long trip to the North Pole so worthwhile. Thank you again and to all of you out in the world, this is Beatrice Carol, wishing you a day filled with kindness at every turn." She waved to the camera.

"And we're off," said her cameraman.

"Beatrice, what a wonderful new signoff," Sandra said immediately. "I really hope that catches on. Thank you for spreading kindness with us at every turn. Being a reporter, you can help spread the word on the power of kindness faster than we can, and I want to express how much your support means to us."

"There are no stories I love covering more," Beatrice said. "And no cause that feels more important."

Her words filled Sandra's heart with love and hope.

CHAPTER 51

Clue Chasing

Location: Latitude 15 degrees, 31' and 05"S

Gunny had been on the sidelines clapping the loudest for the two Santas.

Most especially he had been cheering on the Santa with the long red hair and form-fitting Santa suit. He knew Cappie was at the Pole for a visit and wanted time with Sandra, but he had barely seen her himself since they had done the treasure hunt and he was ready to remedy that. In fact, he needed some time with her. Life had been heavy with concern over the elves, the production levels at the Pole, and most especially with both of his brothers. Love had done both Crow and Ghost wrong as of late, and neither twin was willing, or maybe, even capable, of rising above it. For Ghost, he hadn't seen his fairy girlfriend in weeks and he stewed constantly over nothing changing for her. For Crow, all the dreams he

JingleBelle Jackson

had held for, maybe one day, of having a future with Birdie had melted away when he was slammed into the barn wall and Birdie was whisked off to be married to a man she didn't want. Crow's comfort was in Birdie's last words that she loved him. Such was his agony.

Gunny understood how both his brothers felt and could only imagine that his own response to such a situation would be similar. If fairy boy came in at this point and whisked Sandra away from him, right as he felt they were on the precipice of locking in something really special, well, he wasn't sure how he would channel the feelings that situation would create for him. The only possible thing he could imagine would help was time and that was what he was trying to give his brothers.

From his viewpoint on the sideline, he finally caught Sandra's eye and she came sauntering over, smiling the whole way. He loved seeing her happy.

"Well?" she said. "Aren't you going to swoon over me, too?" she said teasingly.

He could play along. In fact, this was the kind of thing he loved to play along on. "Swoon, huh? I think you have plenty of others 'swooning' over you right now. Besides, this guy here," he said, pointing to himself, "pretty much 'swoons'," he made quote marks in the air, "over this girl here," he pressed a finger to Sandra's shoulder, "every single time he sees her. Frankly, it's ridiculous." Sandra saw such affection in his eyes for her. She reached up and kissed him right there in

282

front of others. It felt natural and great. She liked knowing this guy was proud of her.

"Hey," Gunny said, "you're distracting me." She smiled and stepped back.

"That's really no better," Gunny grinned. "Okay seriously, I could use a break from here for a bit. Any chance you feel the same? Want to change out of that Santa suit and check out the next clue?"

"Give me fifteen minutes and I'll meet you in the hotel lobby," Sandra said, already moving away. Gunny didn't need to ask twice. Sandra needed a break, too, wanted to stay busy and not sulk about Birdie and, most of all, wanted to get those clues done and get her parents back.

"Maybe ten minutes!" she called back to him, now running. "Grab the backpack from my office, please!"

"No fair!" Gunny said, now running himself. "That's a fifteen minute walk back and forth!"

She turned and grinned with gratitude. "Better run faster then," she said.

# # #

"Okay, so any idea where we might be heading this time?" Gunny asked as they got ready to leave.

"Yes, actually," Sandra said. "I looked up the coordinates and it looks like we might be landing smack dab in the middle of the Amazon jun—"

JINGLEBELLE JACKSON

"The blooming Amazon jungle!" Gunny said, cutting her off. "Are you kidding me? That is like one of the last places I ever want to go. I might as well just flat-out tell you right here and right now since there is a good chance you will come to eventually know it, I hate snakes. I mean truly hate them. It's irrational, really, especially when you consider I have lived on a farm all my life where they are regularly found, but there you have it. I hate snakes."

"So, my big cowboy has something he's actually afraid of, huh?" Sandra said, not realizing completely what she had said until Gunny repeated it back.

"Your big cowboy, huh?" he said, cozying up to her close while she stayed steady and didn't back away. "Hearing those words from you made telling you about my snake fear totally worth it."

The two held eyes for a minute before Sandra deliberately broke the spell. This between them was becoming something unique and special but it could wait. Her parents had waited too long. Gunny totally got that and was just as committed to the cause as she was.

"I just want it noted that considering my feeling for snakes and jungles, I need to get some credit for what we are about to do and where we are about to go," he said.

"Well, I could go alone . . ." Sandra said.

Gunny grabbed her hand. "Jungle, here we come."

And that is exactly where they landed – smack dab someplace that was clearly the Amazon jungle by looking around.

284

It was ridiculously hot, even more humid, and there was overgrown foliage everywhere that made even Sandra shudder to think what all might be slinking about. They could hear monkeys and Sandra saw a beautiful blue macaw fly by. "Looks like I should have brought Squawk instead of you," she joked, pointing the macaw out to Gunny, who barely took a glance. His eyes were locked on the ground around them.

"Let's just find the clue and get the jump out of here," he said tensely. "I hope to . . . BUG! BUG!" Gunny hollered, pointing out the biggest centipede Sandra had ever seen crawling by. "I hope to shout that we do not, I repeat, do not, have to do any pacing or backwards walking this time or you might have to come back by yourself after all."

Sandra knew he was mostly joking but she wouldn't have blamed him if he wasn't. It was sort of beautiful there but too humid and too wrapped all around them for the two to appreciate.

"Okay, then let's find this clue and go. The locket usually puts us close so let's look right here where we're at. This is so not funny of Calivon to put seekers through this."

Gunny snorted his agreement as he looked around. They hadn't worn the right clothes and he was sweating something awful but there was no way he was going to take his shirt off in all that vegetation.

After twenty minutes of looking and swatting at the vegetation carefully with the biggest knife in their backpack, they had found nothing but vegetation. Literally nothing that

JINGLEBELLE JACKSON

looked like it could contain, or be hiding, a clue. Another stunning macaw flew by. Sandra stopped to wipe her brow and admire the bird when she spotted what they had come for.

"Gunny, it's there!" she said excitedly, slapping him on the arm and pointing upward. "There's writing on that tree limb! It's hard to see but it's there!"

Gunny peered up where she was pointing and was relieved to see she was right. Thank goodness they could get out of there. Except how were they going to get the clue?

"Can you make it out?" Sandra said, peering hard at it, which wasn't easy to do since despite the thick vegetation, the clue seemed to be lined up perfectly with the afternoon sun filtering through the dense jungle leaves.

"I think I can get most of it," Gunny said.

"Here," Sandra said. "Bend down so I can stand on your shoulders."

"Stand on my shoulders! Are you sure?"

"Well what else are we going to do? I could use the locket to get up there, I guess, but there could be a snake or something else up there and I'd still have to hang over the branch to read it upside down. If you're willing to try the shoulder thing, I am. It might just be enough closer that I can read the coordinates clearly."

Gunny wasn't crazy about the idea. He didn't mind helping her but he wasn't sure he could hold on tight enough or be still enough for her to be safe. Still, the alternatives were limited.

286

"Fine, climb up," he said as he shoved her on up.

"Okay, stay still," she said.

"You're the one moving."

"I just about have it. It's just the last number Yes, I think it's −149.9000." Sandra had no more read out the coordinates carefully and finished with the last one when the two tumbled together...

... and landed sprawled out in a large snow bank!

"What happened?" Sandra mumbled, trying to stand up on the icy terrain they were on. "Where are we? Antarctica?"

"Wrong pole, I think," Gunny said, scrambling to stand on the icy snow and help Sandra up at the same time.

"Why do you think that?" Sandra asked loudly to be heard over the wind that was howling. It was super cold there, she realized. So like Calivon. She felt it must be the South Pole because it was closer to the Amazon jungle than the North Pole was.

"Pretty sure, I'm right," Gunny said with urgency in his voice and grabbing tight to Sandra's hand. "The South Pole doesn't have polar bears and here come two now! Use your locket, Sand! Use your locket!"

Sure enough, Sandra turned to see where Gunny was looking and two polar bears were coming at them faster than she would have ever guessed something that large could move. She grabbed the locket and wished them to home.

. . . where once again they crash landed on the deck of the *Mistletoe,* knocking over a new potted palm plant that Tug had meticulously placed, and sending the dirt scattering all over the furniture, the deck, the two of them and the sputtering elf!

"Wha-wha-what is happening?!" the self-assigned housekeeper elf managed to sputter out. "Your Highness? Mr. Holiday? Where did you come from?" he said, spitting dirt out of his mouth as the two would-be detectives picked themselves up off the deck.

"Uh, sorry about that, Tug," Gunny said, looking around at the mess. "We were running for home and looks like we didn't stop soon enough. Just got a little too exuberant, huh, Sandra?"

"Oh, Tug, I'm truly so sorry," Sandra said, feeling bad about the mess and especially about how covered the elf was in dirt from top to bottom. "Worst of all, I'm afraid we can't even stay to help clean up."

"Of course, Your Highness, of course. I will have this cleaned up in no time."

"Thank you! Thank you, Tug! I am so sorry again."

Sandra waved as the two ran down the dock. They needed to use the locket again and she didn't want to scare the little guy by disappearing in front of him.

"Goodbye!" Tug called out. "Nice to see you!

"Tsk, tsk, how did she ever get along without me?" he pondered out loud as a clump of dirt from on top of his head felt to the deck. He grabbed a broom to clean up what had been sparkling clean just minutes before.

CHAPTER 52

Debriefing

Location: St. Annalise Island

The two adventurers actually headed for the closest beach rather than use the locket right away again. They needed to talk about where they'd been and where to go next.

"So, what just happened?" Sandra said, breathless from all that had just occurred. "How are we ever going to get the next coordinates with those big bears all around?"

"We're going to have to plan ahead and take a gun next time," Gunny said matter-of-factly as Sandra stared at him like she hadn't heard him right.

"No way, Gunny! No way! We are not going to kill anything! That is too much and too far!" she leaped to her feet and was pacing, feeling mad at Gunny for even suggesting it.

JINGLEBELLE JACKSON

He pulled at her hand to sit back down but she was having none of it until he clarified. "A *tranquilizer* gun. Not a real gun. I know you would never agree to kill something."

Sandra plopped back down next to him. "I see your reasoning but I hate to have to do even that."

She gave him another look and reached up to feel her own hair. If she looked anything close to as bad as Gunny did, then she believed she had never looked worse! Their clothes were damp and clingy from the humidity in the jungle. Gunny's hair was pasted to his head from sweat and hers had become a frizzy mass sticking out everywhere. Both of them were covered in dirt and now sand was being added to the mix. On top of all of that, they had welts forming where they had been bitten by oversized Amazon mosquitoes and who-knew-what-other-kind-of-exotic-bugs, the welts were starting to itch unmercifully.

Still, none of that measured up to the anger Sandra felt for Calivon. At each location, they could have been killed! The extreme weather and geographic conditions, combined with the new twist of sending them off the instant the last letter of the coordinates was read out loud, were deliberately jarring and could have been outright fatal.

All sorts of questions had begun nagging at Sandra. She had the advantage of having her locket to get to these places. How was the average elfin with limited powers supposed to get anywhere near these clues? There was no way that they would likely be able to find even the first clue. And why

290

Enchantments A South Pole Santa Adventure

wasn't there more protest by all elfins over not being able to see the original documents on the history of their people? That seemed unnatural as well. Surely some were curious and surely there were historians amongst the elfins? The more she pursued each clue, the more questions she found herself having.

She felt too mentally tired, and was itching in too many places, to talk it out with Gunny right then. One matter, though, was pressing. "How are we even going to get back to the Arctic location?" she lamented. "We didn't write down the coordinates!"

"Rest your very, very messy head on that one," Gunny said, reaching over and pulling what looked like a small tree branch out of Sandra's hair. "I memorized them as you read them out loud." He tapped his head. "A super-duper memory for short notes is one of my super powers." He grinned, hoping nothing gross-looking was stuck in his teeth.

Apparently not in his teeth but on his face as Sandra motioned for him to wipe his cheek. *Gross*, he thought, *that felt like slug slime*. He didn't even look at his hand. He didn't want to know.

"I'd kiss you for that super power." Sandra said. "But I'm going to pass because of, well, you know, that slime there." She pointed. "And that dark spot right over there." She pointed to a place under his eye as she rolled away to stand up. "I think it's moving."

291

JingleBelle Jackson

Gunny jumped up, slapping at his face as Sandra started laughing hard. Until she stopped and started slapping on her own back. It felt like things were crawling on her, too.

"We go nowhere and do nothing else today before a shower. Please escort me home," Gunny said, holding out his hand.

"Well, I would but if it means I have to hold that dirty hand . . ." Sandra teased.

He held out his other that was equally as awful, grabbed her hand, she grabbed her locket, and whisked them away to the North Pole. More exploring would wait for another, cleaner day.

CHAPTER 53

Jason Learns

Location: Jason's Fairy Castle Office

He was king of the fairies and it was doing him no good at all.

He couldn't get cooperation from his own council, he couldn't get the saneer's cooperation and, maybe most frustratingly of all, his status hadn't been of any help in getting closer with Sandra again. "In fact, I think it's only made it worse," Jason said to himself, pondering the situation as he paced around the regal office he'd been given as the king.

"Made what worse?" a voice asked. Jason whirled around. He'd been so deep in his own thoughts, he hadn't heard anyone enter the room.

"I actually did knock," Reesa said, "but it seems I still surprised you."

"Reesa!"

JingleBelle Jackson

She had surprised him with her silent approach, but he realized the biggest surprise might be that he found himself glad to see her. Reesa had challenged him regularly but since an incident where he had saved her life when Calivon had threatened her, she had been also quietly loyal underneath her natural shan fairy haughtiness. She was smart and, unlike himself, had been a fairy her whole life. Well, technically he had been one as well but had only learned he was in the past year. That meant she had insights and advantages that he needed but didn't possess. He was choosing to trust her and hoped his trust was not misplaced.

As happy as he felt to see her, there were two good reasons for why he needed her to leave.

"Reesa, you should go," Jason said with concern clearly showing in his voice. He took her firmly by the elbow to lead her back to the door.

"Your Highness," Reesa started, feeling annoyed.

"We've been over that," Jason said firmly. "I prefer my name."

"If it really was your name, perhaps I would use it," Reesa said. "Jason," she wrinkled her nose as she said it, "is not a fairy name."

"Well, it's the name I have and the name I like whether it is fairy or not, I don't really care," Jason said. "And I'll be keeping it. So use it. That's a royal order if need be." He looked at her sternly.

294

Reesa started again. "Well then, fine, Jason," she said, drawing out the two syllables in his name, drawing away from his strong grip and looking at him directly. "I've come to take you to lunch."

"That is a delicious thought, but I simply have no time right now, Reesa. I'm sorry. I really would enjoy it but I must ask you to leave," Jason said, hurrying her to the door. "Before you go, though, may I ask you something?"

"Of course," Reesa said.

"Why are the saneers so powerful? And what did you mean 'including my own parents'? Did the saneers take my parents?"

"Oh, Jason, even we shouldn't talk of them," Reesa said in a low voice, looking around uneasily and feeling uncomfortable with where the conversation was going. She pushed the door shut and Jason stepped back.

"That's just it. Why not? Why should you, as a powerful fairy in her own right, or me, as the king of fairies for fairies' sake, have to fear anybody, let alone other fairies?" Jason looked at Reesa with such a vulnerable, open expression of appeal as he leaned against his desk that she found herself, very reluctantly, sharing what he wanted to know.

She looked around and sat down on a plush red settee in the room and patted the seat next to her for Jason but he just waved her off and began pacing. She shrugged the dismissal off and started in.

"The story really isn't that complicated. In fact, as stories go, it's fairly mundane," she started slowly. "There weren't always saneers. At one time there were just shans and shanelles."

Jason now had stopped pacing and now had his back leaned on his desk, listening intently.

"Then, during the time that King Fable was our ruler, about three hundred human years past, the king made an unpopular, and some felt, unjust ruling against two shan families. The two families had gone against a declaration made by the king that many, including my family to this day, felt unfairly favored the shanelles." Jason didn't even ask for details. He was pretty sure he would have supported the king's decision. Shans never liked anything that was seen positive for shanelles.

"So then what happened?" Jason prodded from across the room, trying to keep his impatience under wraps.

"Nothing," Reesa said. But, of course Jason knew the answer wasn't that simple so he waited, frowning, for the rest. "At first," Reesa continued.

"The families left from our kingdom and there were many rumors about where they had gone. Finally, after much time passed, they returned and the answer to where they had been was evident immediately to all in the glow of their orbs. They had turned dark. The symbol of dark magic at work! They had sought out, and received, new powers from the dark beings of magic." Reesa stopped for a moment and shuddered, and when she started again, she spoke even softer. Jason moved to the seat next to her to listen and offer a sense of security.

"They took things from the king's family. Things like beauty and time like they have done to the elves and Wistle. The king, of course, threatened them with imprisonment if they didn't undo their enchantments but they had no fear. Not only could he not capture them, each time he tried, they did more damage to his family." Jason could not hold still at the thought and was up pacing again.

"Finally the king gave in to their demands. The saneers, as they had named themselves after one of their original leaders, were given their own part of the kingdom and allowed to be self-governed on some issues. The king intended for them to continue under the fairy kingdom and his reign but they have never acted in that way. They have never since recognized our ruler and are very rarely even seen. Most fairies today are not sure they even really exist and certainly have never seen a saneer." She added with another shiver, "And never want to."

Now Reesa was up pacing a bit, wondering if she had told too much, seeing Jason's level of increased agitation. Still she pushed on.

"In exchange for the concessions made, the saneers released most of the enchantments on the king's family, though never on his wife, who is to this day said to be a star far off in the sky." She paused again before adding to Jason's back as he looked at the currently blue sky thinking on what Reesa had just said. "I will point her out to you on our next clear night." Jason nodded and slowly turned around again as Reesa continued.

"But the saneers' dark magic changes had also cost them a great deal. They were now forced to primarily orb only in the dark – only the most powerful can appear at any time – and it's said that, while they smile all the time, there is no happiness held in their hearts." Jason found himself nodding his head remembering that feeling when he met with them. Surprisingly, he didn't feel despair in this story. He felt hope. There was a lot of work to do but knowing the history, he felt he had the opportunity to bring all fairies back together. Had he spoken the idea out loud, Reesa would have laughed, which would have been highly against royal protocol, even though she was also a friend of sorts. You were free to laugh with your king but not at him.

Instead he changed the topic slightly and asked his other pressing question. "What about my parents? What do the saneers have to do with their disappearance?"

"The story is that they are that tree." Reesa nodded to the window facing out to a magnificent, multi-colored tree in the courtyard.

"WHAT?" Jason demanded, moving toward the window to consider the preposterous claim Reesa had just made. Jason had stood at the window many times admiring its strength and unique beauty. It was like no tree he had ever seen with leaves of multiple colors that changed year-round but never was bare. As he stared at it now with new curiosity, for the briefest moment, he thought he felt a connection. It seemed the tree even shivered for a second as there was a loud rap on

Jason's office door. He whirled around feeling a moment of panic as he looked to the clock and realized time had gotten away from him. Reesa needed to leave. The rest of the story would have to wait for another time. His two good reasons for her to leave earlier had arrived at his door, and without him so much as answering the knock, two dark orbs appeared and there stood the two saneers, smiling insincerely as they always did.

Uncharacteristically, Reesa made a small exclaim of almost fright.

Jason drew himself up fully to feel as large and "kingly" as possible, unhappy with the turn in this planned meeting that he hadn't fully thought out, now knowing even more about how dangerous the saneers were. He placed himself carefully between the saneers and Reesa.

"Tambler and Kilt, you will excuse me while I finish this appointment." He said this with more authority than he felt, but he knew he could show no weaknesses to these two. He was king of fairies and his authority for large and small matters was not to be questioned – even by those who didn't recognize his reign.

He considered calling for the guards posted in the foyer but believed that would only provoke his "guests" and not be effective in any case. He chose to leave the two saneers standing where they were in his office while he pulled Reesa through the door behind him, which led to his private quarters. It wasn't ideal but she could exit from his rooms.

JingleBelle Jackson

As soon as the door closed, he spoke in a loud whisper to her. "Go. Now. Through that door." He pointed across the room. "I will catch up with you later." He turned to go but she did not let go of his arm.

"I can't," Reesa said firmly. "You cannot meet with those two alone. You know you can't! You are the ruler of our kind and they're dangerous!"

"I know they're dangerous. That's exactly why I will meet with them on my own. They have already harmed one of my friends – or have you forgotten about Wistle?" he asked with some disgust. It was not okay for the others not to care about what had happened to the brave fairy.

"Of course I haven't forgotten! I care about her too. I'm going back in with you," Reesa said stubbornly and bravely.

"You won't," Jason said. "Reesa, you are not helping and I don't have time for this. As your king, I am ordering you to release me and leave."

Reesa's faced flashed with anger, which quickly changed to almost a beseeching look for him to change his mind. When she could see in his eyes that he would not, she let go of his arm and walked away.

Jason went right back into the room with the saneers. There was business to discuss.

"What a nice view you have of such a beautiful tree," Kilt said, smiling as Jason closed the door behind him firmly and rejoined the dangerous duo.

CHAPTER 54

Mirror Mirror

Location: North Pole Village

"Sandra?"

"Sandra? Wake up, Sand!"

Sandra had had enough energy after adventuring to the jungle and the arctic for a shower and to get a light dinner with some of the elves. Afterward, she had headed back to her room and landed, clean clothes still on, flat down on the bed. She had slept without moving or dreaming until she started at hearing her name called.

Birdie? It was Birdie! She was here! Sandra struggled to get fully awake to greet her friend. She was groggy but already happy knowing Birdie was back. She pushed up off the bed and looked around to greet her friend, only to realize it had just been a dream.

JingleBelle Jackson

Without moving another inch, she flopped back on the bed and dozed again to sleep.

"Sandra! Wake up!"

That did not sound like a dream.

This time, Sandra sat right up. "Birdie?" she said, groggily, but waking up fast. "Where are you?" She scanned the dark room. "Are you here?" She felt silly talking to the empty room but Birdie seemed so real.

"I'm in your bathroom mirror." Sandra heard the words and laughed out loud. Her imagination was really good sometimes. Still, she pushed herself out of the bed to the bathroom, flipped on the light and . . . screamed! Not at her wild and woolly hair that would scare any sane person in the state it was in, but at seeing Birdie, who was indeed in the bathroom mirror. Sandra whirled around to look behind her but nobody was there. Birdie was just in the mirror.

"Bird?" Sandra asked tentatively, still blinking against the bright lights. "What's going on? Is this really you?"

"It's me, Sand! Wake up! Wake up! I only have so much time!"

"But how is this possible?" Sandra stammered out.

"I'll tell you the details later. For now, just suffice it to say, I found a magical friend who sympathized with me and Sam and is helping me."

"Are you married now, Bird? What did you wear?" Sandra asked with sadness in her voice. She was sad her friend got married without her being there and sad she would be

302

living so far away with new obligations that would mean she would rarely get to see her. Losing Birdie was a very hard loss for Sandra.

"I'm not married, Sand! That's what I wanted to tell you. Tell Crow. You've got to tell him, Sand. I know he hates me now but I still want him to know that they couldn't make us get married in the end."

"You're not married? Birdie, that's great!" Sandra felt wide awake now with such great news. "When are you coming back?"

"Not soon, I'm afraid. That's why you have to tell Crow. I don't want him thinking that just because I'm not there it means I'm married away somewhere." She looked around as if someone was coming, but seemed satisfied no one was, and continued.

"My parents set it all up but when the ceremony time came, Sam never showed. He never showed, Sandra! That night one of the servants at my mother's slipped me a note from him that just said, 'happy wedding present to my bride' and had his initials. He escaped for us, Sand! It just shows what a really great guy he really is. The note almost made me sad we didn't get married."

"Well, I'm sure he'd still be willing if you really feel that way, Bird."

"I said *almost,* Sand! You know I love Crow. Or even if you don't know it, I know I do. I'm really clear about that now."

"So, then, why don't you come back?"

JingleBelle Jackson

"Because my desperate parents are searching the country — maybe the world — for my groom to force him to come back and marry me. And if they find him, and he declines, they're going to lock him up! It's such a mess. I feel terrible for impacting his life so much."

"What can I do?"

"Well, first of all, please tell Crow as soon as you can but not before you do something with your hair." Birdie smiled while Sandra grimaced at her.

"Now? Right now? You tease me about my hair in the middle of the night when you are just a mirror and you need something from me?" Sandra brushed her hands through it to mess it up even more.

"Okay, okay, but I do suggest you consider tying it back tomorrow." Birdie continued her tease.

"Which is today since you woke me up so early," Sandra said. "Seriously though, Bird, is there anything else I can do? Can I use the locket and come get you?"

"I thought about that but so did my parents. They say if I leave or anyone comes and breaks me out, they'll just come get me again and take me back. I know they will so it doesn't make sense. I'm willing to be here a while. It's kind of good to be home, really, and catch up with some friends, but I'm not going to be willing forever and I'm not going to marry Sam even if they find him." She turned and looked toward the door. Her voice was hushed now.

Enchantments A South Pole Santa Adventure

"Sandra, I have to go. Tell Crow, Spence, and the others, too. I want everyone to know that I'm still single, independent me!"

With that she was gone and Sandra found herself just looking at herself. Birdie was so right about her hair. That jungle had really done a number on it. She would tie it back before she went anywhere, and by anywhere she meant straight to Crow.

# # #

As soon as he heard she was there to talk to him about Birdie, the younger version of Gunny was unwilling to hear anything Sandra was trying to tell him.

"No, Sandra, NO," Crow had said firmly and loudly, actually shutting the door on her and not reopening it even after she shouted through it.

"She didn't get married. She wants you to know that she didn't get married. She only loves you."

He still didn't open the door until she finally went to leave, and it cracked open. That's all she needed. She knew he was hurting; she had been through that kind of pain, but he had to have all the facts before he completely shut his heart off to Birdie.

She told him everything that Birdie had told her without leaving out a single detail. When she got done, he asked to hear it again.

JingleBelle Jackson

"So there's nothing we can do, right now," Sandra finished.

"I'm not one to sit around, Sandra," Crow said. He then spilled out a plan while she sat there, impressed again with this classy brother of Gunny's.

CHAPTER 55

Checking in on a Friend

Location: Holiday Ranch

The next trip Sandra took with her locket she took alone. It wasn't back to the Arctic to check for clues. It was down to the Holiday Ranch to see Wistle.

She didn't even bother with politely checking in with Ghost or the Holiday family members. She asked the locket to take her right to Wistle.

"Wistle?" Sandra called out, trying to get her bearings. She knew she was in the ranch bunk room but even in the middle of the day it was very dark. All the shades were pulled and the lights were off. "Wistle? Where you at?"

"Go away, Sandra." Sandra finally heard from a bed in the farthest corner. Wistle had grown so thin that Sandra could barely see her lying there pressed up against the wall in one of the bunks.

307

"Wistle, I can't. You're my friend and I care about you. You're still a fairy, you know. You could use your fairy ball powers and get out of here for some fresh air once in a while."

Sandra moved to the blinds and pulled them open.

"No LIGHT!" Wistle's voice was clear and loud now, and Sandra pulled the shades mostly closed again.

"Fine, but you need to talk to me. C'mon, Wistle, just for a little while. I've missed you. We all miss you. You know we don't care a thing about how you look. We know why."

"Why, Sandra? Why? We probably disagree on why. I suspect you think it was because of the saneers but I think it was because of you!" Wistle said to Sandra in her weak voice. As Sandra listened, the truth of Wistle's words hit her so hard she wobbled where she stood and reached out to steady herself against the closest bunk.

More than anyone, Wistle had tried to talk her out of meeting with the saneers. And more than anyone, Wistle had been affected by the outcome of Sandra's actions. She didn't blame Wistle if she hated her now. She understood and felt a new urgency to fix this. Even if it meant at great sacrifice to herself, she had to fix this for Wistle.

She put her hand back around her locket to go and replied to her friend, "I'll fix it, Wistle. I'll fix it. Please stay strong for a little longer."

ENCHANTMENTS A SOUTH POLE SANTA ADVENTURE

With that, she was gone and Wistle flipped over. She knew no one could fix anything. It was going to last forever.

# # #

If Wistle's outcome was based on the progress Jason was making with the saneers, there was a good chance she was right and it would last forever. His meeting with Kilt and Tambler after Reesa had left had been frustrating at every turn. He had ordered them, as their king, to release their enchantment on Wistle. He had offered them treasures from the royal riches. He had threatened to kick them out of the fairy kingdom. With each thing he tried, he had become more and more frustrated as the two had simply stood there, obstinately refusing to change. Finally, his frustration had driven him to the end of his patience and he ended the negotiating. Instead he had resorted to using a considerable amount of royal magic on them. It had no apparent impact on them at all as they had stood there smiling, this time with a bit of a smug look even showing in their eyes. They were unstoppable it seemed, so he stopped. The two had spoken in their strange way by looking at each other, had given him a last look of disgust, and orbed away without a word.

As Jason yelled out in great frustration at the room, Tambler had reappeared briefly. "Do not summon us again, Jason of St. Annalise. We will not change what is in place,

309

JingleBelle Jackson

and if you continue to disturb us, we will be forced to take action. There is much we know of you and your family that you do not and many good reasons for this to be our last meeting. We give you this warning only in deference to your role as king of most fairies." With that, Tambler disappeared, smiling, as Jason, mighty king of the fairies, leaned back on his desk for support. *What did the saneers know about him that he did not?* The thought made him shudder.

CHAPTER 56

Holiday Ginghams and Paisleys

Location: North Pole Village

To say the elves were excited about the plans for June 24 was to understate the situation. The date marked six months to Christmas Eve and a night where the sun never set at the North Pole. It was always special that time of year, and with all the challenges that had been happening, there had been no time to pull together a May Day Festival. So, instead, Sandra had suggested they have a Happiness Hoedown to celebrate being "hoe"le and happy again! She thought it was a clever play on words. The elves were more excited about everything else. First and foremost, what they would get to wear. Naturally, Diva had taken control of the wardrobe ideas and arranged for a fashion show in the main square two weeks before the event so the elves could preview their choices.

JingleBelle Jackson

"Gunny, I had never even heard of a hoedown before going to the one at the ranch, but now, thanks to you and your family, it's one of the best things in my life at the moment," Sandra said, leaning back against her tall boyfriend before the fashion show started. She hadn't actually called him her boyfriend to anyone else, but she had been practicing the words in her head and liked how they sounded.

"My whole family is excited to be invited to this, blue girl," Gunny said. Then he bent forward and whispered in her ear. "You'd look great in that little green light-up number." They both laughed and she swatted at him. It was not something she would ever wear!

Diva had gone all out on the dresses once she understood what a hoedown dress generally looked like. She had mostly stuck to ginghams and checkered patterns, but she had layered those with Christmas-patterned fabric and big lacy flounces underneath that the girl elves were loving. The dresses looked surprisingly both country and Christmas and even fashion-forward in their way. Definitely Diva originals. She had done something similar for the boys and put each of them in gingham shirts but some of the panels were replaced again with a Christmas-patterned fabric in the same tones of the shirt. They each were matched with a simple pair of blue jeans. The elves modeling in the show all loved what they were wearing, and as each look went down the runway, orders poured in. What put each outfit over the top, though,

312

and what the elves wanted most, was the cowboy boots and hats. Somehow, Diva had managed to get hold of the brightest colored boots and hats ever made. It was doubtful any respectable cowboy or cowgirl would have worn any of them, but these were elves who loved fun and loved color and they loved those boots and hats with a passion. Those happy elves made for two happy Santas.

"What are you going to wear to the hoedown, Santa?" Sandra asked her mentor who had joined them, knowing that Santa's go-to outfit for every occasion, year-round, was his Santa suit.

"Hoe Hoe Hoe!" Santa said adding, "Those are 'Hos' with an 'e' at the end just so you know." Sandra smiled that he was having fun with the occasion too.

"Well, you think about it because I'm pretty sure Diva is not going to let you get off that easy."

"What are you wearing?" Santa asked.

"Something in an aqua blue. In honor of Birdie. It's her favorite color."

"Sounds like an excellent choice," Santa said, nodding his head at the idea.

"I think I'd like to see you, Mr. Holiday, in a pair of boots in that color there!" Sandra pointed to a pair of turquoise-colored boots that Hiccup was modeling as he strode down the runway with a stick pony that Diva had provided to the cowboy models. He stopped right in front of them and grinned. "Giddy-up," he said followed by, "hiccup!" The trio all burst into laughter as Hiccup rode his horse away with a couple of other elf cowboys on stage.

"It's going to be the very best hoedown any of us have ever been to, and I've been to a lot," Gunny said.

"I think you are one hundred percent right even though I've only been to one," Sandra said. She wanted to enjoy every minute till then. June 25, the day after the hoedown, would be a much harder day, but that was something she couldn't share with him or anyone else. Now was a time to focus on fun.

CHAPTER 57

It's a Happiness Hoedown, Y'all!

Location: North Pole Village

The Happiness Hoedown started earlier in the day than probably any hoedown in history because this one involved excited, impatient elves! All elves loved nothing more than a party and most of them hadn't slept at all the night before. Santa had declared the day an official holiday at the North Pole, and even the elves serving in remote places like the South Pole outpost and St. Annalise had been called back – including Tug.

"Hello, Your Highness!" Sandra heard from across the square as she hurried to get another last-minute detail put into place.

"Tug!!" she said, genuinely glad to see her housekeeper elf was there. She wanted every elf to enjoy this celebration. She waved back as he scurried off with some others. "No cleaning today!"

"No, ma'am, your royalness! I don't want to get my new outfit dirty!" Sandra's heart soared seeing how cheerful he and

315

JINGLEBELLE JACKSON

the rest all were. *All the extra work putting this event together was totally worth it,* she thought, feeling happy and satisfied.

By the time Sandra got down to the barn area, Gunny, Crow, and the other helpers had everything set up. They had a big, temporary dance floor in place with hay strewn on it and hay bales for seating all around. Surrounding the dance floor area were booths for food and fun. Elves could enjoy all sorts of typical fair foods. There was cocoa, corn-on-the-cob, and the elves' favorite cinnamon rolls homemade by Cappie. Sandra had baked up some of her own favorite tropical granola bars and brought in kabobs of fruit from St. Annalise in hopes that she could get some of the elves interested in foods that were a little healthier. At least she would have some things she liked, she thought grinning.

" . . . *squawk!* . . . granola bars . . . *squawk!* . . . yum!"

"Why thank you, Squawk," Sandra said, happy to see her big bird. "I'm happy you like them as much as I do."

" . . . *squawk!* . . . even more . . . *squawk!*"

Sandra wasn't just all about health food, though. She loved to make her elves smile and had arranged to introduce a new sugar treat at this hoedown. She had brought in a cotton candy machine and was certain it was going to be the most popular thing there! Spencer and Network Naters had volunteered to run the booth, and Sandra hoped the two of them would be enough.

Like Diva, some of the other elves were especially excited about this new dance event. Ellen had been so excited about

316

ENCHANTMENTS A SOUTH POLE SANTA ADVENTURE

the Happiness Hoedown, she had taken a reindeer express to the Holiday Ranch to learn how to square dance from the Holiday sisters. Glory and Blue had loved having her there! In return, for the first time, the whole Holiday family was visiting the North Pole Village, and, like every first-time visitor ever, they all were in awe of the specialness of the place.

"This day is going to be so special," Sandra said out loud, watching Ellen and the Holidays doing a practice dance on the floor while Buddy and his band played square dance music that sounded suspiciously like a Christmas carol with a country beat and twang put to it. Sandra smiled, loving the perfection of the moment.

"Hope I'm the guy putting that smile on your face right now," Gunny said, coming up and putting his arms around her. It felt natural to have him be like this now. "Well, sort of," Sandra said, leaning back. "It's your family who I'm smiling about now and how glad I am that they're here and how much joy they bring me. And all of that is because of you. So, yes," she said, turning to face him, "I guess you are the guy responsible for putting this smile on my face."

He grinned, looking past her to his family.

"They really are the best, huh? I hit the family jackpot."

"Gunderson Holiday, since when are you on the sidelines?" Gunny's mom called out.

"C'mon, girlfriend, a quick swirl around the dance floor will get us both in the mood!" Gunny grabbed Sandra's hand and lined up with the rest.

317

Before they knew it, the dance floor was full of happy elves in bright ginghams and even brighter hats and boots. Thanks to Ellen's insistence, they had been taking her lessons for the last week and most were doing an excellent job for their very first hoedown. It was hard to hear the dance caller in fact, for all the laughing that was going on.

By noon, there wasn't a spot for one more elf on the dance floor, which was okay, since it seemed the rest were busy playing the carnival games they had set up, taking rides on Em and eating cotton candy. As Sandra expected, the line for cotton candy was the longest of all the booths, and big, puffy cotton clouds could be seen everywhere she looked. Clicker was getting photos of all the happenings and came over to where Sandra had just finished putting up the last decorating touch. This needed to be a picture-perfect event but she herself was not yet even close to picture perfect.

"Oh, please, Clicker, don't click any pictures of me yet! I haven't had time to change. I've got to go get in my hoedown dress, too. Click some of Santa over there. He and Mrs. Claus are looking particularly festive in their red gingham."

"Okay, Sandra, but when you get back, I'd like to have the next dance." He bowed politely like he had seen others doing on the dance floor.

"That would be my honor, Clicker. Thank you." Sandra hurried off with a dance tune in her head and heart.

CHAPTER 58

A Love Lost

Location:

She was alone when she got to the hotel and glad to see that no one was around. It was a day of fun for everyone. In her room, she took her time getting ready. The event was going to run far into the evening and she needed a little bit of time alone. She wanted to look pretty for the day and let her hair sparkle, knowing it would look festive in the lights Gunny and Crow had put into place. She decided she would leave it down for the day and put it up, more formally and less outrageous, for the evening.

She had ended up having Diva make her two dresses. Her daytime hoedown dress was flirty and flouncy and done in shades of green that showed off her eyes, and she had selected a pair of Christmas green boots to go with it. Her evening dress was longer, more subdued, and in Birdie's favorite color of aqua. She loved them both.

She fought back feeling a little nervous about the day, as she put the finishing touches on her outfit. "This is going to be the perfect day," she said to herself in the mirror.

"Sandra."

She knew the voice before she saw the man.

"Jason?" she said, feeling confusion on every level. She hadn't seen him again for weeks. No word at all, and seeing him now, standing at her door, caused her heart to skip a beat. Was it because he was model handsome as fairies all were, she thought quickly, or had he just scared her? She dismissed trying to figure it out.

"I saw you come in and I waited but, well, you haven't come back out and I've never been patient." He walked toward her but stayed back making sure it was okay. "You actually look unbelievable in that outfit and I mean that in a good way." He smiled and she laughed.

"Sit down," Sandra said, motioning to the bed. He just kept walking toward her. "Seriously beautiful, Sandra," he said.

Sandra felt like she couldn't turn away from this man she had loved and lost. She had to shake her head to clear it. "Oh, Jason, you are not one to talk," she said. "You didn't even dress up and you look, well, like fairy life suits you."

"Surprisingly, I think it does," he said, moving away and sitting tentatively on the edge of the bed. "It's ironic, Sand.

I lost you in this room," he said, looking around. "I'm still sorry about that."

Sandra just nodded quickly. She knew he was. She even knew it was okay now, but the pain of it had been hard to overcome and there were still raw pieces in her heart here and there. No matter what was to come in her life, the man before her had been the first boy she had ever loved.

"And I'm here to let go again," he continued, now looking at her as Sandra's heart twanged. "We've both moved on, I think. As much as I have honestly wanted you back, I think I did too much damage. I never, ever meant to hurt you, Sandra. It was only out of confusion and a need to know myself."

His eyes bore into hers, looking for understanding, which he found there, along with a deep and lasting love for this important friend she had. Sandra came and sat next to him.

"I always knew that, Jason," she said quietly. "Deep inside I think I understood it, too. I long ago forgave it."

He reached out and hugged her with so many emotions passing through his mind – regret, longing, love, friendship, hope – but knowing they were both on the right path.

"You will surely find this to be outrageous," he said, laughing with some irony behind it. "I know I sure do, but I think I'm falling for Reesa."

"Reesa!" Sandra burst out. She was surprised to hear it but at the same time it made sense. The fairy was more than just haughty. She was smart and fair and could be Jason's

JingleBelle Jackson

equal. And Reesa knew the fairy world in ways Jason didn't and could have his fairy back in tough times.

"Does she feel the same?" she asked.

"I think so. You know Reesa, she's a hard one to read, but I think I would be good for her, and I'm pretty certain she'd be good for me, too. But I wanted you to know first and not just find out another way. You matter to me, Sand, like I have mattered to you. You always will and you will always be able to turn to me for anything you may need from me or my kind. You know that, right?"

Tears were in her eyes now. Another goodbye from Jason in the same room as the first one, not as agonizing as the first but bittersweet. Goodbyes were not her strength.

Jason saw the tears. "Oh, Sandra, have I hurt you again? I don't mean to. I thought, well it seemed you and Gunny had become close."

"I love him, Jason."

"Yeah, that seemed kind of obvious," he said with a touch of bitterness in his voice.

"Not to him I don't think," she said, reaching for a tissue and blowing her nose.

"Only because he's completely afraid you don't," Jason said. "I've been there. I recognize all the signs."

"This is a weird conversation to be having with you," Sandra said, rolling her eyes back and forth.

"And a good one," Jason said. "It means we can be friends."

"Oh, Jason," Sandra said, now reaching over and letting him hug her in a tight goodbye. "Make sure Reesa knows that too, okay? I'd like us all to be friends and that will take some kind of miracle for sure."

Jason laughed. He knew what she meant.

"She's tough, but underneath it all there's signs of a good heart and she's very loyal. I didn't come here about this, you know I would have already told you if I had, but I've made no progress with the saneers. Despite being afraid of them herself, though, Reesa has been one of the few to stand with me to consider how we can get them to release Wistle. Something they said the last time I insisted we meet has me thinking there's a chance that Reesa may be able to help me with some things I need to know." His sentence drifted off and he looked at Sandra as though he was considering whether to share more or not before he shook his head, smiled and stood up.

"Okay, well you have a 'hoedown' to get to," he said, grinning now. "I have to say, even as breathtaking as you look, I'm not sure I mind missing that occasion. Fairies don't really 'hoedown.' Thankfully this time, I need to get back to the stack of things that seem to never end in my new role." He moved to the door and then came back.

"Sandra, you know I know your lineage. I will always keep that secret and I will defend you in every way I can if you need me. I've learned on my own that you're right to be fearful of it being known. Let that human lunk that you

JINGLEBELLE JACKSON

love," Sandra rolled her eyes at him, "take care of you." He leaned down then and kissed her lightly, gently, bittersweetly on the lips and then moved to the open door and was gone.

Sandra stood there with her eyes closed, processing what had just happened, and when she opened them again there stood Gunny.

"This human 'lunk' loves you back," he said and crossed the room to the Santa he was crazy about, thinking that for the first time ever he actually liked the fairy guy.

CHAPTER 59

A Clever Crow's Plan

Location: North Pole Village

They had been dancing and eating and laughing and making merry for hours. The band played on and the happy part of the Happiness Hoedown was just as present as the dancing part.

"You ready?" Sandra asked him again just to be sure. He nodded and reached out his hand to hers.

Sandra nodded her head to Gunny. "Be right back then," she said. Gunny still wasn't one hundred percent behind this plan but he loved his brother. He gave a solemn tip of his cowboy hat and the two were off.

In what seemed just a blink of time to the handsome cowboy, they were at their destination. Sandra put her finger to her lips to indicate that he not say anything and pointed

325

that he was to stay there while she went to look around. It only took a moment to find who she was looking for.

"Sandra! What are you doing here! I told you not to come! It won't do any good to rescue me – they'll just drag me back, and if my parents find you here, it'll be even worse. For both of us." Birdie whispered loudly as she looked frantically around.

Sandra pulled on her friend's arm and spoke in the same tone of whisper. "I didn't come alone," she said and dragged her friend back to what she assumed was Birdie's bedroom where Crow stood, more handsome than he had ever looked, hat in hand.

Birdie took one look at him and started crying. She crossed the room without hesitation and he pulled her into a hug that she never wanted to end.

"Crow, I, I don't even know what to say," she started. "You can't stay. It will just put you in danger." The cowboy put his fingers to her lips and stepped back so she could see him get down on one knee.

"Ambyrdena Snow, this is a rescue but more than that, this is a proposal from my heart that I hope truly speaks to yours. I love you, Birdie, and I believe you love me. Let's not waste any more time. I'm here to bring you back. Marry me! Tonight! We have everything all ready. All you have to say is 'yes' and we'll make it so. Then it won't matter whether your parents come find you or not."

Birdie looked at Crow and looked over at Sandra who encouraged her friend. "Say yes, Bird," she said sincerely. "You've loved him since the moment you met." Birdie was smiling and crying.

"Yes! Absolutely yes! Not because I have to but because it's what I really want!"

Crow gave a yelp, stood up, grabbed Birdie and reached for Sandra. "If you don't mind, Sandra, this bride and groom have a wedding to get to."

"It would be my absolute pleasure," Sandra said, and in a blink she whisked them away where all of her friends and Crow's family were already gathered around and ready to welcome her. Birdie cried as she hugged each one and Sandra had to pull her away.

"Bird, we have to get you ready! You want to wear a wedding dress, don't you?" Sandra said.

"You even got me a dress?" Birdie said, astonished at her thoughtful friend and amazing groom. She followed Sandra but turned around and ran back for a hot kiss in front of everyone. "That is for my very hunky husband-to-be!" she said, while the Holiday brothers and even the sisters hooted with glee. Every one of the family was there but Ghost, and while Crow understood, it was hard for him not to have his twin there.

Still, nothing, now that he had Birdie in front of him, was going to mar this perfect occasion. "Go get ready, my

JINGLEBELLE JACKSON

beautiful bride-to-be, and get back out here. Not every couple has the top Santa as their officiator!" He didn't add that time was of the essence. He knew he didn't need to. Birdie knew it better than he did.

Cappie, Em, and Breezy were all in Sandra's room, waiting to help Birdie get ready. Sandra loved that the little elves wanted to help too. "Birdie, I know this isn't necessarily the dress you would have picked out for yourself," Sandra said from her closet. "But we have a western theme tonight and you're marrying a cowboy, so we felt it needed to have a little country flair to it. Diva designed it and Cappie sewed it."

"And I LOVE it!" Birdie said, seeing the dress Sandra brought out and slipping into it in an instant. It fit her perfect! It was nothing at all like she had ever imagined for herself the few times she had day-dreamed on a wedding dress, but it was perfect for Crow and this day. It was lacy and flouncy, yet sexy and sparkly at the same time. In keeping with the gingham checks everyone wore for the Happiness Hoedown, it even had a flirty white-on-white gingham layer in amongst its flounces. It fell to just below the knee and allowed her to show the cutest pair of white cowboy boots she had ever seen.

"Crow found those for you," Sandra said, seeing her beautiful best friend looking at them.

Breezy and Cappie fussed with Birdie's hair and make-up, adding just the lightest touches for highlighting her beauty. Sandra got ready in her dress too while Birdie got finished off. She sat and pulled on her boots, and Cappie finished her

Enchantments A South Pole Santa Adventure

off with a short veil, then turned her around to present to her best friend.

Sandra was breathless. Birdie was always beautiful but she completely glowed. "Oh, Bird," was all she could say.

"Don't make me cry!" Birdie said. "And you look so beautiful, too. Thank you for picking my favorite color for your dress." She knew Sandra had done that on purpose.

"Okay, bride Birdie, are you ready to get married?" Sandra asked, finding it hard to believe, but super happy for her best friend knowing this solution that Crow had come up with was exactly the right one.

"Lead me to my groom!" Birdie said, feeling happier than she could remember feeling in her entire life.

Chapter 60

Dearly Beloved

Location: North Pole Village

Everyone there that day knew they were at a very special union. The urgency placed on Crow and Birdie and the way they had, creatively and bravely, decided to work together to set troubles behind them and face the challenges bonded together added a depth to this occasion not usually present at most weddings. Not to mention, there was fun in the air with the hoedown theme and almost all their favorite people there. Crow was missing Ghost, they all missed Wistle, and Birdie felt a pull on her emotions that it would not be her dad walking her down the aisle. But then Spencer stepped up, looking incredibly handsome himself in a green gingham shirt and string tie. He had actually slicked back his hair for the very special occasion and Birdie noted how handsome her friend was becoming as he matured with the rest of them.

"Bird, I know your dad isn't here. Could I do the honor, as one of your best friends who loves you like a sister, of escorting you down the aisle?" Spencer asked, his voice shaking slightly. As a rule, Spencer tried to avoid emotional issues but Birdie meant the world to him and he was struck by what this ceremony meant. The trio of best friends would be changing. He knew it was inevitable, of course, but it was all happening too fast and too soon as far as he was concerned. First she'd been kidnapped and before he could adjust to that dilemma she was getting married. It was almost too much for a simple best friend like him to keep up on. But not too much for him to step up when he was needed like now. He would be there for Birdie – and Crow now, too – in any way the couple would need, starting now with walking this beautiful bride down the aisle.

Birdie could just nod her head up and down, tears sparkling in her eyes at Spencer's gesture. She realized in that moment, how special indeed their deep friendship was to them both. She took his extended arm gratefully. Spencer held strong and covered Birdie's trembling hand with his own so she would know how importantly he was taking the role. "Don't be nervous," he whispered looking right at her and trying to sound stronger and more confident than he felt. "We've got this." She nodded again with gratitude-filled eyes.

Crow's and Birdie's friends and family, with assistance from the North Pole elves, had decorated the barn for this part of the event. It had been closed off, only to be unveiled if Crow had been successful in rescuing Birdie and she had said yes.

The decorations were simple, for the most part, with twinkling white lights making everything look wedding-like and pretty. Sandra knew how much Birdie loved putting the new Academy of Kindness together, and she had blown up into poster size a hundred kindness lists from children to hang all around the walls of the big barn. They looked so special and added so much, she realized she had hit on a good idea that they might never take down. Kindness lists were all about love. This wedding was all about love. The North Pole, the South Pole, and St. Annalise were all about love. Everyone gathered there that day, literally every single person, was all about love.

Maybe the most special touch, though, had been Squawk's idea. He and Birdie had always been especially close because she alone could speak his original bird language. Squawk had suggested they ask in any birds who wanted to attend and honor Birdie's special day, and thousands had answered the call and were there in the barn ready to do a special tribute to Birdie as she walked down the aisle, on the arm of her friend, to her true fiancé.

Gunny marveled at the day it had been as he walked Sandra up the aisle. He knew now, for sure, that the girl he loved, loved him back and he felt himself grinning like a fool at the thought. He had eyes for no one but her. The bride was beautiful but Sandra seemed more stunning than ever. He found himself envying his little brother and hoped someday, when it was right and not hurried, maybe this would be him and the beautiful girl beside him. He squeezed Sandra's hand and she looked over at him like she too knew what he was thinking.

As Birdie appeared, songbirds began their singing. Doves formed lines and flew in front of her. Eagles landed at the end of each row like sentries honoring her. Puffins and colorful macaws, like Squawk, birds of every color and size, flew to the front to a special gazebo that Gunny had built. The beautiful birds sorted themselves into a colorful display unique only to this special occasion. All gathered there were in awe.

That was matched only by the beauty and the smile of the bride who was coming down the aisle. Crow was wowed most of all. She was the most stunning woman he had ever set eyes on and he couldn't believe, first, that he had almost let her get away and, second, that she had agreed to be married to him, a cowboy from Texas, who loved her with all of his heart. He vowed again, as he watched her come up the aisle with her best friend Spence, that he would never let her parents, or anyone else, place her in danger or cause her any harm again.

Santa welcomed them all and conducted a short but meaningful ceremony, with the elves crying all the way through it. Cappie and Mrs. Claus ran around passing out tissues to everybody like they were party favors. When Santa pronounced them husband and wife and Crow bent her over for a long kiss, cowboy calls and cowboy hats all went up into the air. It was all perfect, right up until the happy couple turned to walk back down the aisle together and Birdie saw her parents standing there at the end.

The crowd quickly silenced as Crow stepped in front of Birdie, never letting go of her hand. Gunny and Chance flanked him with Glory and Blue coming to stand by their side. Birdie was a Holiday now and no one, not even parents, were free to do her harm.

Birdie felt completely loved by them all and terrified it would all be ripped away from her by her own parents as fast as it had come her way.

"Mr. and Mrs. Snow," Crow said, refusing to fear them. He realized there was probably a more proper way they were to be addressed but it seemed like the least of what they faced right now. "I understand I am not the son-in-law you had wanted for your daughter and I can't necessarily say that I blame you. I myself wonder how a lowly cowboy from Texas could be so lucky as to have a royal beauty from Africa love him as much as he loves her. I guess somewhere along the way I grabbed the lucky ring.

"The fact is, however, I am that lucky man and with Birdie's full consent we were just now married in a wedding that surpassed any wish I could have had for it, most especially seeing my beautiful bride come down the aisle and then that kiss we just shared. Woo, boy were there sparks at that." He grinned as the room laughed but not his new in-laws.

JINGLEBELLE JACKSON

"I'm going to ask you kindly and earnestly to please not mar this day for us. But if you insist on trying to take my bride, we will do everything in our power to resist, and even if you succeed, I will never stop coming for her."

"Zeentar," Sandra started, but the water wizard put up his hand.

"Ambyrdena, please step out from behind," Zeentar paused, before adding, "your husband." Never letting go of her hand, Crow had Birdie step up to his side so they both faced her parents.

"Ambyrdena, never in all of our dreams and desires for you did we ever imagine ourselves missing your wedding," Zeentar said. Birdie could see that her parents too were holding hands, which was an unusual show of public affection for them.

"And we are so glad we did not, our beautiful daughter," he continued as sobs burst from Birdie at what she was hearing. A miracle was happening here in front of them. "We admittedly came here to take you back but could not interrupt a ceremony that was clearly divined. Crowder, you are not the man we had hoped for our daughter but it seems you are more than that. You are certainly brave and committed, and it is easy to see our daughter loves you. It seems we owe you our thanks and our apologies. Primarily however, we owe our apologies to our only child. Ambyrdena, can you forgive us?" There was not a dry eye in the whole of the North Pole.

336

Enchantments A South Pole Santa Adventure

Birdie ran down the aisle to them, her mother caught her in her arms, the trio hugged . . . and they all disappeared.

"Beware Crow," the stunned crowd heard. "To follow is to die. Our daughter, our way!"

"MY WIFE! OUR WAY!" Crow shouted to the air, running down the wedding aisle to where he last saw his wife and falling to his knees in reaction to the agonizing, duplicitous, conniving deception that had just happened. "BIRDIE!!" he cried out but was met with just deafening silence.

CHAPTER 61

Saneers 1; Sandra 1

Location: The Mistletoe

The days afterward passed as if they were in slow motion. Everyone wanted to help and no one knew what they could do. At every turn they were blocked.

Santa had immediately demanded a hearing with the Esteemed Council of Magical Beings and was just as quickly turned down. The council, Calivon to be specific, sited it as a "domestic matter" that was "not worthy of council attention."

Even before Crow could ask, or Gunny could stop her, Sandra had run down the aisle, grabbed Crow's hand and used the locket to follow them.

. . . and had gone nowhere. The Snows had planned ahead and shielded access to Birdie, and them, from all magic that Sandra and the others had tried, then and since. Much like the saneers had done with Jason and the fairy council members.

JINGLEBELLE JACKSON

For all gathered, it was a stunning end to the most joyful occasion. For Crow, it was agonizing. He had expected the Snows to come after her, but he had never expected them to take her once they were married. Adding agony to the situation, the Snows had timed it just right, the ceremony was over but the papers had not been signed, or filed, leaving room to call the vows null and void. He had even overheard his well-meaning brother Chance, a top-notch Texan lawyer, talking with his mother and saying that all countries had their own sovereign rights and the Snows could choose simply not to honor the marriage in their country. Crow knew that was exactly what they would do.

Sandra tried to spend quality time in her room whenever possible, in hopes that Birdie would reach out to her through the mirror as she had done before. But day after day, night after night, passed with no communications. Every night she tossed and turned, waking to listen and getting very little sleep.

Her sleeplessness wasn't just over worry for Birdie, however. She felt like she was losing friends at every turn. Wistle, Ghost, for the most part, since he refused to leave the ranch and was not good company for anyone, and now Birdie – even Jason to some extent. She was done with it and determined to get at least one of them back. She had planned to take action the day after the hoedown, but the kidnapping had happened and since then, one thing or another had kept her from rescuing Wistle. It was likely fear if she was truly honest, but now she was determined again that she would meet again with the fearsome saneers. Jason might not have had any success with them, but she believed she knew how to reach them. She had started by visiting the UFO hall again on St. Annalise and asking around about them. Then she had been sure to spend part of each night visiting the *Mistletoe*, using her locket and telling no one. Fortunately Tug, Cappie, and Thomas were all still at the Pole so her actions were a risk to no one but herself. She knew it could be devastating and could cause heartbreak to those who loved her, but she also knew it was her own actions that had created the heartbreak Ghost was living under and the devastation Wistle had endured. She needed to make it right, no matter the cost to herself.

She also had to be sure no one else was involved this time so she was going every evening after feigning being tired and needing to turn in early. The truth was, a lethargy had come to everyone after Birdie's kidnapping and no one really questioned her exhaustion.

She was there on the back deck of the *Mistletoe* on her fifth night of trying to meet with the saneers when they finally appeared.

Careful, her mother said in her head, *every word matters with these two.* As always, Sandra took strength knowing her mother was there even if she wasn't physically present. Once again, as Sandra had hoped, it was Tambler and Kilt with their fake smiles and false niceties who joined her on the *Mistletoe's* deck.

JingleBelle Jackson

"Good evening, Sandra Long Name," Kilt said. "We understand you are in need of our services again. This surprised us."

"Oh, it appears that the message was relayed wrong," Sandra said, trying to be very clear. "I'm not in need of your services. I'm in need of this meeting with you to renegotiate the terms you determined when you met with Jason Annalise, the king of your kind."

The two snorted. "Jason Annalise only imagines himself the king of our kind," Tambler said. "As powerful saneers, we answer to no one. I believe he has come to know that."

Sandra had so many things she wanted to lash out at them with that she had to struggle with her own response. *Steady, darling,* her mother said.

"I got it, Mom," she said absently out loud as the saneers looked quizzically at her. She realized her slip and hurried on to cover it.

"I'm here to appeal to your kind side," Sandra said. The two saneers stared at her blankly and said nothing. They turned and looked at each other for a moment and something seemed to pass between them. She assumed they were, like many magical species, speaking telepathically. She didn't know if it was good or bad that they were considering her words.

"You graciously provided me with a clue to find what I had sought from you, though, not in actuality the document

342

ENCHANTMENTS A SOUTH POLE SANTA ADVENTURE

I had bargained for." She was trying hard to make her points and not insult them.

"We trust the clue we provided has proven to be useful," Tambler said.

"In return, you received a month's worth of time from hundreds of elves and incredible beauty from Wistle of the Woods, plus her time, in fact, as she has not been amongst her own kind or any others since that day. I'm here to ask you now, as superior beings from the magical world to release the spell from my friend Wistle. If you truly feel the payment has not been adequate then, please, let's begin the renegotiations with me." She tried not to shake as she said the last and as she heard the alarm in her mother's voice. "*Cassandra!*" Even her mother had not known of her plans.

As her mother exclaimed, Sandra's head throbbed with pain and she grabbed it as the pain pulsed and, thankfully, passed. The saneers said nothing about her motion. They instead faced each other again and then her.

"We have determined that you will receive the release of the spell on your friend. Her full beauty will be restored to her and we will remove the memory of the experience from her because, as you understand, we want only to be fair and we wish to be just," Kilt said while Tambler smiled nodding. Uncomfortably for Sandra, their smiles seemed sincere this time. She had mixed feelings about Wistle's memory on this being erased, but she didn't want to argue and she suspected

JINGLEBELLE JACKSON

Wistle would not actually object. It wasn't something a fairy would ever want to remember.

"Wha-what is the payment you will expect from me in return?" Sandra asked, bracing for whatever it was. She could not give up the *Mistletoe* but anything else within her personal power, most especially her own time, even if the demand was for years, she was prepared to release to them.

"We believe we have received adequate payment as of this date and your contract is now released." The two faced each other again for a moment then they turned again to her. As they did, an envelope floated to her hands.

Sandra looked at them quizzically.

"We have determined, since you have suggested we have a kind side and, as you stated, we did not actually provide the document you sought, to supply you with a bonus clue to what you seek. We find it entertaining that you are seeking this elfin document and believe interesting changes for the magical world could come about from its discovery. This clue will keep you from having to return to the Arctic."

They knew how far along she and Gunny were! She shivered thinking of it but said nothing to provoke them.

"I am grateful for your kindness and this meeting."

"Kindness is not our way. We are fair and our business on this matter is complete."

They turned and orbed. Sandra couldn't help herself.

"Everyone can be kind," she called after them. "Just choose it!"

344

Enchantments A South Pole Santa Adventure

As soon as they were out of view, she checked in her head for her mom who seemed already to have gone. Her parents never got many minutes to hang around, so to speak, so Sandra wasn't surprised she had left. She knew her mother had been upset with her, but thankfully, it had all worked out in the end. Sandra grabbed her locket to head to the Pole but instead aimed it right at the Holiday ranch where a grateful Ghost heard only the words, "the saneers released . . ." before barreling down the hall and finding a confused, but beautiful Wistle standing there in front of her rejoicing friends. The saneers had kept their word! Plus, they had given Sandra an extra clue. Surprises in the magical world, heck, in the very normal human world for that matter, never ceased to exist.

Sandra grabbed her friends and headed to the North Pole. Two friends restored, one friend still to find.

CHAPTER 62

Always a Payment

Location: North Pole Village

Having Wistle and Ghost back helped restore hope and smiles to everyone, even Crow that evening. Everyone, that is, except the people closest to Sandra. When Sandra shared a greatly abbreviated version of what had happened with the saneers, the looks on her friends' faces – most especially Gunny and Cappie's – ranged from upset to fury.

"I have to be able to trust you, Sandra!" Gunny raged in front of everyone, embarrassing Sandra. "I can't believe you met with the saneers without me!"

Sandra had turned to Cappie for support but had found none there. "I believe Gunny speaks for all of us," Cappie had said, looking just about as upset with her as Sandra had ever seen.

" . . . *squawk!* . . . I'm mad too! . . . *squawk!*"

347

"And me, too, Sandra! I am bigger than the saneers and you should have taken me," Em had huffed.

All the anger had caused Sandra to burst out in tears, which made her even more embarrassed but didn't really change how they all felt.

"I know you're right," Sandra said to the room. "I would be just as furious if one of you had done this. Maybe even more so, but you have to understand, *I'm* the one who created the problem and I was the only one who could fix it. To be perfectly honest, it was very frightening. I'm very tired, and I could use your understanding now instead of your anger."

Wistle walked up to her and, hugely uncharacteristically for a fairy, hugged her. "I'm not sure what all the fuss is about but I do know this, if it involved the saneers, then you are one of the bravest people I know."

"As are you, my friend," Sandra said, hugging her too-thin friend back gently. "As are you."

As the saneers had said, thankfully Wistle had no memory of the months she had lost or what the saneers had taken from her, and those who did know about it, primarily the Holiday family, were more than happy to forget. She was restored and beautiful again and just as feisty as any fairy they had ever known. Every fairy, that is, except Quisp, who very simply was one of the bravest, kindest beings Sandra had ever been honored enough to know and she proved it once again.

Sandra was walking back to her room tired but happy after the reunion with the Holiday family members all back together for the first time in months when Quisp popped out of her hair.

"Quisp! Where've you been? Did you hear the good news?" Sandra asked, feeling happy while she tried to squelch a yawn.

"I'm happy for Wistle," the little fairy said. "But I'm worried for you, Sandra. The saneers are never kind. You cannot believe them!"

"Quisp, were you in my hair the whole time I was on the *Mistletoe?*" Sandra asked, now at a full stop and feeling alarmed for the little fairy who nodded yes.

"Quisp! Are you all right?" The little fairy nodded yes again and Sandra felt instant relief.

"Why did you go with me, my tiny friend? You could have been hurt!"

"You could have been hurt, Sandra! I couldn't let you go alone! What if you had needed someone to go for help?"

"Quisp, it is one thing for me to risk myself when I'm the one who created the problem but I never could have forgiven myself if you had been hurt as well!"

"I'm fine, but concerned, Sandra. I believe the saneers scanned your memory and learned things they shouldn't know about you," Quisp said softly. She didn't really want to tell Sandra what she thought but knew Sandra had to know.

Sandra thought about how the meeting had gone and how her head had hurt and what the saneers had said about believing "interesting changes would come to the magical world as a result of finding it." Quisp's theory would explain how the saneers knew about her experience at the Arctic. They hadn't followed her, they had scanned her and stole her memories! That was the payment they had taken!

This shook her to her core and she stumbled to a nearby bench and sat there thinking of all the implications it could have. How much of her memory did they scan? Did they take any of her memories without her permission as they had Wistle's? Did they know about her parents and her secret? How could they not? Would they tell Calivon? Was there anything she could do about any of it if they did?

It was the last question that got her to get up and head for some badly needed hours of sleep. She knew the answer.

No.

She had known the saneers would expect some kind of trade when she dared to meet with them and request that Wistle be restored. Scanning her memories, without her permission, seemed to be what they took in exchange. Tambler and Kilt were conniving and devious, untrustworthy, and dangerous but her dealings with them were over.

There was not a single thing she could do now and worry would help nothing. She would not give the saneers any more of her time or attention.

"Thank you, brave Quisp," she said. "Let's get some sleep."

CHAPTER 63

The Justification

Location: Africa

Birdie could not believe her own parents had kidnapped her. The morning after the kidnapping she had awoke in her childhood bedroom. She was dressed in one of the sarongs her mother favored wearing. Birdie had always felt they were beautiful but she would have traded it now for a tank top and pair of shorts. She went through all the drawers and a closet in the room, looking for her wedding dress and the boots she loved that Crow had selected, but they were nowhere to be found.

Her parents insisted they had an explanation for their radical actions, and that she would see they were justified at what they had had to do. If she would just calm down, they said, and listen, they would explain it to her.

But Birdie would not be calm and would not listen. Her mother told her one day when she was storming around, "Ambyrdena, I am your mother. I love you. You must trust that I know best."

"Love, Mother?" Birdie had replied, appalled that her mother believed her own words. "Love does not look like this, Mother. Not ever. And trust, Mother? How could I ever trust you or Father again? I love you as my parents but you have completely broken my heart and smashed my trust. And to have love without trust is to live in agony," she said forlornly before adding with fire in her voice. "And to be a fool."

Finally, after days like this with her parents wanting to explain their actions and her refusing, she changed her mind and listened. She needed to understand if she ever hoped to escape or negotiate.

The story, while being important enough to her parents to have permanently risked the love of their only child, did nothing to soothe Birdie. She had listened to the whole thing through twice. As her mother told it, the people of the country her mother ruled and the people of the country bordering theirs that Sam's parents ruled (it seemed, he too, was of royal descent, which he had never mentioned to Birdie, implying it meant nothing to him as she felt of hers) had agreed to a treaty long ago to get the factions to quit warring. It was the ancestors of Birdie's mother's family and the ancestors of Sam's mother's family who had drawn up the peace agreement. As thanks, the people of both countries allowed their countries to be governed by monarchy rule. The royal lineage in each country was established at that time.

As part of the documents drawn up, the people, even then – almost 900 years ago – had been forward-thinking and built in an out for their future citizens. They agreed to a clause that said each one hundred years, the monarchies would need to have representatives that joined the two houses together or the people could choose for a democracy and the monarchy would be dissolved.

"This clause has been fulfilled every millennium up to this one," her mother said. "There has been little worry on this issue for many years, for there was no need. My parents', your grandparents', union was sealed with so many decades to go it was of little concern. When your father and I married, there was much consideration on the matter, but the need to include magic back into the lineage, as your father offered to us through his powers as a powerful water wizard, was felt to be more pressing.

"So, when Sam was born in his kingdom and several years later you were born, both kingdoms rejoiced and your betrothal was sealed." She said this as if it was a wonderful thing that Birdie would understand and completely accept.

Instead, Birdie sat there wondering truly if she had ever heard anything more ridiculous. All of this had been decided hundreds of years ago and was being done simply to keep their families in power? A power neither Birdie nor Sam had

JingleBelle Jackson

any interest in holding at all? And both countries, now in a modern world, could release being strict monarchies with royal rule only, and become democracies?

Birdie said as much while adding, "And while both kingdoms rejoiced, did anyone stop to consider what the children who would grow up to be adults would have to say about it? It seems leaving that consideration out of the plans is what has brought us to this point today."

"We are given great privilege, Ambyrdena, and it comes, at times, with great sacrifice as well. Never in our imagination did we expect to be in this position! You have always been such a kind and supportive daughter. I hardly recognize the willful woman who is before us now," her mother said.

"I feel the same about both of you," Ambyrdena said in return. "What has happened to the parents whom I have always loved with all of my heart and I felt loved me in return? Keeping your power over this land is more important than my happiness? Than our love for each other?" She looked at them both to see some glimmer of understanding in their eyes but there was none.

"We do not do this for us," her mother said. "We do it for you and the people of our countries. Someday you will understand that this sacrifice was worth it and will agree that it was the right course for our countries. You are fortunate because you will not have to make this decision for your children.

Enchantments A South Pole Santa Adventure

With one hundred years to come, they will be free to choose whatever partner you approve of for them."

"Are you kidding, Mother? I, and my husband, Crow," she added the last in hopes of irritating both of them and because it was true, "will never, ever assume who is right or wrong for any children we might have. That selection will be their own, as Crow is mine."

"That will be your right as a parent as this is our right." It was her father who was talking now, apparently trying to show support for her mother, Birdie thought. Most of this seemed crazily important only to her mother with her father going along.

"As soon as we locate Sam, the two of you will be joined in marriage, which, according to the governance of both of our countries, cannot be undone. I hope you will think over what we have shared here and be more willing to be support-ive of your responsibilities," her mother said, getting up to leave.

"You said the marriage has to be done every one hundred years?" Birdie asked, still trying to understand.

"Yes," her father said. "We are in the 900th year of this treaty and it must be done by the 300th day."

"What day of the year is that?" Birdie asked.

"It matters not," Birdie's mother said with a sharp glance at Zeentar that implied he had said more than she felt he should have. "Sam will be located soon and, with any luck at

355

all, the two of you will be newlyweds by this time next week and the people of both of our lands will rejoice."

Without another word, her parents left.

"It's so appropriate that you are a princess, Mother," Birdie said behind them. "Because you are living in a fairy tale."

CHAPTER 64

Here Birdie Birdie

Location: The Mistletoe

Maybe, the worst part for both Crow and Birdie of being apart was hearing nothing from each other. Birdie's parents had closed her off to everyone except the two of them. She suspected they had shielded her location or Birdie knew that Sandra would have already been there.

But lonely days by herself with nothing to do but think had led Birdie to a creative way to address the dilemma and that solution had just landed on the deck of the *Mistletoe*.

"Shoo! Go away!" Tug said to the annoying pigeon that had appeared for the second day in a row and threatened to make a mess on his just polished back deck. "Shoo!"

As the days had returned to their normal pace of being busy and full, much of the North Pole group had migrated back to St. Annalise.

357

JingleBelle Jackson

Tug was particularly happy to be back on the island. From his view, the *Mistletoe* had been in such a messy state that he hated to let up on the cleaning at all. True, most visitors, and even Sandra, didn't necessarily notice his efforts but, inch by inch, he could see the difference and had no patience for having another bird on board. As it was, Squawk was just about the main cause of most messes on the tug! The big macaw left feathers and sunflower seed shells everywhere.

"Shoo, now, go!" he said to the persistent bird, which flew in the air and deliberately, from Tug's telling of the story later, left something very messy on the deck rail for him to clean-up. "How rude, you pesky pigeon!" he said as he went to grab a mop and bucket for the clean-up. A quick swipe with a paper towel would have likely taken care of the mess, but Tug was nothing if not very, very thorough with his attention to cleaning. He was busy cleaning on the rails when Sandra found him as she cruised by from working at the barge to grab some lunch.

"Hey, Tug, okay with you if I grab something for lunch?" she said, heading straight to the galley. She was famished. The little elf dropped his mop and ran after her.

"I made you some tomato soup with extra crispy croutons," he called after her.

" . . . *squawk* . . . croutons! . . . yum!"

Tug looked at the big bird with frustration. Sandra caught the look and asked him about it.

"Everything okay, Tug? You seem a little flustered."

"I am, Your Highness, and I apologize that you have noticed," he said. "It's just this very pesky bird keeps landing on the deck and the more I shoo it away, the more it keeps coming back!"

Sandra smiled hearing him tell his story. Tug liked an orderly ship and the *Mistletoe* was many things but orderly was rarely one of them.

"There he is again!" Tug exclaimed as the bird flew right in through the almost always open galley window. "Oh, my stars! Shoo! Shoo! Go on! Shoo!" Tug was chasing the bird all around the galley, knocking things over everywhere he went with Sandra watching in horror at the mess that was coming from it.

. . . crash! . . . thud! . . . wham! . . .

Things were flying off the shelves and landing loudly with messy results on the floor, the counters, the table – even the ceiling!

. . . kerplunk!

A jar of honey smashed, sending the sticky substance everywhere, but nowhere more than directly on Tug!

" . . . ack! . . ." Squawk squawked as a glob landed directly on him.

"Tug! TUG! It's okay. It's just a bird. They come and go around here all the time," Sandra said, trying to calm Tug and both the birds inside the galley before anything else was destroyed. It was chaos! Finally, the bird Tug was chasing flew over and landed in front of Sandra.

JingleBelle Jackson

"That's just it, Your Highness," Tug said, frowning at the bird and dismally surveying the mess he had made. "This one won't go."

"Well, I'm just sorry Birdie isn't here because she would have a good conversation with our persistent friend here. In fact —"

Sandra stopped mid-sentence seeing that this persistent bird had a note tied around its leg. She cautiously reached out and the little troublemaker held up its leg for Sandra. It patiently waited for her to remove the note before flying right out the galley window without a look back. Tug watched in amazement at how easy it had been for her royal highness to get rid of the winged devil.

Sandra carefully unrolled the document the bird had carried, curious to know if it was for her or someone else. *Were children getting creative and sending notes by homing pigeon now?* she wondered, smiling. She wouldn't put it past them. She was always in awe of how creative children everywhere could be.

The smile left her face as she read just the first few words of the note. It was indeed for her. And for Crow. It wasn't something from a clever child but rather from a very clever best friend, and wife, and in its way the note was good news.

"Being held by parents. Long story, but if Sam cannot be found and the two of us married by October 27, my parents will have to release me. Tell Crow not to worry about me — they will not harm me. They would harm him, though, and any of you, so STAY AWAY!

360

The key is keeping Sam away, too. I know he wants the same. Miss you, BFF! -Bird

<u>Sandra, don't read this part.</u> ☺ Crow, come get me the minute the clock strikes 12:01 on October 28 and take me away for the most romantic honeymoon any couple could ever dream of because I dream of it, and you, and our beautiful life together, every minute, of every day. I remain yours forever. Your adoring wife, Birdie"

P.S. I dare not try this again so don't worry if you hear nothing else. Also, DO NOT RETURN A NOTE!!

Of course, Sandra read it all and smiled at how wonderful the words were. She wasted no time and didn't worry about Tug seeing her use her locket this time. He was a family member now and loyal inside and out. She grabbed onto the locket and headed to Crow.

She was gone when Tug looked up from wiping down one of the cabinets. He wondered, as his rag stuck to the honey on the counter, how he couldn't get rid of a pesky bird but couldn't keep track of a beautiful Santa.

CHAPTER 65

Santa Tours the Barge

Location: South Pole Village

The note from Birdie helped. October 27 seemed ages away to the groom who was wronged at the altar, but there was so much to do, even he didn't have time to sulk.

For Sandra, any sulking she was doing was more about being too busy to gather more clues or make any real progress on the hunt for the elfin document. She and Gunny had managed to follow the new coordinates the saneers had provided, which had landed them in the Moroccan Desert in the middle of a vicious sand storm. It forced them back to St. Annalise to get supplies They had grabbed snorkel masks to wear over their eyes and dressed with their arms and legs covered because the sand stung so bad. Despite the near black-out conditions, they had persevered and found the next coordinates scratched on an outcropping of rocks. Those coordinates had

363

JingleBelle Jackson

led them to a disgusting, smelly alley in an unsafe area of New York City where the only coordinates they could locate were actually graffiti drawn on a garbage dumpster. It seemed unrealistic to think that was the clue, but with nothing else even remotely resembling directions in any way, it was the one thing they wrote down. Since then, they had been too busy putting the last touches on the *South Pole Village* barge and loading in supplies. As a result, all of their explorations had been put on hold once again.

Sandra's concerns about her parents, Calivon, and Birdie were countered somewhat by her growing excitement as the barge neared completion. The elves had worked miracles with Gunny in getting the last of the redesign done to accommodate the school, and now last-minute touches were being completed and supplies loaded.

"I really think she's going to be ready for her first sail on the sea with the *Mistletoe* towing her along by next week, Santas," Gunny said, giving his weekly report to the two Santas as they listened while sorting through a pile of the latest kindness lists that children had sent.

"The *Mistletoe* will be ready, too," Sandra promised. In her history with the big tug, the *Mistletoe* had never actually tugged anything, but the big boat had been built as a tug and served as a tug before her parents had made it their home. Sandra knew it could go back to doing it again. "Thomas has been working on making sure she is sea-worthy for the duty.

We used to sail the world together and I'm sure in her bones she's as excited about the idea as I am!"

Thomas and Cappie had offered to captain the *Mistletoe* whenever the big barge was out touring since they knew Sandra would need to spend most of her time on the barge. They were both long-time sailors and both were looking forward to the chance to serve in such a unique capacity.

"So that means we need to plan a press tour and show the new beauty off to the world," Gunny said. He was trying to keep the pride out of his voice. After all, the barge had been built through a lot of hard work by a highly committed team, but he felt particularly proud of how she had come together. He had dreamed up the original idea, helped design her, and then been present to oversee and actually do much of the construction. He knew every room, what still needed to be done, and what special accommodations had been made so that her manufacturing area was set for happy elves working at sea amidst the roll and pitch of waves. He wasn't sure if he would ever get a chance to work on a project so grand and felt a tug of emotion that this phase of the project was coming to an end.

"We do!" Sandra said, knowing exactly how he felt about getting to show off the big barge. She could hardly wait! This was South Pole Village – her equivalent to North Pole Village. It was really special and she was ready to step up and show the world.

365

"I'd like it to be more than just for the press, though. Let's have a party and invite all of our friends, family members, some children even, and the Iceland elves! Oh, and all our friends from the South Pole Santa competition! I know they'll want to see it! Let's have them get here the day before so we can give them an extra-special tour and we can all have some time together."

Both Gunny and Santa nodded their heads as Sandra shared the idea. Her enthusiasm was catching. It was a perfect occasion to plan for a reunion with the other finalists.

"Santa, would it be okay with you if I assigned the details of putting it together to Zinga and Breezy? They're the top at public relations."

"Ho Ho Ho! Absolutely! Remind me what elf volunteered to be the toy factory supervisor?"

"That would be Holly, sir. She's been studying with Tack for the past year. I'm really excited to have her lead the South Pole Village production team."

"Holly will be excellent," Santa said. "Let's have them both available for the tours so they can show off how things work here. It's quite different than what I'm used to."

"One more thing I should add. With all the drama going on around with Birdie and her being gone, we've fallen a little behind on our launch for the AOK," Sandra said as the trio walked down the deck to the stairs. "I think it is all too much to do before Christmas this year, so let's plan the tour and the party and the AOK launch for after Slumber Month. Would that be okay with you, Santa?"

"Ho Ho Ho! Absolutely! Elf production is slightly behind thanks to those saneers and every hour counts to getting us back on track. Now let's see this new production line of yours."

As they walked and talked the factory floor, Santa paused at each new machine put in place and considered the new, streamlined and efficient systems Sandra had chosen to have installed. All of the toys would still be designed, tested, and produced by the elves but their production capacity would be much higher on the barge for its size than at the factory at the North Pole. Some of that was necessary since, even though the barge was very large, it still wasn't as big as the original. In order to produce as many gifts, Sandra's team would need the efficient equipment she had selected.

Overall, Santa seemed pleased with what he saw. He was a traditional toy maker. There were few touches at the North Pole factory that could be called "modern', in a way. Looking at him, however, on this day, Sandra was mentally taking notes. While he was not outright effusive about any one particular production line or new system, he didn't seem to disapprove. Sandra hoped this inspection might be the first step to some needed improvements at the North Pole. She knew Tack would welcome the updates. The patient elf had been envious of the barge factory. Sandra glanced at Gunny,

JingleBelle Jackson

who smiled and gave a quick nod to indicate that he too knew what she was thinking.

"Oh, my goodness, you two!" Sandra suddenly said as she looked at the clock on the factory wall and started for the door. "I promised Christina Annalise I'd be a guest teacher at the school today! I've gotta go! Bye, Santa! Bye, Gunny!"

"Oh Oh Oh, to borrow your term, Sandra," Santa said jollily. "You better run! Christina is as tough a taskmaster as I am!"

"I know, know, know!" Sandra called back, grinning at how she and Santa loved to use their signature laughs in other fun ways.

Gunny was barely paying any attention. He loved showing off the barge. As she ran out the door, Sandra heard him taking Santa down the hall.

"Santa, wait until you see how the recreation area turned out. The pool is shaped like a candy cane!"

Sandra heard the pride in Gunny's voice and suspected she was lucky she was helping Christina. Santa's tour was going to be really long.

368

CHAPTER 66

Come and Get Me

Location: North Pole Village

After all the craziness and drama around her supposed engagement to Sam, marriage to Crow, kidnapping – twice! – by her parents, and the exhausting search for Sam her parents had conducted for months to force the marriage between Birdie and Sam to happen, it all came to a rather anti-climactic, quiet ending.

As the days had counted down to October 27, Birdie's mother had become more and more insistent and fretful, sometimes spending hours alternating between charming Birdie, threatening her, and begging her to contact Sam to keep the promise that had been made between the two countries centuries ago.

"You are too young to understand what it is the two of you are tearing apart with your obstinate ways," Serena stated almost every day in exactly that way. "If you go through with this, you will always regret it. You'll still be royalty, just not the ruler."

"No, Mother," Birdie would calmly reply, sitting quietly on the edge of the bed in the room her own parents kept her locked up in. "I will never regret following my heart. As for the monarchy, these are modern times. I believe our people, at least our young people, will love a democracy and the rights that come with it."

"I blame this ridiculous talk on Christina Annalise and the nonsense they must teach at that school you attended," Selena would say in reply. "No child from here will attend there again if I have some say and I will retain the say when you marry Sam." She would turn and leave the room dramatically, only to return for another version of the same conversation the next day and the next until, at last, October 27 arrived.

That evening both of her parents had come to her room begging her. It had made Birdie incredibly sad to let them down; they were her parents, after all. Knowing they would not be successful in making her marry Sam had helped to release her sheer anger at them. She wanted to love them and wanted to have her family reunited in the future, but she was sure it would take time and not just on her part. In fact, ironically, she suspected it would not be her, the daughter who had been kidnapped and taken away from her husband at her own wedding, who would be the bitter one. She expected that it would be her parents who would be struggling to forge a new direction in the new ways of their old country. She held on to hope that they could "forgive" her and accept the new ways. For her, she could give them the time. She knew she would be caught up in all the wonder of making a new life with her new husband who she loved with all her heart.

She didn't know if her parents knew she was aware of the significance of the October 27 date. They had never named the actual day with her and she had never mentioned it but it had been easy to count the days and figure out what day was the 300th of the year.

Neither of them seemed to notice that evening when they came for a last round of pleading and threatening that she had taken extra care with her appearance and looked especially beautiful. Her husband was coming for her and she wanted to look her very best.

For whatever reason, Selena and Zeentar were nowhere to be found when the clock struck midnight. She was free! The marriage bonds for her and Sam and all generations to come between their two countries had been released! She could hear cheering break out in the city around her and knew it was more than just herself who would celebrate this change.

"Ambyrdena?"

She whirled around from where she stood at the window listening. She knew that voice and she ran to embrace him.

"Sam! Thank you! I don't know how you did it or where you hid but I can never thank you enough for this great gift

371

JingleBelle Jackson

you have given me and Crow," Birdie exclaimed, knowing he too knew it was now safe for the two of them to be together.

"Nor can I," said a very sincere Crow, delivered there by a beaming Sandra who gave a quick wave to her best friend and then, using her locket, quickly disappeared. "I know you made this sacrifice largely for Birdie rather than yourself. We will always be in your debt and call you our friend." The young men shook hands.

"Go on now with yourselves," Sam said, gazing at how beautiful Birdie looked, "before I change my mind and call for a constitutional change of an extended time to make it all legal." He realized he was only mostly joking. Crow was a very lucky man.

But Birdie only had eyes for her cowboy. "Take me away, my groom," she said, pouring herself into his eager embrace and wondering how he was going to make that happen when, once again, her very best friend in the whole of the world briefly appeared, held her locket, and all three were gone.

Sam, too, then disappeared. It seemed there were several things about himself he hadn't shared with his fiancée.

# # #

As Sandra and Crow had agreed upon in their planning, Sandra had taken the love-struck couple back to North Pole Village. There they were given the reception they had missed after their wedding, receiving an outpouring of love from all.

Crow had arranged for the honeymoon and no one but Gunny knew where they were going. Crow had only shared it with his brother as a precaution, but he was very clear that they were not to be disturbed.

Sandra also had taken one extra precaution. She had called Jason. It was still a little early in their new roles of being "friends," but he had said she could call on him, and she needed his help. When he heard her plan, he hadn't hesitated to agree, even welcoming the chance to attend the couple's reception. He had always been friends with Birdie and, of all the Holiday brothers, Crow had always treated him respectfully and as a friend. Jason was happy for them both. He had arrived, however, holding hands with Reesa and Sandra was surprised at the pang of – was that jealousy? She shoved the thought away and decided she would have to sort out her feelings around it later.

"Jason, thank you for coming. And, Reesa, how nice to see you as well." As Sandra greeted the regal fairy, she was pleased to realize she meant the words. Their friendship was not traditional in any way but there was respect between the two young women.

Jason wasted no time. "Before we join the festivities, may I have a minute with you, Sand?" he asked with a look over at his date to be sure it was okay with her, as Gunny walked into join them. Reesa's response to Jason's look was to reach out and hug Gunny in a feigned greeting (too tight, both Sandra and Jason were thinking). Jason knew that was Reesa's way

JINGLEBELLE JACKSON

of saying "be quick about whatever it is you need to do" and "what you do is of no matter to me." He respected her independence but could have lived without her hanging on his least favorite person after the saneers. Jason might not have minded so much if he knew how unbearably uncomfortable Gunny was being hugged by the fairy. The last time they had met he believed Reesa had called him "disgusting." (In fairness, at the time, he really rather was.) At the moment, he was thinking he actually preferred that to this and he looked over at Sandra for help. She just giggled and walked to a separate area with Jason.

The king of fairies got right to it. "I was able to do what you asked, Sandra. The honeymoon couple is now under my protection," Jason said, feeling pleased at being able to offer something important as a wedding gift, thanks to his new powers and role. Helping others was how he most wanted to use any power he had in his role as king. "Bird's parents will not be able to find them or take her again."

Everyone had doubted Birdie's parents would actually steal her away again at this point. But no one wanted to underestimate what the out-played couple might choose to do in their anger at their daughter and her new husband. Being under the fairy king's protection guaranteed that no one, or nothing, would be able to harm the guarded couple in any way. The gift, given so generously by Jason for his friends, had flooded Sandra with gratitude and appreciation for the gifter. It was such a relief to know that Birdie and Crow would be safe! She grabbed and held Jason almost as tight as Reesa had embraced Gunny. Jason wrapped his arms around her, realizing how strong the pull to her remained before he remembered himself, where they were and who they were each now with, and stepped back.

"It was my honor to be of service to you, Ms. Claus dot dot dot," he said, trying to add some frivolity to shake off his emotions before returning to the other room and back to Reesa. "Time for some reception fun, my fairy wonder," he said, as Reesa gave Sandra a look across the room that could have melted metal. It caused Sandra to shiver.

The two wandered off as Sandra watched them and Gunny watched her.

CHAPTER 67

Happy Birthday!

Location: St. Annalise Island

The month of November was flying by as fast as the others that had come before it. Christmas Eve was now just a month away with so much to do, but first there was another occasion to mark. It was Sandra's birthday and she knew just what she wanted. A day off.

"*squawk* . . . happy birthday! . . . *squawk!*" Sandra awoke that morning to her favorite birthday greetings from her longest friend of all.

"Why, thank you for remembering, Squawk," she said cheerily. "Even if it is a little early." She had hoped for a rare day of sleeping till seven, but when you lived with an early bird, you knew from the start that would be unlikely. He had greeted her early at every birthday she had been lucky enough to celebrate since she was small.

"Happy Birthday, Sandra!" Em came flying into her room before Sandra could even sit up in bed, followed by what seemed like every elf at the North Pole all coming to wish their favorite South Pole Santa a happy birthday on her day. "We brought you breakfast!" Em exclaimed and at that, Gunny came along bringing a trolley full of cinnamon rolls and hot chocolate that disappeared before Sandra could get to either one. It was the absolute best start to a birthday even if it was too early.

Once they all had managed to eat every crumb and drink every drop, the room cleared of the giggling elves, and Sandra was left with just her handsome suitor standing there smiling at her, holding out a gift.

"For me?" Sandra feigned smiling, knowing presents often came on birthdays. This was the first gift she had received from a boyfriend and she was extra excited about it. She couldn't remember Jason ever giving her a gift to be unwrapped. Ironically, his birthday was the same day as hers. Thoughts of Jason flashed through her mind but she set them aside. Reesa would have to be sure he had a happy birthday this year. It was not her place.

She sat up fully and pulled her mop of hair back to get it out of her way. She knew she must look a fright but didn't care. When people came early, they got what they got from her.

She scooted over and patted the bed so Gunny could sit with her. He watched her open the gift with anticipation and saw the tiny expression of disappointment pass her face when she saw what it was.

"Dang it, Sand, I knew I should have gotten you jewelry! I know that's a standard kind of boyfriend/girlfriend gift but you have your locket and you don't really wear any other. I wanted something that was more true to me."

"Really, Gunny, it's very nice. The nicest hair brush I think I've ever seen. Definitely the biggest and you know I need it." She politely reached up and pulled the brush through her unruly curls as Gunny burst out laughing.

"Now, I see!" he said, still hooting it up. "I am so used to working with this, it never occurred to me you would think it was for you! Ha! Wait till they hear about this back at the ranch!" He was laughing so hard he rolled back on the bed as she held the big brush in her hand wondering what it was for if it wasn't for her. She did think of one other use for it. She swatted him with it.

"Hey, whoa!" he cried out, still laughing, grabbing the brush from her and catching her close. "Okay, I'll tell you what this is for." He paused for drama. She rolled her eyes at him waiting.

"This, my girlfriend," he said that part just because he loved saying it, "is for brushing the horse I got you that is now part of the Holiday Ranch herd."

"A HORSE! You got me my own horse? What's his name? What's her name?" Sandra was leaping all around the room.

The brush was for brushing a horse, not her own hair. That was soooooo much better! Gunny got her a horse of her own.

"A her," he said in response, smiling a mile-wide smile. "And her name, appropriately, is December."

"December! No way! Gunny, I love it! I love you and I love her! When can I meet her?"

"How about now?" he asked, totally loving Sandra's reaction. He had hoped she would be excited and this had exceeded his hopes. He loved to make her happy.

"Now would be so perfect but can it be later? Now I have somewhere else in mind I'd like to go." She reached over to her nightstand and waved a small piece of paper at him. He knew what it was. She wanted to go check out the next clue location. He did too.

"Yep, later is better. It's your birthday and you get to decide what we do. Uh, before we go though, maybe you should use this brush." He grinned at her, teasingly indicating her hair.

She came over but instead of grabbing for the brush, she grabbed for a kiss. "I love my gift, Mr. Holiday," she said.

"Well, now you're making me feel like it's my birthday," he grinned, feeling ridiculously happy.

CHAPTER 68

The Final Clue

Location: Somewhere in Asia

Sandra marveled, ever so briefly when they landed, at how one minute you could be so excited about what you were setting out to do and the next you could be so miserable and as frightened as you could ever remember being.

The coordinates had brought them smack dab to the middle of a very rickety, very high suspension bridge crossing a deep canyon between two formidable rock formations. It seemed they were high on a mountain range, and judging by the look of a building off in the distance that she suspected was a temple of some sort, it looked like they might be in some Asian country, but neither of them had any idea of which one. Nor did they care. They were both too busy trying to hang on and not drop through one of the very sparse boards that passed for decking on an apparently still-used bridge, though it was hard to imagine.

The very old suspension bridge was made of worn rope and fragile boards spaced unevenly across the width of the canyon. There were small flags tied along each rope rail. They appeared to have been brightly colored at one time but now were long-faded and largely flapped in tatters in the steady wind that blew.

"Sandra, don't move!" Gunny called out to her from his spot a few feet away.

No problem there, she thought.

"Gee, Gunny, I was thinking this might be a great time to take up jogging." Sarcasm sometimes came to her under nerve-wracking conditions. She would apologize later. If they lived.

Sandra seriously wasn't sure she *could* move. At all. She was pretty close to petrified from fear. Gunny felt similar but managed to swallow his dread and step forward to get closer to Sandra. His step rocked the whole bridge and Sandra screamed out for him to stop moving.

"That's not exactly possible," Gunny said, trying to talk to her calmly while his heart raced. This was the worst place the clues had taken them, yet and they needed to get out of there. "Think, Sandra. Concentrate. Where would a clue be here? We need to find it and get out of here." He took another step forward and the bridge rocked perilously to one side.

"Gunny!" Sandra cried out scared.

"I know, I know," he said, scared out of his mind too. "Sandra, we need to make it to the rock there." He didn't point – no way was he letting go – but nodded with his head at the rocks behind Sandra. They weren't close but closer than the ones behind him. "It's probably where he put the clue."

Sandra looked at the rock and looked at the bridge and shuddered. "Are you sure, Gunny? What if it's on the other side?" She didn't want to move toward either side.

"Maybe we should use your locket and come back later?" Gunny suggested.

That seemed to help Sandra with her courage. She didn't want to have to come back another day. She was tired of the tricks and time Calivon was taking from her and her family. "Okay, let's try for the side by me." She took a deep breath and a step forward to the next board – and heard it crack as she stepped on it!

She clung to the rope rail as Gunny tried to stride closer to her, knowing they dared not share the same step but also knowing he needed to be close enough for her to reach in order to get them both out of there safely.

"Gunny, I think there's a number here," Sandra said, feeling stunned as her step and the resulting reaction of her clinging to the rail had brought her eye to eye with one of the faded flags. She reached to move it gingerly and get a better look. "It is! It's a number!" She read it out to Gunny as he put it in his memory. This time, there was no way they could write it down so memory would have to do.

JingleBelle Jackson

"It's not complete," he said, stating what Sandra already had realized. It forced her to take another step to the next flag. "There's just an N here," she hollered out as she reached the next flag. It made sense knowing that it would be added to the number they had, but it also meant she would have to take at least one more step forward to get the rest of the coordinate. *Someday I will get even, Calivon*, she thought, as she forced herself forward. Gunny did the same and the bridge rocked perilously. They both clung to the flimsy rope rail on opposite sides in an attempt to keep the bridge balanced.

"There's nothing here!" Sandra cried out in despair, looking at the flag she was at.

"Is it just faded?" Gunny asked hopefully, wanting to keep her from having to move forward again.

Sandra looked at it closely. She said nothing in response but instead stepped forward again. Gunny did the same and took one more step before having to stop the bridge from rocking too much.

"Don't move, Sandra!" he shouted at her. She felt like she couldn't. Not because she so fervently didn't want to but instead because the gap between the next two steps seemed wider than either one of them could manage. It was over. They were so close and they would never be able to find her parents. The wave of despair hit her as hard as the fear of the bridge and she clung there feeling defeated for the first time. Calivon and the saneers were going to be victorious.

Gunny suspected what she was feeling and hastened to speak. "Don't move, Sandra! I have the other coordinate! It's here on this flag on this side! No, wait, these don't seem right." He looked at them again looking puzzled. He took a fragile step forward to see the next flag but it contained nothing and he took a step back to check the one before. "These must be them," he said, sounding immensely relieved. "I've got the other half!"

Relief flooded through her as she pulled together her courage to reach Gunny. With fingers barely linked, she released her other hand from the rotting rope rail to wrap it around her locket just as the board she was standing on gave way and they both went tumbling toward the canyon floor far below.

# # #

When they landed alive on the deck of the *Mistletoe*, Sandra's overwhelming feeling was of outrage over what they had just been through. Each clue had been found somewhere dangerous and perilous but this one had gone too far! Gunny understood but now that they had made it through, he was ready to put it behind them and try out the next clue. They had to — he didn't want to forget any of the numbers or letters they had retrieved.

"We've got to do this, Sand," he said. "We have time and I don't want to forget the coordinates."

He had scrambled to write them down when they arrived but he could only make sure they were right when Sandra spoke them and she was still shaken from the shaking bridge.

"But what if it is even worse than what we just came from?" she demanded. "What then?" Gunny knew she wasn't really asking him. She was just working out her fear and frustrations with the whole process. He worked to calm her.

"Then we will handle it – like we have with every location," he said. "None of them have been easy or fun, island girl," he threw in a nickname now in hopes of getting a smile, "but we've made it through them all. We can do it."

Sandra just looked at him, without a smile, but knowing he was right. *What a way to spend a birthday,* she thought. She reached out her hand for his, read off the coordinate, and off they went.

CHAPTER 69

A Dewey of a Clue

Location: Scotland

The extra "coordinate numbers" Gunny had found made sense immediately as soon as they arrived at their destination. They were at a library and the duo realized the extra number referred them to a book. Sandra couldn't contain her excitement.

"It's a call number! For a book! Of course it is. How did we not figure that out? We've done it, Gunny!" she exclaimed, clapping her hands together and grinning with joy. Gone was her outrage and trepidation. "I can feel it. This is finally the last stop. This is where I'll find the papers that have been hidden in plain view for centuries and release my parents — and really all of the elfin people in some ways." Once she read the elfin documents, her parents would be free and Calivon would lose his place of power, changing everything

JINGLEBELLE JACKSON

in the magical world for the better. Sandra had butterflies in her stomach thinking about it all. She wasn't sure if they were from excitement or nerves.

Gunny wanted to be excited for her but kept his optimism in check. They were dealing with Calivon here and it was almost impossible for him to believe the guy would let Sandra be successful on this mission. On the other hand, maybe Calivon couldn't keep her from it. Either way, they were going in and finding the book.

Sandra went straight to the front desk to show the librarian the call number she had and listened carefully as the woman told her where to find that section in the library.

"Hmmmmm," the older woman said, putting on a different pair of glasses to look closer at the number and typing it into the computer in front of her. "The Book of Elfin," she read out loud as Sandra struggled to contain her excitement. She didn't want to draw any attention to herself or the book.

"Yes, that is the book I'm looking for," Sandra said as calmly as she could, as her heart beat so loudly she thought it could be heard throughout the entire building.

I've worked here 43 years, and I don't recall ever seeing this book," the librarian said, now looking hard at the young woman in front of her, growing a little suspicious of a student who wanted something she didn't know about. That was a very rare occurrence at this point in her long service to the library. Especially in the historical periodicals where she prided herself on her knowledge of them. "It's in row six,

Enchantments A South Pole Santa Adventure

shelf five in the historical periodicals section," she read to Sandra. "Perhaps I should go with you." But when she looked up, the girl with the unruly red hair was gone.

"So impatient," the librarian muttered and then moved on to the next reader in line at her desk.

Sandra and Gunny took the big staircase two stairs at a time. Sandra had briefly considered using her locket but knew the stairs would get her there and the use of magic in such a public space would be highly frowned upon by most, including her parents. She checked in her head but could find no sense of either of her parents there. Nonetheless, she sent out a mental call to her mother. *Mom, I'm close, I know it.*

Gunny, with his long legs, beat her to the shelf. He looked at the paper in his hand with the call number and looked at the shelf, running his finger along each book to check. He looked again, checking the paper and each book on the shelf and then looked at Sandra with an expression that said he didn't know what to say to her. There was no book.

"It's not here, Sand," he said. "I'm so sorry."

Sandra wanted nothing to do with his words or his sadness. She couldn't handle any more despair. She wanted to have a crying fit right there in the bookshelves but instead she made her way to the shelf to see for herself where it should have been.

She took the book call numbers from Gunny and, like him, started checking each book on the shelf with her fingertip touching each as if to mark it off as seen. When she got

389

JingleBelle Jackson

to where the *The Book of Elfin* should have been, it was. It was there! Right in front of her! A golden book that shined.

"Well I'll be hoodwinked," Gunny said under his breath as Sandra gave him a victorious smile. They both had seen that the book hadn't been there for him and it was there for her. Clearly it also explained why the librarian had never seen it either – it wasn't there for her to see. Undoubtedly, it had been enchanted to be hidden to anyone who was not at least part elfin.

Sandra carefully pulled the book out. At first glance it appeared to look like most any book, except for its gold glow. Naturally, at St. Annalise, Sandra had seen – and worked with – magic books before but this was more than just a simple book of magic. This was THE top book of the unseen magical world and contained answers and information not meant for the human world. Gunny instinctively knew that and out of honor for the magical world he stepped away to allow Sandra to review the book on her own. She appreciated his thoughtfulness.

Despite all the magic the book was sure to hold, Sandra was only interested in one part of it. Toward the back she found an old parchment carefully folded. It was somehow sewn into the book but she could unfold it. She saw the words that were scrolled on it in the boxy way of writing in ancient writing and knew it was what her parents had sent her to find. She had, at last, found what she had been seeking. She snapped the book shut smiling. She would take it somewhere safe and private for the reunion with her family! She turned to find Gunny and saw him there looking frantic, shouting but not saying a word. For a moment she couldn't understand what was happening until Calivon and three other elfins stepped into her view!

Run! She heard her mother shout in her head, but the top elfin had done something, cast some kind of spell, and she could go nowhere. In fact, as Sandra looked wildly around for some help, she realized Calivon had enchanted the whole or the library and only she and Gunny, and the four of them, seemed aware of what was happening at row six, shelf five.

Calivon began clapping. "Bravo, bravo, Sandra," he said with no real sense of enthusiasm. "When I hid those clues with my 'assistants' here we never, ever, imagined that anyone would find them, let alone the book, and yet, here you are. How is that possible? You claim to have no magic. Clearly that brutish human you seem to prefer has none, so how, exactly, are you here?"

Sandra made no response except to tighten her grip on the book.

"Go away, Calivon," she said. "I found it fair and square after going to all the awful places you hid the clues. All elfins should get to have access to the knowledge here. I know you're the one who took my parents. Now I'm going to get them back and tell all of the magical world what you've done."

With those words Calivon came racing up to her much faster than she ever could have imagined as Gunny squirmed to get free. Sandra was scared, but refused to flinch or show she was afraid of the fearsome elfin leader. She knew she shouldn't but couldn't help herself from speaking to him boldly.

"When they're back, you'll be the one who will be gone for years. In prison!"

The elfins scurried forward but Calivon waved them away. He looked at Sandra with deep hatred and then stepped back, a neutral look restored to his face, as if he had caught himself and this was all just an amusing game.

"I suspected all along who you were, Miss Long-Named Santa Claus. I just couldn't prove it. I'm still wondering how your clever mother was able to hide you so well. That is something I still need to figure out.

"But that is actually for another time. I simply can't keep all these humans waiting," he waved in the general direction of the rest of the library. "So I'm afraid I must ask you to release the book so that we can be on our way." Sandra went to hold it even tighter and realized she was holding nothing. Instead, it was Calivon who now held it in his hands.

CHAPTER 70

Words Remembered

Location: Scotland

He had taken the book! After all the places they had been, the challenges she and Gunny had faced, and now Calivon had ripped all of it away. It was too much. The frustration, the anger, the emotions all were threatening to boil over in Sandra but something stronger was tapping at her. Something she realized was what he had feared. She, too, was powerful and she had seen the words! As she thought about the page, she realized even though she had only seen it once, she somehow knew the words printed there. And speaking the words, her mother had said, was all a Leezle had to do to stand in his or her power. As the smug elfin turned to walk away with his guard elfins, but before they all disappeared, Sandra called after him.

"I am a Leezle born to this land. I am elfin from birth and royal by destiny. Elfin magic flows through my veins. I'm strong and smart, compassionate and fair. I stand united with my kind and claim the birthright that is mine."

As he heard Sandra chant, Calivon turned with both rage and fear showing on his face.

But nothing happened. Sandra started again this time not mumbling, but speaking strongly, loudly, and standing tall and proud. As she spoke, she was joined by the voice of her mother, not just in her head this time, but ringing through the whole of the library room.

"I am a Leezle born to this land. I am elfin from birth and royal by destiny. Elfin magic flows through my veins. I'm strong and smart, compassionate and fair. I stand united with my kind and claim the birthright that is mine."

As they chanted, the room reverberated and began to spark. Calivon was shouting at his henchmen. "Seize her! Keep her quiet!" He was trying one magic attack on Sandra after another but from the minute she began chanting the words, nothing could hurt her. She spoke the words again, with even more confidence knowing this was for her family and knowing her mother stood somewhere chanting the same. A third female voice now joined in. Sandra was unsure of who it was, but she too spoke the words.

"I am a Leezle born to this land. I am elfin from birth and royal by destiny. Elfin magic flows through my veins. I'm strong and

smart, compassionate and fair. I stand united with my kind and claim the birthright that is mine."

As they finished, the room burst into light, and anything standing was sent flying. Sandra landed hard against one of the bookshelves that teetered as if it would come tumbling down but somehow stayed righted. Her head was ringing as she struggled to sort out what had happened. Whatever had happened, win or lose, she knew she had given everything she had to get her parents back.

"Cassandra!" She saw Gunny scrambling to get to her through her barely opened eyes. *Why was he using her full name?* she thought, too confused and tired to figure it out.

"Cassandra!" he said again.

But it wasn't Gunny saying her name. It was her dad. It was her dad who was picking her up in his arms. It was her mom who was sobbing next to him, kissing her face.

"Sandra? Sandra? It's your mom, darling," her mom was saying over and over.

"And your dad," Sandra's dad added, bringing just the slightest smile to Sandra's mouth.

"I sort of figured if it was Mom, Dad, it must be you, too," she managed to whisper weakly.

"You always were smart, Cherry Top," her dad said, setting her gingerly on a table. "We need to check you, sweetheart. Are you hurt anywhere?"

"Pretty much everywhere," she mumbled back.

JINGLEBELLE JACKSON

Her mother began to quickly touch each part of her while talking quietly. "You did it, darling! You did it. You released Calivon's hold on us and restored the Leezle line! You were so brave through everything and you did it. There, done. How are you feeling?" Her mother stepped back a bit. Sandra stretched her arms and legs and realized her mother's magic was at work already healing her pains. Sandra was able to open her eyes fully and found both of her parents' worried faces within inches of her own.

"You're hovering. I think this is what they call 'helicopter parents'," she joked, as both of her parents burst into happy tears and reached to hug her close in the best hug Sandra ever remembered receiving. Her parents were hugging her! They were alive and here and hugging her! They could be a family again. She started looking around.

"What about Clementine? Did she make it?" Panic was taking over again. As much as she wanted her parents back, she didn't want her little sister to live without her parents like Sandra had had to do for far too long.

"She did," Sandra's mother said, motioning behind Sandra as she moved to sit up on the table. "Sandra, I'd like you to meet your little sister, Clementine. TinTin, this is your sister, Cassandra. Sandra, actually, as she has always been called by all but your father when he had chores for her to do." Her mom smiled trying to add a little levity to this very emotional moment. It wasn't every day two sisters met for the first time and Cassie knew this meeting was going to be a

ENCHANTMENTS A SOUTH POLE SANTA ADVENTURE

little more complicated than Sandra could have been ready for under even the best of circumstances.

But Sandra felt ready. She had been given enough time over the past months to get used to the idea of having a little sister and was looking forward to all the things she would be able to introduce her new little sis to on St. Annalise and the South Pole Village barge. Her mind raced with those ideas. The elves would be so thrilled to get to know her, plus TinTin could play with the children going to Kindness Camp, in between classes at St. Annalise, of course, and . . .

"Hello, Sandra," a shy voice said. "Mom and Dad have told me so much about you."

Sandra saw a strange look in her mother's eyes as Sandra turned to greet the voice. Was it a look of worry or concern? Either way it contrasted with the smile on her mother's face. *What was that?* Sandra thought passingly but let it go, feeling more excited to hug her sister than worry on the look.

She turned to greet TinTin with arms wide open and understood the look she had seen from her mother at once. Sandra's smile froze on her face, trying to comprehend.

"Clementine?" she asked, not understanding and turning to her parents. "Mom? Dad?" They both were nodding their heads with enthusiasm, almost willing her to accept without question the girl in front of her.

The pretty girl standing there looked almost nothing at all like Sandra. She had short messy hair that sparkled like Sandra's but was almost white in color. Her pale skin looked as if she had never been out in the sun and Sandra realized that she probably hadn't. Sandra could see, though, even from a few feet away that TinTin's eyes were as green as her own. She was plainer than Sandra but striking in her simplicity. Almost none of this registered with Sandra, however, as she tried to match what her mother had told her, and she believed to be true, with who stood there now.

"How old are you?" Sandra finally asked TinTin directly. She knew it was a rather rude question to ask upon first meeting someone but she had to know.

"Nineteen, I think."

"Nineteen? You think? Mom and dad told me you were nine!" Sandra said, talking just to TinTin now, feeling completely misled by her parents.

"I am," TinTin said. "Or I was. But then I changed and I was older. It's okay, though. It wasn't that much fun being little where we were at."

"What?" Sandra said, hopping down from the table and backing up to put some distance between her and her parents. Gunny came over to put his arm around her for support. He had stood back and didn't know exactly what was going on, but whatever it was, he wasn't going to let her face it alone.

"Cassandra," her mother said, talking calmly but fast, in a run-on sentence likely brought on from nerves. "I know this part is hard for you but there was nothing you could do and it wasn't your fault, and the three of us have come to accept it. After all, elfins have very long lives and we're all so happy to

Enchantments A South Pole Santa Adventure

be here now with you." Sandra's dad and TinTin both nodded their heads.

"When?" Sandra said quietly, needing to know the answer and dreading it at the same time. "When did she change?"

Her mother's answer came as her father held TinTin close. "TinTin went from nine to nineteen overnight. The night –"

"The night I met with the saneers," Sandra said more to herself than anyone else there. "They scanned my memories and took time from someone I cared about! I did this!"

She shook off Gunny's arm and ran from the room.

CHAPTER 71

A Gift for a Santa

Location: St. Annalise Island

It had taken hours of talking and the magic of the Christmas season, but day by day, Sandra was slowly forgiving her part in what had led to TinTin's childhood being stolen away. The little family had managed only bits and pieces of time together since Sandra and Santa were so busy.

In the weeks that had followed their release, no one had been able to locate Calivon. It wasn't for lack of trying. An extensive, continuing search had been launched and it seemed all of the magical world was looking for the shamed ex-leader.

Fortunately, in Calivon's haste to get away, he had dropped the Book of Elfin. Sandra's mom had been able to return it to its place of distinction in the magically protected Elfin High House where it would be, once again, open to all elfin to review. The Magical High Council had heard the family's story

JINGLEBELLE JACKSON

and had responses ranging from pure outrage from Laile to a sense of amusement from Reesa. While Cassie had sought to hide from her responsibility as a Leezle, and therefore the leader of the elfins, she now understood that had never been realistic or responsible. She had been crowned immediately as the top ruler of the whole of the magical kingdom, which had rippled out in many ways. One of her first acts was to eliminate both Calivon and Zeentar from the Council. She would look for replacements with integrity that lived with a focus on fair and kind.

Some of Sandra's own friends had been surprised by exactly how powerful her family really was. Those closest to her, though, had always known Sandra was extraordinary. Her kindness, her ways of thinking, her commitment to others, even her beauty – all were elevated from most. Sandra was quick to remind them each that nothing about her had changed just because her parents and new sister had been rescued. She was still exactly the same person she had always been – royal Leezle or not. In fact, much to the skepticism of Wistle and some of the others, Sandra insisted that what made her most special of all was her human side because humans had the biggest hearts. Her parents, especially her very human, non-royal dad, had beamed with pride hearing her words. They believed it was true as well.

The reunion between Sandra's parents and Cappie had been full of tears and thanks. It was almost impossible for Cassiopola and Sanderson to feel they could ever thank Cappie enough for raising their daughter so lovingly in their place. For her part, Cappie didn't need or even want any thanks. It had been her greatest gift ever to have the privilege. In fact, having them back had led to some surprisingly bittersweet moments for Sandra and Cappie who both realized the changes it meant again. Neither would have wished for Sandra's parents to be gone but both felt they had been lucky for the very special time together.

While the reunion with Cappie was emotional, the reunion with Squawk was just crazy! Cassie was the one who had made it possible for Squawk to talk. He loved the ability and loved Cassie so when she walked onto the deck of the *Mistletoe,* well, the big bird fainted. He fainted! It was just too much for him all at once. Sandra panicked seeing Squawk lying there flat and lifeless and started screaming. This completely frightened Tug who threw a beautifully decorated, four-layered birthday cake he was carrying, that he had made just for Sandra, high in the air, landing upside-down, frosting-first all over him! Once Squawk had awakened, Tug was checked to be sure he was all right and part of the cake was salvaged, Sandra had declared it the best birthday – and cake – that she had ever had.

The *Mistletoe* was almost crowded with the full family on board plus Squawk and Em and Tug and even little Quisp seemed to be there with them most of the time. For Sandra, it had never felt more like home but something important was tugging at her, and in this case it actually was the big tug boat.

JINGLEBELLE JACKSON

She cornered her parents for a quick talk as soon as she could get them all to herself.

"I love the *Mistletoe* so much. She's been the place I have felt safe and close to you," Sandra said to her parents who disconcertingly had taken to smiling at her all the time – almost like the saneers except sincerely. She knew it was just that they were so happy to be with her because she felt the same way – and probably looked the same way. But not that afternoon. She was doing no smiling.

"Oh, honey, we know. We love this big tug, too," her dad said sincerely.

"But you would have done the right thing," Sandra said dismally, causing her parents' smiles to change to looks of concern.

"What right thing is that, sweetheart?" Sandra's mother asked.

"You would have given it to the saneers like I should have!" Sandra blurted out with despair in her voice. "If I had just given the *Mistletoe* to the saneers when they asked, nothing bad would have happened! The elves wouldn't have lost time. Wistle wouldn't have lost her beauty. and most importantly of all, TinTin wouldn't have lost her childhood!"

"Oh, Sandra!" both her parents exclaimed, reaching in to hug their agonized child. They had no idea how she had been feeling. "Nobody blames you, darling," her mother said. "We all understand."

404

"I blame me!" Sandra said, pushing back and now pacing around her parents. "Yes, I love this big boat, but not more than my friends and family. It's a place and my home but I've realized more than ever lately what matters most to me. Home is wherever the people I love are. I have several homes now, in fact." She paused thinking about how much she loved St. Annalise, North Pole Village, and the new South Pole Village barge along with the *Mistletoe.*

"I just really want you and TinTin and the elves and Wistle to know that if I had it to do it again, I would have given the saneers the *Mistletoe.* I'm so sorry. I love her but I love you all more and I know we can live anywhere as long as we're all safe and together." She looked at her parents willing them to understand, which, of course they did.

"Cassandra Penelope Clausmonetsiamlydelaterra dot dot dot," her father started in sternly. He only used her full name when a missive of some sort was coming. "Never in our entire lives have we not been proud of everything you've done. If, and only if, you had a selfish moment where you wanted to keep your home and the place you feel most safe from the perils that have been lurking and frankly, taken a great deal from you, there is no one who wouldn't understand. All of the people affected love this big boat like home too. She has a way of casting a spell. Was that your doing, my dear?" he asked, smiling at his wife.

"Not me this time," Cassie quipped with her hands in the air, palms open, feigning innocence. "She has magic of

JingleBelle Jackson

her own in these well-worn boards." She patted the side of the tug.

"I'm so glad you shared this with us, Sandra, and now it is time to let that guilt go," her mom said seriously to her daughter. "Lingering regret has no place in a healthy life. We learn from each choice and we move on with the wisdom we gain. Like your father said, we are always only proud of you."

Sandra felt relief flooding her whole body. The guilt of her decision had been eating away at her happy feelings and sharing an apology and being forgiven had made her feel better immediately. She would apologize to the elves and Wistle, too, and suspected now that they too would forgive her as well.

The trio had hugged and hugged and moved right into talking merrily on their Christmas plans. This year, the family and friends planned to spend Christmas Day together. It had been a huge year for them all and being together was the gift they all wanted. Both sets of newlyweds would be there, Spence and his family, all of the Holidays, Christina Annalise (and she was hoping for Jason), and even a smattering of elves and fairies. At the very least, representing the elves, would be Em and Tug who, it seemed, were both now permanent family members. Tug cleaned and shined every day, often the same spot over and over, content as can be. Happily, there had been plenty of messes with so many people now living on-board for the hardworking elf to clean up.

406

After a few precious hours spent together on St. Annalise, Sandra had to get back to work. It seemed the month of December flew by even faster than ever. As Sandra landed back at St. Annalise with Em after the long night of delivering gifts on Christmas Eve, she wasn't surprised to see her parents waiting for her patiently on the beach.

"Happy Christmas Eve to our Santa daughter, and you, too, Em!" called out Sandra's dad.

"Happy Christmas Eve!" Sandra called back.

"Happy Christmas Eve, Sandra's mom and dad!" Em said, getting in on the good vibes. Sandra grinned at her little friend. She loved how Em had taken to her parents.

"We tucked TinTin in for the night but wanted to be here on this Christmas Eve to greet you two," said her mother, smiling, with a pretty package held out in her hand. "We have a present for you, Sandra."

"A present?" Sandra said, surprised. "You don't want to wait and have me open it later?"

"No," said her mother, shaking her head. "It requires discretion. We trust Em completely."

Em nodded at them solemnly. She would never tell a secret that was important to keep.

Sandra untied the bow and lifted the lid to the pretty box to find a star charm that sparkled even in the moonlight.

"It's beautiful," Sandra said sincerely, not sure why it needed discretion but loving the gift.

JINGLEBELLE JACKSON

"It's a wishing star," her dad said. "We thought you could wear it on the same chain with your locket."

"Sure," Sandra said. "It will look great with it."

"Sandra, it's a wishing star with real wishes," her mother said. "As the royal head of elfins and a descendant of the Leezles, I alone can grant magical gifts. For your bravery, your service, and your loving heart, you are being gifted with this wishing star. Its power is strong, and while I am making it possible, even I cannot tell you the number of wishes it contains. Each star is unique and chooses its own amount of power. Perhaps it contains only one wish or perhaps it contains many. It is for the star to know and you to discover. Whatever number it is, however, each time you choose to use it, you should think carefully about what your wish is, for it could be your last. Do not use the star lightly, but thoughtfully and wisely. Ultimately, you can use it any way you like as a token of thanks for all you have done for the seen and the unseen world.

"There's no time limit on using your wishes so do not feel hurried and please do not let others know of your gift. There are many who would take it, I fear, and the wishes can be used by whoever holds the star."

"We won't tell anyone," Em said solemnly as Sandra smiled and quickly removed her locket, added the wishing star and slipped it back on her neck.

"What an incredible gift. I'm so honored to receive it," she said with love in her eyes as her parents beamed.

Enchantments A South Pole Santa Adventure

"Sandra, do you know what you'll use your wishes on?" Em asked. "Maybe you could wish for a candy castle!"

"Oh, Em!" Sandra exclaimed as they all laughed at the earnest little delgin. "Maybe I could, maybe I could." A candy castle was one idea, but she was already thinking on other possible ways on how she could use them.

"I love it, Mom! I love it, Dad! I'm going to use it to wish TinTin back to her real age," Sandra said, feeling ecited about this unexpected chance to make things right.

"Oh darling," Sandra's mother said. "I wish the wishes could be used for that. I'm afraid whatever the saneers have done is not so easily undone. Believe me, I've tried." She looked at Sandra with sadness and concern. Sandra frowned at the news. She seemed ready to object when, instead, she shook off whatever she was thinking and reached over to give her parents both a big hug and pulled Em in.

"Let's not worry about it on this perfect night," Sandra said.

As the little group headed for the *Mistletoe*, out of habit, Sandra held her locket as she often did when she was happy. It gave her comfort and brought her joy. Her thoughts shifted as she touched the new addition. A wishing star with real wishes. "Not to be used lightly . . ." her mother had said.

No problem, Sandra thought to herself, smiling. Since she couldn't use them to help her sister, she knew exactly how she was going to use her wishes whether it was one or many.

JingleBelle Jackson

She believed in kindness and forgiveness, but too much had been taken from her family and others. She would use her star charm to help make Calivon and the saneers pay for all that they had taken. It was the best gift her mother could have ever given her.

CHAPTER 72

Great List, Great Life

Location: The Mistletoe

Sandra sat in the rocking chair on the deck of the *Mistletoe* for a few minutes, alone, enjoying the night sky and the twinkling Christmas tree. It had been a perfect Christmas Day full of family and fun and gifts and joy in abundance. Now everyone in the whole world, it seemed, was tucked in bed at the end of this magical season. She rocked in the chair, thinking on how this was the best Christmas she could remember. So much had made it special and Sandra doubted there could ever be one so grand again. She loved thinking about everything she had to be thankful for. She thought through the items in her head and counted them off on her fingers to keep track.

- Her parents were back
- She had a new sister

JingleBelle Jackson

- They were all living on the *Mistletoe*
- Cappie and Thomas were just a dock away
- Squawk, Rio, and Em were happy
- The South Pole Village barge was done and ready to sail
- The Academy of Kindness was ready to launch
- Spencer was doing great
- Wistle was back to being beautiful and she and Ghost were in love
- Quisp was safe
- Birdie and Crow were living happily ever after
- Sandra and Gunny had a promising relationship
- She and Jason were friends
- Christina Annalise seemed content and worry free
- The elves were healthy and happy
- Santa and Mrs. Claus had made it through another Christmas
- Most children around the world were on the Nice List
- And best of all, perhaps, she was South Pole Santa and got to deliver gifts to children every Christmas Eve.

"Eighteen big things," she said out loud, smiling. "And those are just for starters." Every single thing in her life felt perfect at that moment.

ENCHANTMENTS A SOUTH POLE SANTA ADVENTURE

"Merry Christmas!" she whispered loudly to the immense, star-filled, tropical sky with her arms wide open and her face raised to the nearly full moon. "Oh Oh Oh! Thank you for my life!"

Epilogue

A Meeting of Mean

Location: Somewhere Dark

"Gentlemen, something important has been taken from me and I could use your help. I know we have never officially met, but I believe we have a mutual acquaintance – a certain Miss Claus and her annoying parents," Calivon said, feeling surprisingly nervous now that he was face to face with who he had sought out. No one searching had found him because he had hid in a place that kind and good people chose never to go.

The two saneers smiled. "Perhaps we can be of service," the one named Tambler said.

The End (for now ☺)

Yummy Elf Treat

Recipe created by Betsy Chan
16-20 Treats

    4 cups oven toasted "square" corn cereal*
½ cup chopped pecans
6 tablespoons butter
½ cup golden brown sugar
¼ teaspoon pure vanilla extract
¼ teaspoon kosher or table salt
2 tablespoons light corn syrup
4 cups mini-marshmallows, lightly packed**
1/3 cup mini green and red (or any color) candy-coated chocolate candies

---

* 4 cups freshly popped popcorn can be substituted (remove all unpopped kernels before mixing)

** The elves counted about 100 mini-marshmallows per cup...but there's really no need to count them ☺

Directions:

In a large bowl, add the cereal and nuts; set aside.

In a medium saucepan, melt together the butter, brown sugar, vanilla, salt and corn syrup. Bring to a boil on medium-high heat, stirring to mix well. Reduce heat to low; add marshmallows and cook for 5-7 minutes, stirring until marshmallows are melted and smooth. Remove from heat, let sit for up to 1 minute.

Pour marshmallow mixture onto the cereal and nuts. Carefully mix together, while sprinkling in the candy, until cereal is evenly coated.

Using a hand wearing a disposable plastic glove (or a hand wearing a quart-sized baggie like a glove), grab a portion of the mixture that's slightly larger than a golf-ball, and gently squeeze into a ball. Drop onto waxed or parchment paper to cool. Repeat until all the mixture is used. Store in airtight container.

Acknowledgements

Thank you to all of my wonderful friends who, once again, helped make this book happen! **Tina Fischer Mitchell,** you are the best of the best. None of the books would be as close to as much fun without your magical covers.

The book would be unfinished and unpolished without the insightful help of my book coach, **Brie Vennard**; the patient read-through for correcting my punctuation and mis-spellings by **Diana Kwong**; and the extra special touch of an original recipe by **Betsy Chan.** (Make the Elf Treats! So good!) I also get supportive design and photography help from **Krysta Rasmussen** and **Wendy Parris**.

Thank you all so much!

Don't miss these other adventures from JingleBelle Jackson:

The Search for South Pole Santa
Sandra Claus...
The Santanapping
Unwrapped

Thank you for reading!
If you enjoyed *Enchantments* and/or any of the other books
in the *South Pole Santa* series please tell your friends
and spread the word! I welcome your review on any of
the websites that provide room for a review! I also love
to hear from readers. You can reach me and find out more
about Sandra and her friends, kindness, fun and magic
at www.jinglebellejackson.com. Or come on over and
join me on Facebook and Twitter. Oh Oh Oh!

Made in United States
Troutdale, OR
12/08/2023

15559077R00260